PIGEONS ON THE GRASS

WOLFGANG KOEPPEN

Pigeons on the Grass

translated from the German
by Michael Hofmann

A NEW DIRECTIONS
PAPERBOOK ORIGINAL

Originally published in 1951 by Suhrkamp Verlag as *Tauben im Gras*
First published as a New Directions Paperbook (NDP1483) in 2020
Manufactured in the United States of America

Library of Congress Cataloging-in-Publication Data
Names: Koeppen, Wolfgang, 1906–1996, author. |
Hofmann, Michael, 1957 August 25– translator.
Title: Pigeons on the grass / Wolfgang Koeppen;
translated from the German by Michael Hofmann.
Other titles: Tauben im Gras. English
Description: New York : A New Directions Book, 2020.
Identifiers: LCCN 2020021694 | ISBN 9780811229180 (paperback ; acid-free paper) |
ISBN 9780811229197 (ebook)
Classification: LCC PT2621.O46 T313 2020 | DDC 833/.912—dc23
LC record available at https://lccn.loc.gov/2020021694

10 9 8 7 6 5 4 3 2 1

New Directions Books are published for James Laughlin
by New Directions Publishing Corporation
80 Eighth Avenue, New York 10011

Contents

Preface

Pigeons on the Grass was written just after the currency reform of 1948, when the German "economic miracle" got going in the West, when the first new cinemas and insurance offices overtopped the ruins and the temporary premises, at the height of the occupation, when Korea and Persia kept the world in suspense, and the sun of the economic miracle looked as though it might shortly go down in the East a bloody mess. It was the time when the new rich were still nervous, when the black marketeers were looking for places to invest their gains, and savers were paying for the war. The new German money might look like dollar bills, but on the whole people still had more confidence in goods, and there was a lot of need around still to be satisfied; bellies wanted filling, heads were still spinning with hunger and bomb blasts, and the senses sought their gratification, ideally before the next show. This was the time, the foundation of the present day, that I was writing about, and I must assume I did a reasonable job, since people took my novel to be a mirror in which many individuals who were by no means in my thoughts claimed to recognize themselves, and a handful whom I would never have supposed to be in such straits as I had chronicled felt, to my dismay, offended by me, who had merely done what an author does, which, in the words of Georges Bernanos, is "to filter my living heart, drawing from it the secret essences of balsam and poison."

WOLFGANG KOEPPEN
MUNICH, 1951

Translator's introduction

Wolfgang Koeppen's novel *Pigeons on the Grass*, first published in 1951 as *Tauben im Gras*, is among the earliest, grandest, and most poetically satisfying reckonings in fiction with the postwar state of the world. What have we done to ourselves? what may we hope for? is life from now on going to be different? is it even going to be possible? These are the unasked and unanswerable questions that hover around this great novel composed in bite-sized chunks, a cross section of a damaged society presented—natch!—in cut-up. I once described it as a "Modernist jigsaw in 110 pieces," but it is as compulsively readable as Dickens or Elmore Leonard. The form catches the eye, but the content is no slouch either. It must be one of the shortest of the universal books, the ones of which you think: if it isn't in here, it doesn't exist.

The setting is Munich, a place to which Koeppen had first come toward the end of the war. It is where, in his own words, he "lay low and made himself small," where he met Marion Ulrich, his much younger wife (they were married in 1948), and where he lived until his death in 1996, at the age of almost ninety. More to the point, it is "the little town out of which death sprawled over the classroom map," as Joseph Brodsky calls it, the epicenter of the developments that an Austrian corporal and failed watercolorist had initially set in train with the Munich Putsch of 1923, developments that, it is calmly suggested near the end of the novel, might be on the point of getting going again. Amid the destruction and the rebuilding, the novel, set in that same 1948, is looking for early signs of a pattern. Is the cycle of violence, exhaustion, and resentment about to get going again, as happened after World War I (as Koeppen, born in 1906, knew very well from personal experience); or is there some higher meaning in it, as Mr. Edwin the visiting poet-intellectual would have us believe; or is there perhaps no meaning at all, is it all random patternlessness, "pigeons on the grass," as Gertrude Stein wrote, or, as she is ignorantly—and rather well—paraphrased by Miss Burnett, the visiting Massachusetts schoolmistress: "the birds are here by chance, we are here by chance, and maybe the Nazis were here by chance, Hitler was a chance, his politics were a dreadful and stupid chance, maybe the world is a dreadful and stupid chance of God's, no one knows why we are here, the birds will fly off and we will walk on"?

Into this place and this time, caught as we have been almost entirely since—with the small exception of the 1990s, when the world briefly promised to be "unipolar" and history to have "ended" (with whatever different hellish consequences that might have had)—between hope and despair, divided in two or more armed camps, enduring or soliciting occupation of one kind or another, engaged in small-scale conflicts or preparing for the Big One, blithely or grimly minding our own business or sleepless with fear and disgust, Koeppen introduces his dramatis personae of Germans and Americans, of soldiers and civilians, whites and blacks, women and men, young and old, celebrities and nonentities, greater and lesser villains. (Who is "good" here? Maybe Hillegonda, maybe Washington, maybe Philipp? But nothing is made of it—it's not an interesting category. We are crooked timbers. We crash singly, we crash together, and we crash en masse.) Elsewhere, Koeppen writes of the same period and the same atmosphere:

In those days, war and peace hung in the balance, only we didn't know. We didn't hear about the cataclysm that threatened us until much later, in newspapers that hadn't yet been printed. Whoever could, ate well. We sipped our coffee and our brandy; we worked hard to earn money, and if the circumstances were favorable, we slept with one another.

Recollecting London at much the same time and in much the same condition, the painter Frank Auerbach has remarked: "There may be some feeling of that turmoil and freedom in those pictures that there was in London after the war. There was a curious feeling of liberty about because everybody who was living there had escaped death in some way. It was sexy in a way, this semi-destroyed London. There was a scavenging feeling of living in a ruined town." Metaphorically, or in microcosm—and, coincidentally or not, there is just such a scene in *Pigeons on the Grass*— we are standing at a set of lights—probably, come to think of it, a rather recent development for 1948—waiting for it to be "our turn." "Fates, conspire," says John Berryman.

After that, it is just a matter of threading and linking incident, cueing the pieces, plotting the entanglements, devising the superconducting phrases or tropes that will end a passage and—via a misunderstanding, it has been pointed out, in some different sense, almost homonymically—begin the next one. People live their lives, confront or ignore their difficulties, head off toward— another phrase from *Death in Rome*—"the next fraudulent little transaction." (The condition of civilization is too rudimentary for honesty to be a policy at all.) Some of these have more carry, more scale, more applicability, some less; but to the characters, and to the book, they are all there is, they all come alike, and they are all the same size. There is not a central plot and flanking subplots, a principal figure and subsidiaries; everything is in equal measure major, everyone gets their moment in the book's light and dark, its night and day. In their sum, they are the totality of existence. Everything teeters and winks, dangling its binary yes/no. It is in the balance. It will come about, or it won't. Fates, conspire: Frau Behrend wanting her coffee and her groceries; Ezra the stray dog; Alexander the "great actor" a little peace; Washington a life somewhere with Carla and their baby carried to term; Hillegonda salvation; Emilia a sale; Susanne a night to remember, or at least not to forget; the astonishing narcopathic Schnakenbach his magic formula; Josef the price of a drink; Mr. Edwin (who seems maybe three parts T. S. Eliot and one part Auden or Spender) the success of his talk and a piece of rough trade afterward. And so on, and so on.

The book is a panopticon (much like Dylan Thomas's *Under Milk Wood* from 1953), and it tells the stories of people in all their myriad circumstances wanting love, or maybe to be comforted. Koeppen is effortlessly all-seeing, all-knowing. Nothing human is alien, etc. Everyone is an Everyman (or Everywoman). Love and death stand at the exits. The future shyly intimates, the past unpredictably looms. Back in the day, Amerika Haus is a Fascist building, the American visitors are beguiled by the Nazis' favorite Badenweiler March, the Hofbräuhaus takes all comers, Odysseus Cotton and Susanne ("since she was Circe and the Sirens and maybe also Nausicaa") fall into their timeless, mythic roles. The book is full of repurposed locations, make-do-and-mend, second acts, moving parts, old situations, old signals.

*

A great mystery to me, and maybe what draws me to Koeppen more than anything else, is how he can write some sentences that are verbless stubs, and others that go on for dozens or scores of lines, and it all sounds like him, and it all is him. It is not style—because style changes, and he comes in different styles—but it is perhaps distance or tone, compounded from coldness, information, certitude, indifference, a certain propensity to label, to repeat, to talk up or slang down. Susanne, who in this book successively appears in a lesbian floor show, steals some perfume, possibly kills Josef, picks up, robs, and rescues Odysseus, is likened to a Homeric figure; the boy Ezra sees everything from the vantage point of his own personal fighter-bomber; Philipp, shy and ineffectual as he is, is indestructible; Emilia's groping pawnbroker Unverlacht is styled as a frog. The prose is sumptuous and cadenced, built to be read aloud; the sentences begin briskly, purposefully, then they are distractible, suddenly ferocious, briefly learned, encounter a mantra, loop and repeat, work themselves free. Then a run of nothing but curt blurts. It is as though Koeppen unites in himself the virtues of wildness and sleekness. These are not books the reader makes; they are written with uncommon decisiveness.

*

Koeppen was himself far too impulsive and unorthodox a character to have done such a thing on purpose, or to have planned it thus far in advance, but *Pigeons on the Grass* turned out to have been the first part of a novel trilogy. In 1953, he published a second part called *The Hothouse*, in 1954, the third called *Death in Rome*. All three books are set at the time they were written—they are all "live." Together, they are known as the "postwar trilogy." They were the last novels he wrote in his life. He lived another forty years and wrote no others. Now, you may say, nothing easier than to have written three novels and then call them a trilogy, or five and a quincunx, or ten and a decalogue. "What's that when it's at home?" my skeptical friend Paul Muldoon might quip; I would probably once have been dubious too. I don't like poems in parts, or paintings in parts either. But having long been inside all three books myself, I have to say I am positively in awe of their parallelisms and congruencies.

First, there are no major overlaps among the books: no shared characters, no internal references, nothing like that. The first is set in Munich, the second in Bonn, the small town on the Rhine that had recently pipped Frankfurt to become the capital of the Western half of the divided Germany, the third in the Eternal City, Rome. *Pigeons on the Grass* is a polynarrative, numerous turning cogs and wheels, like a piece of clockwork; *The Hothouse* is a monodrama, the story of a Social Democrat member of the Reichstag on the day of a big rearmament debate; *Death in Rome* brings the four members of a German family, two brothers-in-law and their respective sons (representatives of four great German trades: murder, bureaucracy, theology, and music), to an unintended reunion. The first book is impersonal (we guess Philipp is our point of identification, but we're not told, and he certainly has no privileges); the second is all personal, with Keetenheuve imagining his decisions and actions reflected in headlines, in italics; in the third, the artist figure, Siegfried Pfaffrath, is given a monopoly on the first person, but only in his sections. So, it's not the setting or the conception or the machinery of the books that are shared. What is it? First, it's that in each book a public event is trailed, and built up to, and takes place: in *Pigeons on the Grass*, it's Mr. Edwin's talk; in *The Hothouse*, Keetenheuve's speech in the debate; in *Death in Rome*, it's the concert of new serial music composed by Siegfried. Each book observes the unities of time and place; the first two happen within twenty-four hours, *Death in Rome* in the space of two days and a night.

But what I am talking about is more inward than that. Each novel seems to be rendered from the postwar atmosphere; it is as though impalpable things—as I say, atmosphere—have concretized themselves or been precipitated against cold glass. (Hence, in part, I think, the title *The Hothouse*.) Either that, or three different mosaics have been assembled—bricolaged—from the same rubble. The same ingredients make three dishes; the same breakage makes three different books. Everything is real, but we are having three go-arounds on a ghost train as well, which means they are metaphysical, and devices. A bewildering number of the same things, properties, Maguffins, recur in all three: Cars, big luxury cars. Showers—for Alexander, for Frost-Forestier, for Judejahn. Newspaper-criers and newspapers. Newspapers, magazines, and radio. Dictaphones or recorders for Philipp, for Frost-Forestier, for Siegfried. Onions. Beer. The books kill off and pair off, bring unexpected deaths and asymmetrical loves. Fast food: *Weisswürste* in one—"white veal sausages. Klett the hairdresser peeled the skin off the whitish filling with his fingers and popped it in his mouth. *Candy-I-call-my-sugar-candy*. Klett smacked his lips and grunted contentedly"—meatballs in another—"there was Helen, envied, reviled, eating her meatballs and mashed potatoes with the head of the working group on agricultural land degradation"—hamburgers in the third—"The waiter brought food. The men must have ordered it. Fried onions sizzled on large meat patties. They ate. They stuffed themselves. The men liked the onions. Judejahn liked the onions."

Cheese. Wine. Buildings. Tunnels and bridges. Cats and dogs. A room above the city, for sex. Ruins. Male prostitutes. Gangs of children. Tribades. The cinema. The German forest. History. Mythology. Literary references, ringing the horizon of all the books: Gertrude Stein (the title here), Kafka (the ending of *The Hothouse* from *The Judgment*), Thomas Mann (title and ending of *Death in Rome* from *Death in Venice*.) Fish. How much Edwin would have liked otherwise to discuss the *Physiologie-du-gout* with the chef and watch the pretty kitchen boys shucking gentle gold-gleaming fish."—"The matjes was a longtime inmate of salt barrels."—"They brought him a plate of sea creatures fried in oil and batter. He gulped them down; they tasted like fried earthworms to him, and he felt nauseated. He felt his heavy body turning into worms, he felt his guts squirming with putrescence, and in order to fight off his disintegration, and in spite of his nausea, he polished off everything on the plate." These things—and I have no doubt there are dozens of others—are deliberately deployed. They have a deteriorating tendency that suggests forward planning—I don't know how Koeppen did it. He had never been to Rome before a chance invitation in 1954; his Bonn book he wrote in Stuttgart. They don't deplete or detract from the realism of the books, they are merely a further formal challenge for the author, and a complicating, delaying, enriching thing for the reader. After all, everything that resists limits extends the life of a book, toward infinity, where it belongs.

*

I translated *Death in Rome* in 1992, *The Hothouse* ten years later. I translated earlier Koeppen (*A Sad Affair*) and later Koeppen (*Youth*). In 1994 I was lucky enough to spend a rather ghostly evening with the man himself in his apartment on Widenmayer Strasse overlooking the Isar and at his local Italian. It was always my dream to translate all three of his principal novels, and to have them all available at the same time, published together in one volume, or in three. In the summer of 2004, in Feldafing outside Munich (where the middle-aged Koeppen, a tenant of the Ulrichs, had courted the young Marion among the ruins and various Allied headquarters), I translated *Pigeons on the Grass*. I thought I owed it to the circumstances. I did it for myself, or on spec, or to keep my hand in. I would like to thank my *gute Fee* Barbara Epler of New Directions for publishing it now, and on this occasion to pay tribute to the various other publishers of Koeppen in English over the past thirty-odd years: Daniel Halpern of Ecco (who offered) and Bob Weil of Norton who did; Alexandra Pringle of Hamish Hamilton and Paul Keegan at Penguin; Neil Belton and George Miller from Granta; and John O'Brien of Dalkey Archive. Last and far from least, I'd like to express my gratitude to David Ward, whose (perfectly good) translation of *Pigeons on the Grass* appeared with Holmes & Meier in 1988, for so graciously allowing the present book to appear.

MICHAEL HOFMANN
HAMBURG, 2019

Pigeons on the Grass

Planes were over the city, birds of ill omen. The noise of their engines was thunder, was hail, was storm. Storm, hail, and thunder, every day, every night, landing and takeoff, death exercises, a hollow roar, a flinch, a tremor of memory in the ruins. For the moment, the bomb bays of the planes were still empty. The soothsayers smiled. No one looked up at the sky.

Oil out of the arteries of earth, stone-oil, "petr/-oleum," jellyfish blood, deposits of dinosaur lard, lizard carapaces, the green of giant fern forests, pewter grass from the time before *homo sap.*, the buried inheritance guarded by dwarfs, by evil, greedy mages, the mythical devil's hoard: it was lugged up to the light of day, it was put to use. The newspapers, what did the newspapers say? *War over Oil, Conflict Escalates, The Popular Will, Oil for the Natives, The Fleet Running out of Oil, Attack on the Pipeline, Troops Guard Derricks, Shah to Wed, Intrigues Surround Peacock Throne, Shadowy Russian Presence, Aircraft Carriers in the Gulf.* It was oil that kept the planes in the sky, that kept the presses in their state of breathless excitement, it worried the people, and with moderate explosions it drove the newspaper deliverymen's puttering mopeds. With clammy hands, depressed, cursing, wind-rattled, rain-soaked, beer-dulled, tobacco-seared, overnighted, nightmare-tormented, on their skin still the whiff of their mate or their other half, feeling the tear in the shoulder, the rheumatism in the knee, the vendors took receipt of the latest editions. It was a cold spring. The news did nothing to make it any warmer. *Tension, Conflict,* people lived in the forcefield of tension, Eastern world/Western world, they lived on the join, on the crack as it might be, time was precious, there was a break in hostilities for the time being, they had barely had a moment to draw breath, and already they were rearming, the armaments drove up the cost of living, armaments clouded joy, here as there people were stockpiling gunpowder to blow the planet to smithereens, *Atom Tests in New Mexico, Atom Plants in the Urals*, they drilled boreholes in the patched-up masonry of the bridges, they spoke of rebuilding and made plans for demolition, they allowed further cracks to creep into what was already fissured: Germany was broken in two. The newspaper smelled of overheated machinery, of grim news, violent death, wrong verdicts, cynical bankruptcies, of lies and chains and squalor. The soiled papers stuck together, as though they had oozed fear. The headlines shrilled: *Eisenhower Visits Troops in Federal Republic, Calls for Increased Defense Contributions, Adenauer Comes Out against Neutrality, Conference Reaches Impasse, Displaced Persons Bring Charges, Millions of Slave-Laborers, Germany to Offer Most Potential for Future Forces Levy.* The color magazines were stuffed with the memoirs of brave airmen and generals, the confessions of decent fellow travelers, the protocols of heroes, the upright, the honest, the innocent, the bewildered, the outwitted. Over collars marked with leaf of oak and cross of iron, they glared back off the kiosk walls. Were they trying to shift copies for the prints, or were they recruiting for a new army? The airmen who were droning up above, they belonged to the other lot.

The Archduke was getting dressed, he was being assembled. Here a medal, there a ribbon, a cross, a glittering star, the webwork of fate, chains of power, the shiny epaulets, the silver dress belt, the golden fleece, order of the Toison de Oro, Aureum Vellus, the lambskin on flint, given to the praise and glory of the Savior, of the Virgin Mary and Saint Andrew and to the protection and promotion of the Christian faith and the Holy Catholic Church, for virtue and public morality. Alexander was sweating. He felt nauseous. The high collar, the tinsel, all that Christmas tree crap tormented and constricted him. His dresser was scrabbling around at his feet. He was putting the Archduke's spurs on. What was a dresser compared to the highly polished top boots of an archduke? An ant, a groveling ant. The electric light in this dressing room, this plywood cabin they had dared offer Alexander, was at odds with the dawn. What a morning! Alexander's face was whey-pale under the makeup; it was a curdled milk face. Brandy and wine and lack of sleep were setting up their toxic ferment in Alexander's bloodstream; they pounded against his skull from within. Alexander had had an early call. The titaness was still abed, Messalina, his wife, the mare, as they called her in the bars. Alexander loved his wife; when he thought of the way he loved Messalina, then his marriage became a thing of beauty. Messalina slept, the puffy face, the smudged mascara, the eyelids as though blackened by punches, the coarse-pored skin, a cabbie's complexion ravaged by drink. But what a personality! Alexander bent down over the personality. He fell to his knees, bent down over the sleeping Gorgon, kissed the skewed mouth, breathed in the smell of drink issuing like a double distillation from the lips: "Wass matter? You going? Oh, leave me alone! I feel so ill!" That was what she gave him of herself. On his way to the bathroom, he trod on some broken glass. On the sofa, Alfredo, the little painter, was asleep, tousled, cute and curled up, exhaustion and disappointment etched in her face, crows' feet round her closed eyes, inspiring sympathy. When she was awake, Alfredo was funny, a torch that burned swiftly down; gurgling, joking, a raconteuse, sharp tongued, entertaining. The only person he knew who could make him laugh. What was it

5

the Mexicans called lesbians? Tortillas, tortilleras, something to do with those maize-pancakes, must be because they were flat chested and dried out. Alexander couldn't remember anymore. Too bad! It might have come in handy. In the bathroom stood the girl he had picked up, whom he had seduced with his fame, with that wry smile that everyone knew. Headlines in the film magazines: *Alexander to Play Archduke in New German Superproduction, The Archduke and the Fisher Maid*, well, he had fished her up, his little dish. What was her name again? Susanne! Susannah at her bath. But dressed already. Cheap off-the-rack dress. Rubbed her laddered stockings with soap. Had splashed herself with his wife's Guerlain. Was feeling grumpy. Mouthy. They always were, afterward. "Well, how was I?" He didn't know what to say. He was embarrassed. "Asshole!" That was it. They were after him. Alexander, the great lover! Oh, sure. And now he'd better have a shower. The car outside was honking like crazy. They couldn't do without him. Who else was a draw? Apart from him. *Alexander, the Archduke in love.* People were fed up; fed up with the times, fed up with the ruins; they didn't want to see their fears and worries, their day-to-day existence, their misery reflected back to them. Alexander stripped off his pajamas. The girl Susanne took in his various sagging flesh with disappointment and curiosity and malice. He thought: Go on, take a good look, tell them anything you like, they'll never believe you, you know they idolize me.— He gasped. The cold spray of the shower lashed his loose skin. They were honking again, downstairs. They were in a hurry, they needed their Archduke. There was a girl crying in the apartment, Hillegonda, Alexander's little daughter. She was crying, "Emmi!" Was she crying for help? Fear, desperation, abandonment were all to be heard in that cry. Alexander thought: I ought to make time for her, I ought to look in on her, she's been so peaky lately.— He called out: "Hille, are you awake already?" Why was she awake so early? He puffed and gasped the question into his towel. The little girl fell silent, or else her voice was drowned out by the furious car horn. Alexander was driven to the studio. He was dressed. He was booted and spurred. He stood before the camera. The lights went up. The medals sparkled in the light of the thousand candlepower bulbs. The screen idol turned it on. They were shooting the Archduke, *A German Superproduction*.

The bells sounded for early morning Mass. *Can-you-hear-the-bells-ringing*? Teddy bears listened, dolls listened, a stuffed elephant on red wheels listened, Snow White and Ferdinand the Bull on the patterned wallpaper listened to the sad song that Emmi, the nanny, sang in a plaintive, drawn-out way, as she scrubbed the thin body of her charge with a coarse brush. Hillegonda thought: Emmi, you're hurting me, Emmi, you're scratching me, Emmi, you're pinching me, Emmi, your nail file's digging into me, but she didn't dare tell her nanny, a rough country girl, in whose wide face simple peasant piety had congealed into something more unpleasant, that she was being hurt, and that she was suffering. The song of the nanny, the *can-you-hear-the-bells-ringing*, was a continual admonition that meant: don't complain, don't ask, don't be happy, don't laugh, don't play, don't dillydally, make use of your time, because we are all doomed to die. Hillegonda would rather still have been asleep. She would rather still have been dreaming. Or, failing that, she would have liked to play with her dolls, but Emmi said: "How can you think of playing, when God's calling you!" Hillegonda's parents were wicked people. Emmi said so. So she had to do penance for the sins of her parents. That was how the day began for her. With church. The streetcar braked for a young dog. The dog was scruffy and collarless, a stray. The nanny gripped Hillegonda's little hand. It was no friendly, supportive grip; it was the firm and implacable hold of the warder. Hillegonda watched the little stray amble off. She would sooner have followed it wherever it was going than gone to church with her nanny. Hillegonda pressed her knees together, fear of Emmi, fear of the church, fear of God, all squeezed her little heart; she dawdled, she made Emmi pull her to lengthen the journey, but the warder's hand pulled her on. It was still so early. It was still so cold. So early, and already Hillegonda was on her way to God. Churches have portals of stout planks, heavy wood, iron frames, and copper bolts. Is God scared as well? Or is God trapped too? The nanny gripped the curved handle and opened the door a crack. You squeezed in to see God. He had a smell of Christmas and candles. Was the miracle in preparation here, the terrible, predicted wonder, the forgiveness of sins, and the acquittal of her parents? Actors' child, thought the nanny. Her bloodless lips, the lips of an ascetic in a peasant face, drew a thin line for all eternity. Emmi, I'm scared, thought the girl. Emmi, the church is so big, Emmi, the walls are going to collapse, Emmi, I don't like you anymore, Emmi, dear Emmi, Emmi, I hate you!— The nanny splashed holy water on the trembling girl. A man pushed through the crack in the door after them. Fifty years of toil and anxiety, and now he had the face of a persecuted rat. He had lived through two wars. Two yellow teeth moldered behind his mumbling lips; he was embroiled in an unending conversation; he was talking to himself; who else would listen? Hillegonda followed her nanny on tiptoe. The pillars were gloomy, the masonry was scarred with shrapnel. A chill breath, as from a grave, wafted over the little girl. "Emmi, don't leave me, Emmi, Hillegonda's frightened, nice Emmi, naughty Emmi, kind Emmi," prayed the child. Take the child to the Lord, the Lord punishes to the third and fourth generation, thought the nanny. The faithful were kneeling. In that lofty space they looked like fretful mice. The priest read out the Mass.

The transubstantiation. The little bell clanged. God-forgive-us. The priest shivered. Transubstantiation! The power bestowed upon the church and her servants. Vain dream of the alchemists. Fanatics and swindlers. Men of learning. Inventors. Laboratories in England, in America, in Russia. Devastation. Einstein. A peek into God's kitchen. The wise men of Göttingen. Photograph of the atom: ten billionfold magnification. The sober priest was suffering. The whispering of his congregation of mice trickled over him like sand. Sand of the grave, not sand of the Holy Sepulcher, sand of the desert, desert mass, sermon in the wilderness. Mother Mary pray for us. The mice crossed themselves.

Philipp left the hotel where he had, barely sleeping, spent the night, the Hotel Lamb in a little lane in the old town. He had lain awake on the hard mattress, the bed of commercial travelers, the flowerless meadow of rushed couplings. Philipp had given himself to despair, which was a sin. Fate had driven him into an impasse. The wings of the Fates beat against the window with the wind and the rain. The hotel was a new building; the fixtures were fresh out of the factory, glossed wood, clean, hygienic, shoddy, and cheap. The curtains, too short, thin, and narrow to exclude the noise and the light of the street, were printed with a Bauhaus pattern. At regular intervals, a neon sign flashed into the room, intended to lure visitors into a gaming club over the way: a four-leaf clover unfolded itself over Philipp and vanished again. Outside could be heard the cursing of gamblers who had lost their money. Drunks staggered out of the Bräuhaus. They pissed against the walls and sang "The Infantry the Infantry," dismissed, defeated conquerors. There was a continual coming and going on the hotel steps. The hotel was a fiendish hive, and everyone in its hell was condemned to sleeplessness. Behind the drafty walls, there was muttering, belching, the flushing of toilets. Afterward, the moon managed to break through the clouds, gentle Luna, a rigor mortis.

The hotel manager asked him: "Will you be staying another night?" He asked it crudely, and his cold eyes, deathly bitter in the smooth rancid fat of appeased greed, of quenched thirst, lusts curdled in the matrimonial bed, took in Philipp distrustfully. Philipp had come to the hotel the night before without any luggage. It had been raining. He had a damp umbrella, and apart from his damp umbrella nothing else. Would he be staying another night? He didn't know. He said: "Yes." "I'll pay for two nights," he said. The cold, deathly bitter eyes relinquished him. "It says here you live in the Fuchsstrasse," said the manager. He looked at Philipp's check-in form. What's it to him, thought Philipp, what's it to him, so long as he gets his money.— He said: "Yes, I'm having my apartment painted." It was a laughable story. Surely no one could fail to realize it was a story. He will think I'm a fugitive, he will think there's something amiss, he will think they're after me.

It had stopped raining. Philipp left the Bräuhausgasse and stepped onto the Böttcherplatz. He hesitated outside the main entrance to the Bräuhaus, a closed maw in the morning, reeking of vomit. On the opposite side of the square was the Café Schön, the American Negro soldiers' club. The curtains behind the large plate glass windows were drawn. The chairs were on the tables. Two women were swilling the filth of the past night onto the street. Two old men were sweeping the square. They swept up beermats, paper streamers, the silly paper hats of the drinkers, crumpled cigarette packets, and popped balloons. There was a tide of dirt that was advancing on Philipp with every jab of the men's brooms. Philipp found himself enveloped by the dust and stink of the night, the rotted detritus of pleasure.

Frau Behrend had made herself comfortable. A log was crackling in the stove. The janitor's daughter brought the milk. The girl was overnighted and hungry. She was hungry for life, the way it appeared in the movies, she was a princess who had fallen victim to a curse, forced to do labor. She was waiting for the messiah, the fanfare of the prince come to the rescue, the millionaire's son in his sports car, the tailcoated dancer in the cocktail bar, the technical genius, the futuristic builder, the victor by knockout over those enemies of progress who had stayed behind, the youthful Siegfried. She was narrow chested, had rickety limbs, a scar on her belly, and pinched lips. She felt exploited. In a whisper through pinched lips she said: "Your milk, Frau Obermusikmeister."

Whispered or shouted, the form of address evoked the memory of beautiful days. The music master strode erect through the city at the head of the regiment. The march rang out from brass and calfskin. Cymbals hissed. Flag aloft. Goose-stepping. Arms swinging. Herr Behrend's muscles strained against the cloth of his tight uniform. The army band in the bandstand! The master was conducting the *Freischütz*. Checked by his extended baton, Carl Maria von Weber's romantic sounds rose in a muffled pianissimo to the tops of the trees. Frau Behrend's bosom rose and fell like waves at sea, at the garden table. Her hands in their lace gloves rested on the checkered tablecloth. For the duration of this one hour of culture, Frau Behrend saw herself adopted in the circle of the regimental ladies. Lyre and sword, Orpheus and Mars became sworn brothers. The Frau Major kindly shared what she had brought with her, the cake she had baked, the sandwich cake with three varieties of jam, pushed into the oven, while the Major sat his horse, supervised the barrack yard, the left-right march, and the drum roll of the Wolfsschlucht.

Couldn't they leave us in peace? Frau Behrend hadn't wanted

any war. War was a plague on the men. Beethoven's severe, pale death mask scanned the tiny garret. A bronze-bearded and beret-wearing Wagner wobbled in dudgeon on a stack of classic piano tunes, the yellowing leftovers of the music master, who in some Führer-occupied and Führer-lost part of Europe had found favor in some painted trull and was now playing "When I Get to Alabama" in some godforsaken dive, patronized by Negroes and harlots.

In fact, he never made it to Alabama. He stayed in the country. The lawless times were over, the times announced *Gruppenführer Found as Rabbi in Palestine, Former Hairdresser Director of Women's Clinic*. The participants had been rounded up; they were behind bars, doing time, far too little time: concentration campers, victims, deserters, con men. There were once again judges in Germany. The music master was paying for the garret, he was paying for the log on the fire, the milk in the bottle, the coffee in the pot. He paid it out of the wages of sinful Alabama. A tribute to decency and honor! What's the good of it? Everything's getting dearer, and once again you need roundabout ways to get at the good things of life. Frau Behrend drank Maxwell House coffee. She bought it at the Jew's. At the Jew's—those were the dark-haired people who spoke hardly any German, undesirables, aliens, flotsam, the ones who looked at you balefully and accusingly out of their dark, liquid, night-threaded eyes, who probably wanted to broach the topics of gas with you and mass graves, and execution sites at dawn, creditors, survivors, who could think of nothing better to do with their saved lives than set up booths and drafty stalls and sell you black market goods on the rubble squares of the bombed-out cities (why bombed? my God, why were we beaten? what sin were we guilty of? my home in Würzburg, five rooms on a south-facing slope, view over the city, view across the valley, the glittering Main, morning sun on the veranda, *The Führer Pays a Call on the Duce*, my God, why?). "They don't leave us anything," said the manageress of the emporium, "nothing, they want to wipe us out." The Yanks were living in the manageress's villa. They had confiscated it and had been living there for four years now. They passed it along, one lot to the next. They slept in the double bed of flamed birch, in the wedding present bedroom. They sat on the rustic chairs in the "Germania" living room, surrounded by the magnificence of the 1880s, parked their feet on the table, eating their cans of corned beef, their conveyor belt diet, *Chicago Processes a Thousand Head of Oxen per Minute*, as their press liked to crow. Down in the garden played the foreign children, paper-bag-blue, egg-yolk-yellow, flame-red, dressed like clowns, seven-year-old girls painted their lips like prostitutes, their mothers slopped around in pants, the bottoms rolled up, gypsies, frivolous people. The coffee in the emporium, tax on it and duty, was moldering away. Frau Behrend nodded. She never forgot the respect she owed the manageress, the fear she had got used to in the hard school of the voucher period, *order for sixty-two and a half grams of soft cheese*. And now you could get everything again. At least in this sector. Though who could afford it? *Forty marks allowance*. Savings honored at a rate of 6 percent, and the remaining 94 written on the wind. Charity began at home. The world was hard. A world of soldiers, for soldiers. Soldiers knew no half measures. Proved themselves. The weights were accurate once more. How long for? There was a run on sugar in the shops. In England, meanwhile, they didn't have meat. Where is the victor, that I may bestow on him his wreath? *Bacon* was their word for speck; *ham* is what they called Schinken. Fatty the smoked wares in the window display of Schleck the slaughterman. "Lean, if you have any." The long knife parted the yellowy-white fat from the reddish fibers at the core. Where is the victor, that I may bestow on him his wreath? The Yanks were rich. Their automobiles glided along like ships, like Columbus's caravels back from the New World. We discovered their country for them. We populated their country for them. Solidarity among the white people. It was nice to belong to the rich. Relatives sending you parcels. Frau Behrend opened the romance she had been browsing in last night, before going to sleep. An exciting story, a true fiction: *Destiny Reaches for Hannelore*. Frau Behrend wanted to know what happened next. The three-color title page showed the picture of a young woman, good, innocent, touching, and in the background were the clustered villains, tunneling away like destiny's voles. Life was full of perils, the way of decency and respectability full of holes. It wasn't just Hannelore that destiny was reaching for. But in the last chapter, the good will prevail.

Philipp no longer understood the functioning of time. The present moment was like a tableau vivant, the silly subject for a scene, a plaster cast of existence, acrid smoke fluttered around it like a mocking arabesque, and Philipp was a little boy in his sailor suit, with the legend s. m. schiff grille on his hatband, and he was in a small town, sitting on a chair in the Germania Hall, and the ladies of the Luisenbund were up on stage performing scenes from the history of the fatherland against a forest backdrop, Germania and her children, that went over well in those days, or perhaps people pretended to like it, the rector's daughter held the cauldron of burning pitch that was probably meant to give the scene some element of ceremony, durability, timelessness. The rector's daughter was long dead. Eva, he had used to throw burrs in her hair. The boys were dead, all the ones who had sat with him on the chairs of the Germania Hall. The town like so many of the towns in the East was a dead town, a town somewhere in Masuria, but you couldn't go to the station and buy a ticket there anymore. The place was destroyed. Curious: the streets were deserted. The classrooms in the gymnasium were silent and empty. Crows built their nests in the windows. He used to dream about it, dreaming through his lessons: how life had died in the town, how the houses were empty, and the streets, and the market was silent and empty, and he, the only survivor, had got into one of the cars left abandoned on the side of the road, and driven through the dead town. The backdrop from his dream had appeared in life, but Philipp wasn't acting in front of it anymore. Did it hurt when he thought of the dead, the dead places, the buried companions? No. Sensibility stiffened as if confronted by the tableaux vivants of the Luisenbund, the notion was pompous and sad and somehow repugnant, a Siegesallee made from laurel stencils and stucco, but more than anything it was boring. At the same time, time that appeared to be standing still was racing by, and Now was a moment ago, this time of seemingly unending duration flew by, if you thought of time as the sum of all the days there had ever been, the alternation of light and dark that is given us on Earth, it was like the wind, it was both something and nothing, it could be measured if you knew how, but even then no one could explain what he was measuring, it flowed round the skin, formed a man, and fled away again, ungraspable, fled whither? whence? And then, to make matters worse, he, Philipp, was standing outside this process of time, not strictly speaking expelled from it, but summoned to watch, an honorable position it appeared, because he had been entrusted with keeping watch over everything, but then the silly thing was that it had made him dizzy, and he was incapable of watching, of observing anything, and ended up seeing nothing but a sea surge in which a few dates were lit up like signals, no longer natural signals, of course, but artfully and artificially set-up buoys in the sea of time, swaying memorials to mankind on the untamed waves, but from time to time the sea would freeze, and the waters of infinity would spew up a frozen image for people to laugh to scorn.

The Engellichtspiele allows its clients to flee the light of day early, in the a.m. *The Last of the Bandits* is a hit film. The owner of the cinema wires the attendance figures to the distributor. House record figures, arithmetical prestidigitation as once in the rubric *gross tonnage sunk.* Wiggerl, Schorsch, Bene, Kare, and Sepp stood under the loudspeakers, under the torrent of words, victory, and fanfares, little Hitler Youths, scout troops, brown shirt, shorts, brown thighs. They shook their collecting tins, roused the pennies, rattled their tin insignia. "For the Winterhilfe! For the Front! For the Führer!" At night, the sirens yowled. The ack-ack guns were silent. Now the fighters were going to pick a fight. Jewels in the form of an Iron Cross. Bombs. Lights flickering. Get your head down! Water surged in the cellar pipes. Next door, everybody drowned. Schorsch, Bene, Kare, and Sepp are watching the last of the bandits. They jam their bony behinds deep into the hollowed-out, farty cinema seats. They don't have apprenticeships, and they don't have jobs. They don't have money, but they've got a mark for the bandit show; somehow they got hold of it, don't ask them how. They're skipping trade school, because they don't have any trade, or the trades they know aren't those that are taught at school, but on street corners, in the doorways of the money changers, in the alleyways of the ladies, in the avenues of friends in the shadow of the court, the trade of nimble fingers that take without giving, the handiwork of stout fists for smashing and hitting, and the soft allure, the profession of melting glances, swinging hips, jiggling asses. Wiggerl is away overseas, with the Legion, with the Annamites in the jungle, with the snakes and lianas, the crumbling temples, or with the Frenchies in their fort, with floozies and wine in Saigon, in barrack-reek, in the punishment cell in the casemates, lizards sunning themselves. Whatever. Wiggerl is fighting. He sings: *Raise-high-the-flag*. He falls. *The soldier's death is the best death*. Heard it so many times, dinned into you in childhood, the example of fathers and older brothers, mothers comforted by their tears, the phrase is never forgotten. Now, Schorsch, Bene, Kare, and Sepp are waiting for the drummer. They're waiting in the dark cinema. The last of the bandits. They're prepared; prepared to obey, prepared to fight, prepared to die. They don't need a god to summon them, a poster on the walls will do the trick, a rousing tune, a copyrighted bit of facial hair, no smiling priest, the robotic mask of stamped tin, a sub-average face, no promise in the eyes, empty waters, blank mirrors showing always only you, Caliban, from whom the geniuses turned away, the synthetic ratcatcher, and his call: prove yourselves, blood, pain, and death, I will lead you to yourself, Caliban, you have no need to be ashamed of being a monster. The cinema is intact; the cash streams into the cash register. The town hall is intact; the entertainment tax is entered on the ledgers. The town is still growing.

The town is growing. *Stop on incomers lifted*. They flow back, a tide that had ebbed away, dribbled into the countryside, into the farmers' parlors, when the cities were burning, when the asphalt melted on the road they walked every day, becoming the waters of Styx, scorching and singeing, where the little shoes trotted to school, where they walked as bride and groom, the stones of home quaked, and then they squatted in villages, lost their household bits and pieces, lost the nest where their brood had been born, lost the things they had always kept, the what-you-were, the youth stashed away in the bottom drawer, a boyhood snapshot, a school class, a drowned friend, a letter's fading script, Farewell, then, Fritz, Goodbye, Marie, a poem, did I compose it?—

The body of the doctor—small delicate taut, well-drilled in exercises of athleticism and agility—lay on the wax cloth–covered table, and from a vein in his arm the blood flowed to another human being not visible and not near, no receiver of the new life thanked the donor with a warm glance, Dr. Behude was an abstract sort of Samaritan, his blood was transformed into a number, a chemical formula, expressed in the sign language of mathematics, it flowed into a Kilner jar where it was labeled, raspberry syrup or strawberry jam, the blood group was on the label, the juice was sterilized, and the preserves were ready to be dispatched, through the air, over the water, anywhere there happened to be a battlefield, and you could find those if you looked, an erstwhile harmless landscape, nature with her changing seasons, a plowed field with seed and harvest, where men had marched and driven and flown for the purpose of killing and maiming one another. There they lay all pale on stretchers, the Red Cross banner fluttering in a strange wind, reminding them of the ambulances hurrying with sirens wailing through the streets of the traffic-choked city, the city they had come from, the tetanus jab burned, and then Dr. Behude's good blood was pumped into their lacerated bodies. Dr. Behude was paid ten marks a pop. The money was paid in cash at the clinic cash desk. The young doctors, who had already carved and sawed and injected and stitched together the men of World War II, and were now stuck in unpaid traineeships and assistantships, forced to realize that they were redundant and far too many, far too many war doctors, they too lined up to sell their blood, it was the only thing they had to sell. For his part, Dr. Behude also needed the ten marks, but that, money for blood, wasn't the only thing that drew him to the transaction. Dr. Behude was chastening himself. It was a kind of monastic mortification to which he liked to subject himself, and the blood, like the weights, the morning runs, the knee bends, the breathing exercises, represented an effort to produce an equilibrium between the strengths and the demands of the body on the one hand and the soul on the other. While he lay on the cool oilcloth transfusion table, Dr. Behude analyzed himself. He wasn't a giver, a charitable man; the blood left him, became a medical product like other medical products, it could be shipped, traded, could be used in the saving of lives, none of it touched Dr. Behude; he was cleansing himself, preparing himself. Before long, the rooms of his practice would be filled with needy people wanting to tap him for courage and strength to go on. The half-crazed horde loves Dr. Behude and they beat a path to his door, the neurotics, the liars who don't know why they are liars, the impotents, the queers, the pedophiles who leer at children, follow short skirts, bare legs, the writers who have fallen between all kinds of stools, the painters for whom the colors of life are paid out in geometrical stripes, the actors who choke on dead words, great Pan was dead, dead a second time, they all came, all those who needed their complexes as they needed their daily bread, the frightened and the incompetent, not even competent to sign up with a medical practitioner, or to pay a bill.—

They had got away with their lives, a useless existence, they were squatting bitterly in tiny hamlets in woods and fields, in huts and farms, the smoke cleared, they listened to the mechanical diggers reaching into the rubble, listened from a distance, shut out of Nineveh, of Babylon, of Sodom, of their beloved cities, the great warming metropolises, fugitives condemned to a continuing summer in the country, penniless trippers, looked at askance by the locals, frantic with nostalgia for the stones of home. They returned home, the barriers were raised, the hated decree banning movement to the cities fell, their exile was at an end, and they streamed back, they flooded in, the level of the city rose *City the Focus of Housing Shortage*. They were back at home, they settled down, they felt each other up, took advantage of each other, traded, worked, built, founded, sired, sat in the old bar, breathed the familiar fug, eyed the district, the coupling zone, the new kids on the asphalt streets, the laughter and squabbling and radio of the neighbors, they died in the municipal hospital, were driven out by the funeral institute, were put in the ground at the southeast corner of things, surrounded by the dinging of the streetcars, the vapor of petrol, happy to be home. *Superbombers stationed in Europe.*

Odysseus Cotton walked out of the station. A little suitcase dangled from the swaying arm, from the brown hand. Odysseus Cotton was not alone. A voice accompanied him. From the suitcase came a voice, mild, warm, soft, a low voice, sighing breaths, a puff of velvet, hot skin under an old ripped auto blanket in a corrugated tin shack, shouts, noise of bullfrogs, night on the Mississippi. Judge Lynch rides over the land, the day of Gettysburg, Lincoln takes Richmond, forgotten the slave ship, durable the brand in the flesh, Africa, lost earth, the density of the jungles, voice of a negress. The voice was singing *Night-and-day*, and with its sound it was protecting, insulating the suitcase carrier from the square in front of the station, it enveloped him like the limbs of a lover, kept him warm when he was in foreign lands, covered him with a canopy. Odysseus stood there irresolutely. He surveyed taxi ranks, looked across to the Rohn department store, saw children, women, men, who were they, the Germans? what did they think? how did they dream and love? were they enemies? friends?

The heavy door of the telephone booth clanged shut behind Philipp. The glass shielded him from the bustle outside the station, the noise was just a murmur in the background, the traffic a play of shadows on the ripple-patterned walls. Philipp still wasn't sure what to do with his day. The hour gaped. He felt like one of the empty packages that the broom has swept up with the trash, useless and now without a role. What role, anyway? Had he had a role, had he left his role, and was that possible, granted there was such a thing as a role anyway, could you leave your role? *The century in the stars, the weekly horoscope, Truman's and Stalin's fortunes.* He could have gone home. He could have gone back to the Fuchsstrasse. Spring was on the way. Weeds were flowering in the villa's neglected garden. Home? a sort of leaky shelter: maybe Emilia would have calmed down overnight. The doors would have been scuffed, holes punched in the plaster, china smashed. Exhausted by her tantrum, tired after her dreams, battered by her fear, Emilia lay on the pink heirloom bed, the deathbed of her grandam, who had lived a fine life, Heringsdorf, Paris, Nice, on the gold standard and in the glory of the Actual Privy Commercial Councilor's title. The dogs, the cats, the parrot, jealous enemies of one another, but united in a common front against Philipp, a phalanx of treacherous looks, in the way that everything in that house hated him, his wife's relatives, her fellow inheritors, the crumbling walls, the scraped parquet, the gurgling, wheezing pipes of the broken-down heating and the decrepit tubs, the pets occupied the furniture like high ground in battle, and watched over their mistress's sleep through half-open eyes, the sleep of the victim to whom they were chained, and whom they guarded. Philipp rang Dr. Behude. Nothing! The psychiatrist was not yet back at his practice. Philipp had no great expectations of a meeting with Dr. Behude, no diagnosis, no illumination, neither encouragement nor a return of self-confidence, but it had become a habit with him to go to the nerve doctor, to lie down in the darkened treatment room, and give his thoughts free rein, a stream of pictures came over him in Dr. Behude's presence, a kaleidoscopic shuffling of places and times, while the soul-therapist did what he could with his gentle, sleep-inducing voice, to free him from guilt and remorse. In the treatment room at the hospital, Dr. Behude buttoned up his shirt. His face looked pale in the white-framed mirror on the wall. His eyes, which were said to have hypnotic force, were dull, tired, and slightly inflamed. One hundred cubic centimeters of his blood were cooling in the hospital fridge.

Night-and-day. Odysseus Cotton laughed. He was happy. He swung his little case. He bared his strong white teeth. He was confident. The day was ahead of him. A day that offered itself equally to all. On the station forecourt waited Josef the porter. His red porter's cap sat straight and stern across his bald head. What was it that had bent Josef's back? The suitcases of travelers, the luggage of decades, half a century of bread in the sweat of his brow, Adam's curse, marches in jackboots, his rifle over his shoulder, his equipment belt, the sack of hand grenades, the heavy helmet, the heavy killing. Verdun, the forest of Argonnes, Chemin-des-Dames, he'd got through it all unscathed, then back to suitcases, heavily accoutered travelers, taking tourists to the Alpine station, taking tourists to hotels, to the Olympic games, the world's youth, and then more flags, more marching, he was toting officers' baggage, his sons left never to return, the world's youth, sirens, the old woman died, mother of his children gobbled up in the war, the Americans arrived with their colored bags, their canvas caryalls, their light luggage, the cigarette currency, the new mark, savings blown away like chaff, seventy years almost up and what was left? The position outside the station, the number on his cap. His body was shriveled up, but his eyes still twinkled alertly behind his steel-framed glasses, laughter lines radiated out from the corners of his eyes, vanished into the veteran gray, the suntanned and beery redness of his face. Colleagues took the place of his family. They left Papa the cushy jobs that sometimes came along in between the heavy carrying, a letter to be posted, flowers to be bought, a lady's handbag to be carried. Josef picked up such commissions humbly, but also with guile. He understood people. He knew how to get on the right side of them. Occasionally, a bag would be given to him to carry when that hadn't been the intention. He put his faith in the day. He spotted Odysseus Cotton. He eyed the little case from where the music played. He said: "You, mister, I carry." He didn't let the singing bother him that built up the shelter around Odysseus, he reached out his hand for the strange world, the *Night-and-day* world, pushed the brown hand away from the handle, pushed himself, small, modest, assertive, friendly, against the dark giant, King Kong, who loomed above him, trackless the never logged, ancient forests. Josef was not charmed or melted by the voice, voice of the broad, sluggish, warm river, voice of being woven in, voice of the mysterious night. Like logs on the river, one went on to the other; totemic animals round the kraal, a taboo round the deserter from the tribe, Josef felt neither pleasure nor dismay, nothing tempted, nothing frightened him away: no libido, Odysseus stood in no affective relation to Josef, Josef was no Oedipal surrogate to Odysseus, love and hate were not involved, Josef sensed generosity, he pushed himself forward gently and insistently, he saw a snack, saw a beer, *Night-and-day*—

The parrot squawked, a lovebird, Kama, the god of love, comes riding on a parrot, the tales from the parrot book, fantastic and obscene, the little girl stole them down from her father's bookshelf, concealed them under her bed, the parrot in ancient representations of the Holy Family, symbolizing the immaculate conception, it was a plump rosella, plump as a successful old actress, red, yellow, agave green, steel blue its feathers, its plumage that it shook crossly, freedom was forgotten, a dream, forgotten, no longer true, the bird cawed, cawed not for freedom but for light, asked for the blinds to be pulled up, the heavy curtains to be drawn aside, the rending of the dark room, the end of the artificially prolonged night. The dogs and cats also grew restless. They leaped onto the sleeper's bed, squabbled, tugged at the worn silk of the coverlet, and down like snow whirled unseen in the darkness in the room. Emilia still lay under the cover of night, which outside had been over for some hours. Her consciousness was still occluded by night. Her limbs lay in deep night as in a grave. The black tomcat put out its pink tongue and licked the ear of the young dead girl. Emilia stirred, thrashed about her, rolled over on to her back, felt the electric fur of the cat, grabbed the head of a dog, gurgled, "what's going on, what's the matter now?" where did she return from, what dark abysses of sleep? She heard the perpetual gurgling in the pipes of the house, the sootfalls of plaster, the snorting, purring, padding, and tail-swishing of the animals. The animals were her friends, the animals were her companions, they were the companions of the happy childhood from which Emilia had now been evicted, they were the companions of the solitude in which Emilia lived, they were play and fun, they were harmless, devoted, and lived for the moment, they were harmless and momentary creatures incapable of deceit or calculation, and they knew only the good Emilia, an Emilia who was good to them. The bad Emilia had it in for humans. She sat up and shouted: "Philipp!" She listened, her features half-woebegone, half-embittered. Philipp had abandoned her! She switched on the bedside lamp, ran naked through the room, switched on the overhead light, silvery candlebulbs swaying on verdigrised medlar branches, wall brackets lit up, light given back by mirrors, multiplied and tinted by colored shades, in red and yellow, falling in red and yellow splotches on the skin of the woman, on her almost undeveloped body, long legs, small breasts, smooth, supple stomach. She ran into Philipp's room and the natural light of the murky day entering through the undraped window suddenly made her pretty form look pale. Her eyes had a sickly luster, there were dark rings round them, the left eyelid drooped as though it had been detached, her small stubborn brow was furrowed, her black hair hung down into her face like a straggly mane. She looked at the desk with the typewriter, the sheets of empty white paper, the paraphernalia of work, which she loathed and from which she expected miracles, fame, riches, security, all overnight, in one night when Philipp would compose some important work, but not over many days, not like the grind of office work, not with the persistent clatter of the little type-writer. "He can't do it. I hate you," she whispered, "I hate you!" He was gone. He had run away from her. He would be back. Where else was he going to go? But he was gone; he had left her all alone. Was she so unbearable? She stood naked in his study, naked in daylight, a streetcar drove past, Emilia's shoulders sagged, her collarbones stood out, her flesh lost its freshness, and her skin its youthfulness, it was as though it had had old sour milk poured over it, it was like cheese, crumbly and sour. She lay down on the cracked leather sofa, which was as firm and cold as a doctor's couch and therefore frightened her, and she thought of Philipp, she conjured his return, forced him back into the room, funny, incompetent Philipp, unbusinesslike, her loved and hated companion, the violator, her violated. She stuck a finger in her mouth, moistened it with her tongue, played with herself, and then she pushed it inside her, and fell into the deep intoxication of pleasure, which allowed her, already exposed to the day and its hostile light, another little installment of inner night, a handsbreadth of secrecy and love, a procrastination—

Night-and-day. Odysseus looked down at the porter's red cap, the stained and worn material, he saw the peak of the cap make a martial line over the glasses and the eyes, he saw the brass number, understood the tired shoulders, the threadbare wool of the jacket, the frayed ribbon attaching the apron, and finally he saw the little belly, barely enough of it to be worth mentioning. Odysseus laughed. He laughed like a child who makes friends quickly, childishly he thought the old man was like an old child, a playmate for the street. Odysseus was pleased, he was cheerful, he welcomed his new companion, he agreed to give him something of his momentary abundance, something of the victor's aura, let him take his case: the music, the voice, now dangled from the old porter's hand. Bravely, like a small, frail shadow, Josef strode across the station forecourt next to the tall, broad form of the soldier. Out of the case came shrilling, squalling, squeaking: "Limehouse Blues." Josef followed the black man, he followed the liberator, the conqueror, followed the occupying and protective power into the city.

A shrine, an altar, a grave shadow, crust of mold from an old, now-rejected faith, of threat looming (now less so), of wellspring of hope, deceptive font for the man athirst: with its wings thrown open, the bookcase was an unholy triptych of script behind the naked Emilia. For whom was she sacrificing herself, priestess and doe in a single form, corrupt Iphigenia, unprotected by any Artemis, switched to no Tauris? The inherited books, deluxe editions of the 1880s, untouched gilt-edged pages of the German classics and the Pharos-by-the-sea-of-life for Madame's salon, the fight-for-Rome and Bismarck's-memoirs-and-reflections for the drawing room, with the special shelf for cognac and cigars, the library of her forefathers, who had made money and didn't read, next to the collection that Philipp the tireless reader had brought into the house, full of disquiet and dismemberment, the heart laid bare, and the analyzed compulsion. And in front of them, in front of the gorgeously bound and the falling apart and vainly consulted volumes, before their eyes, so to speak, and at their feet, rested the naked heiress, her hand jammed between her still girlish thighs, trying to forget what now went by the name of reality and adversity and struggle for survival and social integration, and Behude liked to talk about the failure to integrate with one's surroundings, and surely all that that meant was that it was a shitty life, a cursed world, and the privileged exemptions lost their fortunate status, the fall into the nicely feathered nest, what good was it now, the soothing flattering hubbub around her years? You're rich, my lovely, you're beautiful, all this will one day etc., you will inherit Grandmama's fortune, the Commercial Councilor's factory millions, he was thinking of you, the careful, foresightful paterfamilias was thinking of his granddaughter, still unborn, he showered her with rich gifts, richly securing her future in his will, you are blessed, my girl, ever onward and upward, you won't need to do anything yourself, he did so much, you won't need to trouble yourself, he took the trouble, he and his eight hundred employees, "for you, my dove, so you bob along" (but what bobs along? what bobs along on top of a pond? frogspawn, birdcack, moldy wood, iridescent paints and oils, restless specters of grease and mud and decomposition, the corpse of the young lover), you can celebrate, my dear, throw parties, have garden parties, my pretty, you'll always be the queen of the ball, Emilia!— She wanted to forget, forget the worthless stock, the expropriated rights, the Reich treasury bonds on deposit, paper, all paper, so much paper, forget the crumbling real estate, the mortgaged stones of the walls she wasn't allowed to sell, the tethering to officialdom, the forms, the granted and subsequently revoked moratoriums, the lawyers, she wanted to forget, wanted to run away from the cheat, but it was too late, get away from the material, give herself now to the intellect, to which thus far she had paid little mind, here was a new savior, with gravity-defying forces, *les fleurs du mal,* flowers grown from nothing, consolation in attics, how-I-hate-poets, the scroungers, the freeloaders, intellectual comfort in crumbling villas, oh-we-were-rich-once, *une saison en enfer: il semblait que ce fût un sinistre lavoir, toujours accablé de la pluie et de noir,* Gottfried Benn, *Morgue, Early Poems* is—darksweet—onanie, *les paradis artificiels* up a gum tree, Philipp up a gum tree, perplexity in the shrubbery in Heidegger's mantraps, the scent of bonbons never tasted again on the excursion with her girlfriends, the Lido at Venice, the children of the rich *à la recherche du temps perdu,* Schrödinger *What is Life?* the nature of mutation, the behavior of atoms in an organism, the organism not a physical laboratory, a stream of order, you will escape decay in anatomical chaos, the soul, yes, the soul, *Deus factus sum,* the Upanishads, order from order, order from disorder, the transmigration of souls, the hypothesis of multiple reincarnations, I'll-come-back-to-life-as-an-animal, I'm-nice-to-animals, the-calf-on-the-rope-that-shrilled-outside-the-slaughterhouse-at-Garmisch, animal birth, Kierkegaard's Fear-and-Trembling diary-keeping Don Juan not going to bed Cordelia, Sartre's nausea, well, I'm-not-nauseated, I am performing darksweet onanie, the self, existence and the philosophy of existence, millionairess, used-to-be, once upon a time, Grandmother's travels, Actual Secret Commercial Councilor, onanie my dark my sweet, Auer's gas illumination hums, if-only-they-had-invested-everything-in-gold, the beginning of state insurance, must-I-stick-stamps-against-my-old-age, billionfold inflation, gold-oh-if-only. Immediate Aid Ordinance, that was Nice, onanie, the Promenade des Anglais, the heron-feathered hats, Shepheard's Hotel in Cairo, Mena House Hotel by the pyramids, the renal cure of the Actual Secret Commercial

Councilor, drying out the silt deposits, desert climate, picture postcards, *carte postale* Wilhelm-and-Lieschen-on-camelback, the ancestors, Luxor, hundred-gated Thebes, the necropolis, the field of the dead, the city of the dead, I-shall-die-young, Admetus the young Gide in Biskra *L'immoraliste* love and no names, the Actual Secret died, his *pompes funèbres*, millions, million-not-in-gold, the depreciation-share, the Temple of Ammon, Ramses the something-or-other in the rubble, Cocteau the Sphinx: I-love, who-will-love-me? the gene, the nucleus of the fertilized egg, I-don't-need-to-take-precautions-twelve-times-regular, the moon, no doctor, Behude's nosy, all doctors are creeps, my cunt, my-body-belongs-to-me, not to suffer, sweet dark beastliness—

Exhaustion beaded on her brow, each pearl a microcosm of the underworld, a squirming of atoms, electrons, and quants, Giordano Bruno at the stake sang the song of infinite space, Botticelli's Spring matured, turned to summer, turned to fall, was it already winter, or a new spring? the embryo of spring? Water collected in her hair, she felt damp, and before her shining eyes, swimming in moisture, Philipp's desk once again struck her as being the magical place, a hated place, of course, but the site of the possible miracle: wealth and fame, for herself as well, distinguished wealth and security. She reeled. The security of which the times had robbed her, which the promised, nibbled, and now-devalued inheritance denied her, which the houses no longer granted her, the cracks in the walls, cracks in the material everywhere, would this lost dream of security, that had swelled up and then gone *phut* like a confidence-trickster, would the weak, impoverished Philipp, tormented by dizziness and palpitations, would he be able to afford them, who at least, and this was new for her, was in communication with the invisible, the idea, the spirit, the art, who had put his stake on a blank square here, but perhaps had property in the spiritual realm? But for the moment there was no security. Philipp said there had never been any such thing. He lied! He didn't want to share what he had with her. How could he live without security? It wasn't Emilia's fault that the old security had collapsed, in whose bosom two generations had made themselves at home. She wanted the party responsible! She demanded her inheritance from anyone who was older than her. At night she had gone running through the house, like a fragile Fury, pursued by her bestiary, the little darlings speechless and therefore lovable, yesterday, when Philipp was ducking, when he couldn't stand her screaming anymore, her pointless traipsing up and downstairs to the janitor in the basement, her fists and feet against the bolted door: "You Nazis, why did you elect him, why did you elect misery, why the abyss, why the end, why the war, why did you send my fortune up in smoke, I had money, you Nazis," (and the janitor, lying behind the bolted door, holding his breath, not daring to budge, thought, it'll pass, it's a tempest, it'll blow itself out, and then we'll have quiet again), and the other Nazis behind other doors in the house, her father behind the secure deadbolt lock, a coinheritor, "you Nazi, you fool, you wastrel, you had to march, get in step, run along, you fellow traveler, swastika on your breast, the money's gone, couldn't you manage to keep quiet? did you have to bark?" (and her father sat behind the door, didn't hear her cry, didn't face prosecution, justified or not, held the share certificates in front of his face, the bank papers, the IOUs, the notes of deposit, and calculated, I still have this and that portion and the other, and a fifth of the house next door, and maybe the mortgaged property in Berlin, but that's in the Eastern sector, so who knows *US against Preemptive War*). Why did Philipp not worry himself? Perhaps because he was living off what little she still had, given her by the god of her grandparents, and his own god was a false god? If only she could know everything! Her pale face twitched. She reeled, reeled naked to the desk, plucked a sheet of paper from the virginal stack, from the little stack of the immaculate conception because it had never happened, ran it into the typewriter, and with one finger carefully typed: "Don't be angry with me. I love you, Philipp. Don't leave me."

He didn't love them. Why should he love them? He took no pride in his family. He was indifferent. Why should he feel moved? No particular emotion constricted or expanded his heart. The ones who lived down there didn't engage Richard's interest any more than other historic peoples: superficially, maybe. He was here on duty; no, that's what they would have said, the people down there, the barracks clan, the old noble servants, he was here to make himself useful, at the direction of his country and his age, and he thought it was his country's turn now, a century of purified instincts, of useful order, of planning and administration and thoroughness, and, in addition to his duty, there would be a sort of ironic-romantic tour of the world and castles. What they might look to him for was candor and unsophistication. It was their chance. Augustus didn't take ship for Hellas out of charitable feelings for the Greeks either. History forced Augustus to take an interest in their muddle. He created order. He tamed a little clutch of fanatics, enthusiasts, and parish-pump politicians; he supported common sense, the moderates, capital, and the academies, and did what he could with the crazies, the sages, and the pederasts. It was his interest, and their opportunity. Richard felt free of enmity and prejudice, unburdened by hatred and contempt. These negative feelings were poisons that civilization had overcome, historic diseases like the plague, cholera, and smallpox. Richard had been vaccinated and decalcified, he had received a hygienic upbringing. Maybe he would be condescending, without wishing to be condescending because he was young, and being young went to his head, he looked down, down on them in their actuality, he looked down on their countries, their kings, their frontiers, their quarrels, their philosophers, their graves, their whole aesthetic, pedagogical, philosophical loam, their continual wars and revolutions, he looked down as on a single tiny battlefield, the earth lay spread out beneath him, as on an operating table, cut to ribbons. Of course, that wasn't really how he saw it; he saw neither kings nor frontiers where for the time being there was just night and fog, nor did his mind's eye picture them to itself, it was just what he had learned at school that saw the continent that way. History was the past, the world of yesterday, dates in books, torment for children, but every day created fresh history, history in the present tense, and that meant being there, becoming, growing, acting, and flying. You didn't always know where you were flying to. It wasn't till tomorrow or the next day that it would all be given its historical name, and acquire with the name a purpose, and then it would become real history, it would weather in schoolbooks, and this day, this today, this tomorrow, would one day turn into what he would call "my youth." He was young, he was curious, he wanted to take a look at it: the land of his fathers. It was a visit to the orient. They were Crusaders of order, knights of commonsense, practical solutions, and moderate middle-class freedoms: they weren't after any Holy Sepulcher. It was night when they made landfall. In the clear sky ahead of them shone a frosty light: the morning star, Phospheros, Lucifer, the light-bringer of the antique world. He became a prince of darkness. Night and fog lay over Belgium, over Bruges, Brussels, and Ghent. Cologne Cathedral loomed out of daybreak. Rosy-fingered dawn touched the curved eggshell of the world: a new day. They flew up the Rhine. *Lieb Vaterland magst ruhig sein fest steht und treu die Wacht am Rhein*: his father's song when he was eighteen, Wilhelm Kirsch's song in classrooms and barrack rooms, on exercise grounds and route marches, the watch of his father, the watch of his grandfather, the watch of his great-grandfather, the watch on the Rhine, the watch of brothers, watch of cousins, watch on the Rhine, grave of ancestors, grave of kin, watch on the Rhine, watch neglected, watch misunderstood, it-mustn't-fall-into-their-hands, whose hands was it in, the French, of course, the people on the river, boatmen, fishermen, gardeners, wine growers, tradesmen, factory owners, lovers, the poet Heine, whose hands should it fall into? anyone's who wants it, whoever's there, so did he now have it, Richard Kirsch, US airman, eighteen years old, looking down on it from above, or was he in fact coming to take over the watch on the Rhine, in good faith, as they were, and perhaps once more caught in the trap of misunderstanding a historical moment? He thought: If I was a bit older, say, if I was twenty-four or something and not eighteen, then when I was eighteen I could have been flying here, I could have been doing damage and dying here, we would have had ordnance on board then, we would have dropped ordnance, we would have lit up a Christmas tree, we would have laid down a carpet of bombs, we would have been their death, we would have soared into the clouds out of reach of their searchlights, when will that day come? where will I practice what they taught? where shall I bomb? whom shall I bomb? here? right here? farther along? others? back a bit? others again?— Over Bavaria, the land grew hazy. They flew over clouds. When they landed, the earth had a damp smell. The airfield smelled of grass, petrol, exhaust fumes, metal, and of something new and different, it was a baking smell, a doughy, fermenting smell of yeast and alcohol, stimulating and giving you an appetite, it was the smell of barley mash from the great breweries of the city.

They moved through the streets, Odysseus leading the way, a great king, a small winner, young, powerful-hipped, innocent, supple, and Josef followed after him, wizened, bent, old, and tired, but canny, and with his canny little eyes looking through his cheap-skate state glasses, he watched the black back in front of him, in hope, in trust, the light load, the good assignment in his hand, the musical suitcase, Bahama Joe with his sounds, Bahama Joe with his music-rattle, vocal prattle, Bahama Joe with his muted cornets and snares and hi-hat, the squeaking and yowling and the rhythm that filled the air and took hold of the girls, the girls, they thought, the nigger, the cheeky nigger, nasty nigger, no, I wouldn't do it, Bahama Joe, and others beside him thought, they've got money, loads of money, one of those black soldiers gets paid more than a chief inspector does with us, a US private, we girls have picked up a bit of English, we've gone to classes at the Mädchenbund, can you marry a nigger? there's no race laws in the USA, they just get ostracized, no hotel would take you, the half-black babies, occu-pation babies, poor wee things, not knowing where they belong, it's not their fault, no, I wouldn't do it!— Bahama Joe, saxophone squeal. A woman stood in front of a shoe shop, she saw the Negro pass reflected in the window, she thought: Those sandals with the wedge heels, I wouldn't mind them, it would be fun to try, they have incredible physiques, so strong, I went to a boxing match once, my old man was fit to drop afterward, he wasn't— Bahama Joe. They passed drink stalls, outdoor bars, forbidden to allied troops, and from out of the wooden hidey-holes out they crept, the touts, the pimps, the scabs: "Hey, Joe, dollar? Joe, you got gas? Joe, wanna girl?" They were already sitting in the booths, the goods, over lemonade, over Coca-Cola, over acorn coffee, reeking swill, the staleness of bed, the smell of last night's embraces not yet washed off them, the splotched skin powdered, the dead dollybird hair bleached and dyed till it looked like bundled straw, they were waiting, hens fresh daily on order, looking through the glass to see what their macs were up to, whether they would give them a wave, a black man, they were cheerful and generous, and so they should be too, mind you, the way they tore up your insides: "they ought to be happy to get a white woman, it's humiliating for us, disgusting and humiliating." — "Hey, Joe, you got something for me there?" — "Hey, Joe, you looking to make a purchase?" — "Joe, I got something!" — "This way, Joe!" They swarmed round them: maggots in bacon, whey faces, sharp, hungry faces, faces that God had forgotten, rats, sharks, hyenas, newts, barely disguised by human skin, padded shoulders, plaid jackets, dirty trench coats, gaudy socks, thick crepe soles under the greasy pigskin shoes, parodies of American low style, poor bastards as well, homeless drifters, war losers. They turned to Josef, to Bahama Joe: "Does your nigger need German money?" — "We'll change money for your nigger." — "Is he looking to score? There's three marks in it for you. You can stay and watch, old fellow, you can be in charge of the music." Bahama Joe, music with its silver sound. Josef and Odysseus heard the whispering, and they didn't hear it, Bahama Joe: they cut a swathe through the whisperers, the hissing serpents, Odysseus pushed them aside, gently and forcefully as a whale, shouldered past them, the little smalltime rogues, the pimple faces, the stinknoses, the clapped-out fucks. And Josef followed the mighty Odysseus, scuttled along in his wake. Bahama Joe: on they went, past the newly rebuilt cinemas *Immortal Passion Gripping Doctor Drama*, the newly rebuilt hotels *Roof Garden over the Ruins Happy Hour*, got chalk dust sprinkled over them, got cement spattered over them, walked through the shopping streets set up in rubble fields, left and right of them the flat shacks flashing with chrome details, neon tubing, and mirror glass: perfume from Paris, Dupont nylon, pineapples from California, Scotch whisky, brightly colored newspaper stands: *Shortage of Ten Million Tons of Coal.*

The lights were on red and prevented their crossing. Streetcars, cars, bicyclists, wobbling three-wheelers, and heavy American military trucks streamed over the crossing.

The red light was in Emilia's way. She wanted to get to her pawn-broker's, who closed at noon, and then to Unverlacht, the junk dealer in the damp arcade, who would reach up her skirts, to the plaintive antique dealer, Frau de Voss, she wouldn't buy any-thing, but at least she wasn't far from Unverlacht's, and finally, she sensed it, she knew it really, she would have to sacrifice her pearls, her moon-pale necklace, she would have to go to Schellack the jeweler. The shoes she had on were well-cut and real snake-skin, but they were down at heel. Her stockings were as sheer as could be, because Philipp loved sheer fabrics, and would get all excited when she came home in winter in a sharp frost with chill calves, but oh woe, some of the threads had worked loose in the ladder-proof mesh, and were running down like little rivulets from her knee to her ankle. Her skirt had a triangular tear in the hem: who was going to repair it? Emilia's fur jacket, too warm for the season, was of finest Siberian miniver, all wrinkled and torn, but there was nothing to be done about it, she didn't have an autumn coat. Her young lips were painted, the pallor of her cheeks lifted with a dab of rouge, her hair was loose in the rainy wind. The things she had brought with her were all wrapped in an English traveling rug, the sort of thing lords and ladies carried their lug-gage in in the satirical funnies and in Wilhelm Busch. Emilia made heavy weather of the frills and furbelows of the old humorists. Any weight exacerbated the rheumatic pain in her shoulder. Any complaint made her tetchy and filled her with stubbornness and bitterness. She stood petulantly under the red light and stared crossly into the stream of traffic.

In the Consul's automobile, in the silent and well-sprung Cadillac, the conveyance of the wealthy on the side of the wealthy, of the statesman, the nouveau riche, the plan manager, if appearances weren't completely deceptive, in a spacious black-gleaming coffin, Mr. Edwin rolled across the crossing. He felt tired. The journey, which he had at least spent lying down, if not sleeping, had strained him. He peered into the dismal day discouraged, discouraged into the foreign street. This was the land of Goethe, the land of Platen, the land of Winckelmann, Stefan George had walked across this square. Mr. Edwin shivered. All at once he saw himself as washed up and alone, as old as his years. With that, he pressed his old, if boyishly slender body back into the soft upholstery of the car. It was a gesture of kenneling up. The brim of his black hat flipped up against the seat-back, and so he set his hat, a featherlight product of Bond Street, in his lap. His noble face, expressive of asceticism, breeding, and self-scrutiny, grew mean. Under the carefully combed and parted, long, silk-soft gray hair, he acquired the sharp features of an old buzzard. The Consular Secretary and the literary impresario of America House, who had been dispatched to meet Mr. Edwin at the station, sat opposite him on the tip-up seats of the car, leaning toward him, and felt obliged to try and entertain their celebrated guest, their laureate, their queer fish. They pointed out the alleged sights of the city, talked about the way they had publicized his lecture, chattered away—it sounded like charwomen indefatigably swishing wet rags over a dusty floor. To Mr. Edwin's ear, the two gentlemen were using the familiar demotic with him. That was irritating. Mr. Edwin was not averse to using the demotic himself, say, in the presence of beauty, but here, with these two well-educated gentlemen from his own class—my class? what class is that? without prejudice to any man, a classless outsider, no common points, none—this demotic, this American they were chewing like gum, was excruciating, lowering, discouraging. Edwin slid farther into his corner. What did he have for this land, what did he have for Goethe, Winckelmann, Platen? They would be sensitive here, perhaps receptive, they had been defeated, doom would have sharpened their senses, they would have intuitions, be that much closer to the brink, that much more on a level with death. Did he come with news, did he bring solace, could he account for suffering? His theme was immortality, the imperishableness of the spirit, the deathless soul of the West, and now? Well, now he wondered. His news was old news, his understanding he had got from books. It was from books, but it was also select, a distillation of the spirit of millennia, drawn from every language, the Holy Spirit versed into the different dialects, select, precious, a quintessence, sparkling and distilled, bittersweet, poisonous, curative, almost an explanation, but only an explanation of history, and finally doubtful even as that, the beautifully formed, clever strophes, sensitive reactions, and yet: he came empty-handed, without gifts, without solace, hope, grief, tiredness, but with sloth, an empty heart, and empty hands. Wouldn't he be better advised not to speak? He had already seen the ravages of the war, who in Europe hadn't? He had seen them in London, in France, in Italy, terrible, gaping wounds in the cities, but what he saw now in probably the worst-affected place of those he had been to, through the window of the consular car, suspended on rubber, compressed air, and canny springs, protected from dust, had been tidied, ordered, plastered over, freshly rebuilt, and for that very reason so horrible, and so infirm: this could never be made good. His theme was Europe, he was to talk of Europe and for Europe, but did he secretly desire the destruction, the devastation of the robes in which the beloved, the intellectually so fervently beloved continent showed itself, or was it the case that Mr. Edwin, setting off late on his travels, to cash in on his late fame—produced from who knows what misunderstandings—to have himself celebrated, that he knew the meaning of the offense, he was a friend of that bird the phoenix, who had to be consigned to the flames, his gaudy feathers to the ashes, these shops, these people, makeshift all of it, the demotic in his automobile—it was all foolish: what was he to say to them? Maybe he would die in this city. A piece of news. A stop-press for the evening editions. A sheaf of obituaries in London, Paris, New York. This black Cadillac his coffin. They brushed a bicyclist. Oh dear, he's going to fall, he's wobbling—

He kept his balance. He regained his balance, pedaled on, steered his bicycle into the open space ahead, Dr. Behude, specialist for psychiatry and neurology, he stepped on the pedals, and he made progress, tonight he will go to America House to hear Mr. Edwin give his lecture, his talk about the intellect of the West, his talk about the power of the mind, the triumph of mind over matter, mind defeating illness, illnesses psychosomatic in origin, symptoms psychically treatable. Dr. Behude felt dizzy. The siphoning off of his blood had really taken it out of him this time. Perhaps he allowed himself to be tapped more often than was good for him. The world needed blood. Dr. Behude needed money. Triumph of matter over mind. Should he pull over, dismount, go to a bar, have a drink, and be cheerful? He bobbed along in the flow of traffic. He suffered headaches that he told his patients to ignore. He cycled on, on his way to Schnakenbach, the tired trade schoolteacher, the gifted fiddler with formulae, the night school Einstein, a Pervitin- and Benzedrine-addicted shade. Behude was sorry he'd refused Schnakenbach the pills last night, to keep the teacher awake. Now he wanted to deliver the addiction-satisfying, the miserably life-enhancing and yet also -destroying prescription to his house in person. He would have liked to ride out to Emilia. He liked her: he thought she was more at risk than Philipp, he'll get through everything, he'll even survive his marriages, a tough heart, neuroses, schneuroses, a pseudo–angina pectoris, it's all much of a muchness, but a stout heart, you wouldn't have thought it, but Emilia never came to his clinic, and Philipp hid away when he called at the house. He failed to spot Emilia standing at the crossroads waiting for the light to change as he cycled by. He was hunched forward over the handlebars, his right hand poised on the brake, his left forefinger on the bell: a mistaken ring might have fatal consequences, betray a professional shortcoming, the mistaken ring of the night bell, now, did he understand his Kafka?—

Washington Price drove his sky-blue limousine over the crossing. Should he or shouldn't he? He knew that the petrol tankers in his depot had secret taps. The risk wasn't great. He just needed to go fifty-fifty with the tanker driver, turn in to the German petrol station, where they knew all the petrol drivers, and take a few gallons on board. He was certain of making good money. And he needed money. He didn't want to lose. He wanted Carla, and he wanted Carla's baby. He didn't have any points on his conduct book. He believed in honesty. Every citizen deserved an even break. Every black man too. Sergeant Washington Price, US Army. Washington had to get rich. He had to get at least temporarily rich; here and today he had to be rich. Carla would have faith in the color of his money. She would have faith in his money before she had faith in his words. Carla didn't want to carry his baby to term. She was scared. My God, what was there to be scared of? Washington was the best, the strongest, the quickest slugger on the famous Red Stars baseball team. But he was past his peak. That murderous running round the bases! It did him in. He couldn't breathe anymore. But he was still good for another year or two. He could still do his bit in the arena. A rheumatic pain spasmed in his arm; that was a warning. He wouldn't chance the thing with the petrol. He had to drive to Central Exchange. He had to buy Carla a present. He had to make a call. He needed money. Now—

Now hop off the 6 onto the 11. She would just catch Dr. Frahm. It was good if she arrived just after the end of consulting hours. Frahm would have time for her. She had to get rid of it. Now. Washington was a decent fellow. How scared she was! Her first day in the black soldiers' barracks. The Lieutenant had said: "I don't know if you'll stay." They pressed up against the pane of glass in the door, flattened their already flat noses like rubber against the glass, one face next to another. Who was sitting in the cage? who represented the species in the zoo? herself behind the glass? or those others in front of the glass? was it such a long way from the German Wehrmacht office, as secretary to the commandant, to these black soldiers with the US Transport Unit? She wrote quite passable English, bowed her head low over the typewriter, not to see the strange being, the dark skin, the lithe ebony lissomness, not the man, not hear the guttural sound, only the words he was dictating, she had to work, she couldn't stay home with her mother, with Frau Behrend, she thought she was wrong in her judgment of the music master, she had to look after her kid, his father was on the Volga, perhaps he was drunk, perhaps he was dead, buried in the steppe, no more greetings to Stalingrad, she had to do something, they were close to starving, those awful hunger years '45, '46, '47, starving, she had to, why shouldn't she? weren't they people too? And in the evening, there he was. "I'll take you home." He led her through the barracks corridor. She felt naked, was she naked? The men stood in the corridor, dark in the evening shadow, their eyes were fluttering like restless white bats, and their glances stuck to her body like round adhesive disks. He sat beside her, at the wheel of a jeep. "Where do you live?" She told him. During the drive he didn't speak at all. He drew up outside her house. He opened the door for her. He gave her chocolate, canned goods, cigarettes, an awful lot for those days. "Goodbye." And that was it. Every night. He picked her up from her office, walked her down the corridor past the waiting, staring, black men, drove her home, sat next to her in the jeep without speaking, gave her some present, said: "Goodbye." Sometimes, they would sit around in the car for up to an hour in front of her house, the motor off, in silence. Back then, the streets were still full of rubble from the bombed buildings. The wind whipped up dust. The ruins were like a cemetery, beyond the reality of the evening, they were Pompeii, Herculaneum, Troy, a lost world. A shattered wall collapsed. A cloud of fresh dust settled round the jeep. By the sixth week, Carla couldn't stand it anymore. Her dreams were full of Negroes. She was raped in her dreams. Black arms reached out for her: they emerged from the bombed basements like slithering snakes. She said: "I can't stand it anymore." He came up to her room with her. It felt like drowning. Was it the Volga? Not icy, a burning river. The next day, neighbors came, acquaintances came, her former Wehrmacht boss came, they all came, wanting cigarettes, cans, coffee, chocolate, "tell your friend, Carla"—"your friend in Central Exchange, Carla, in the American shop"—"don't forget to tell your friend, Carla, soap": Washington Price remembered it and got it and brought it. Her friends thanked her offhandedly. It was as though Carla were buying them off. Her friends seemed to forget that all those goods in the American stores cost money, cost dollars and cents. Was it funny? was it nice? something to be proud of? Carla, the benefactress? Before long, she couldn't tell one way or another, and thinking about it hurt her head. She gave up her job at the transport barracks, moved into a different house, where other girls lived with other men, and she lived with Washington, and was faithful to him, even though she had many offers of sex, because everyone, whether black or white, German or foreign, thought that, because she was now living with Washington, she would go to bed with anyone, it turned them on, and Carla wasn't certain of her feeling, and she wondered, do I love him? really love him? strange, strange, but I'll be faithful to him, I owe that to him, to be faithful to him, I won't have anyone else, and in her idleness she got used to the picture-world of endless color magazines that showed her the way a lady lived in America, the automatic kitchens, the miracle detergents and dishwashers that got everything clean while she lounged in the Lay-Z-Boy, watching the television, Bing Crosby was piped into every home, the Vienna Boys' Choir alleluia-ed in front of the electric stove, you rode from East to West on the plump cushions of a Pullman car, in streamlined automobiles you enjoyed the show of lights flickering under the palms of San Francisco Bay, security of every kind was offered her by drug manufacturers and insurance companies, no nightmares to trouble your rest, *you can sleep soundly at night* with Maybel's Milk of Magnesia, and the woman was a queen, whom all there served and worshiped, she was *the gift that starts the home*, while the children had dolls that cried real tears; and they were the only tears that were wept in this paradise. Carla wanted to marry Washington. She was ready to follow him back to the States. She got her former boss, the commandant, who was now chief clerk at a law firm, to have her husband missing on the Volga declared dead. And then along came the baby, a little black creature, stirring in her belly, too soon, it made her ill, no, she didn't want it, Dr. Frahm had to come to her aid, had to get rid of it, right now—

"The center you see before you was completely demolished. In the space of just five years, the return of democratic government and Allied generosity have made it once more the flowering focus of trade and business." *Marshall Plan Assistance Extended to Germany, ERP Funds Cut, Senator Taft Criticizes Expenditure.* The tour bus with the travel group of schoolmistresses from Massachusetts passed the crossing. They were traveling incognito, and never knew it. It didn't occur to any German, seeing the women behind the bus windows, to take them for schoolteachers. They were ladies, sitting on the red leather seats, well-dressed, prettily made-up, youthful-looking where they weren't young, so they thought, rich, well cared for, idle ladies, whiling away their time with a tour of the city. If you hadn't set the city on fire, there might have been something worth looking at here, and you wouldn't be here to see it, soldiers are one thing, but women on an occupation forces ticket, that's something else, that's just hangers-on. An American teacher earns—whatever she earns—many times more than her German counterpart in Starnberg, the poor, cowed thing, don't want to give offense, a bit of powder on my face, and it might draw unfavorable comment from the vicar, and the school inspector might make a note of it in my personnel file. Education in Germany is a grave and gray affair, remote from pleasure, certainly not no thanks all the same to glamor, and it remains eternally unimaginable, a lady in front of a German class with cosmetics, with scent, taking her holidays in Paris, taking research trips to New York and Boston, my God it makes your hair stand on end, we may be a poor country, but we have our pride. Kay was sitting next to Katharine Wescott. Kay was twenty-one, Katharine thirty-eight. "You've fallen for Kay's green eyes," was what Mildred Burnett said. Green eyes, cat's eyes, untrustworthy eyes. Mildred was forty-five and she was sitting in the seat in front of them. They had one day to see the city, and two more for the rest of the American Occupation Zone in Germany. Katharine wrote everything down in her notebook that the American Express guide standing next to the driver said. She thought: I'm sure I can use it in my history classes, this is a historic moment, America in Germany, the Stars and Stripes over Europe, I'll have seen it for myself, I'll have witnessed it.— Kay had given up keeping a record during their tours. They didn't get to see much anyway. It wasn't until they were back at the hotel that Kay copied out the most important items from Katharine's shorthand notes into her travel diary. Kay was disappointed. Romantic Germany? This was grim. The land of poets and thinkers, or music and song? People looked the same as everywhere else. There was a Negro standing at the crossing. A little portable radio was playing Bahama Joe. It was no different from Boston; just like one of the poorer parts of Boston. This other Germany must be an invention of her college German professor. Kaiser was his name, and he'd lived in Berlin until '34. Then he had been driven out. Maybe he's homesick, thought Kay, this is his home after all, he doesn't feel about it the way I do, he doesn't like America, he thinks everyone here's a poet, they're not as businesslike as we are, but they drove him out, wonder why? he's nice enough, but in America we've got our own poets, Kaiser calls them writers, important writers maybe, but he sees a distinction: Hemingway, Faulkner, Wolfe, O'Neill, Wilder, Edwin lives in Europe, he turned his back on us, same as Ezra Pound, in Boston we had Santayana, the Germans have Thomas Mann, but he's living with us, funny, he's exiled too, I suppose, look at their poets, let's see, they had Goethe, Schiller, Kleist, Hölderlin, Hofmannsthal, Hölderlin and Hofmannsthal are Dr. Kaiser's favorites, Rilke's elegies, Rilke died in '26, I wonder who they have now? sitting in the ruins of Carthage and weeping, I ought to try and get away from the group, maybe I'd meet someone, a poet, I could talk to him, me, an American, I'd tell him not to be sad, but Katharine keeps an eye on me, so annoying, after all I'm a grown woman, she didn't want me to read *Across the River*, she called

it an immoral book that should never have been printed, I wonder why that is, because of the little Contessa? I wonder whether
I could ever fall for someone as quickly as that.— A dull town,
thought Mildred, and the women very badly dressed.— Katharine
wrote: "The oppression of woman still clearly noticeable, clearly
no equality of the sexes here." She would give a talk on the subject to the Women's Club in Massachusetts. Mildred thought: It's
silly traveling all women together, we must stink, woman as the
feeble sex, a tiring journey, and what do we see? nothing, every
year, I have to trot out the same stuff, dangerous Krauts, slayers
of Jews, every German in a steel helmet, well, I can't see much
sign of it, peaceable people, poor, I bet, military people, *Warning
against Pacifist Propaganda*, Katharine doesn't like Hemingway,
made such a fuss, the hinny, when Kay wanted to read the book,
dreadful book, countess beds old major, I'm sure Kay would go to
bed with Hemingway *like that*, but there's no Hemingway here, so
she takes chocolate to bed with her, Katharine, besotted with Kay,
those green eyes have bewitched her, what's that I see? a urinal,
didn't it have to be, I never seem to see monuments, only ever
that sort of thing, wonder if I should go into analysis? what for?
it's too late, in Paris, those places have corrugated tin surrounds,
like little Hottentot grass skirts, I'm surprised those fellows aren't
embarrassed?—

Green light. Messalina had spotted her. Alexander's nymphoma-
niac wife. Emilia tried to get away, but her flight failed: on the
corner there was a urinal, as Emilia only realized when she was
met by a succession of gentlemen buttoning up their trousers.
Emilia stumbled, stunned also by the severe smell of ammonia
and tar, with her heavy plaid, the humorous plaid of the carica-
turists, she was on the point of blundering into the backs of the

men passing water, backs over which heads turned to look at her, blank elsewhere eyes, simple faces slowly assuming expressions of bewilderment. Nor did Messalina relinquish her prey, once spotted; she waved away her taxi, her hired car that was to take her to the hairdresser, where she was to have her hair bleached and bouffed: and now she stood poised outside the urinal. A blushing Emilia came running out of the men's lavatory, and Messalina called out: "Emilychild, if you're looking for a boy to pick up, I can put you on to Hänschen, you know, Jack's little friend, you remember Jack, don't you, they see each other at my house. Well hello, how are you, can I give you a kiss, you've got such a tempting complexion, so pink. You don't get out enough, I think, I want you to come to my house tonight, you know I'm giving a party, maybe Edwin the poet will come, he's supposed to be in town, I don't know him or his stuff, but apparently he's won some big prize. Maybe Jack will bring him along, I think it would be nice if he met Hänschen!" It made Emilia squirm when Messalina called her Emilychild, and she hated it when Philipp came up in her talk, every one of Messalina's remarks offended and embarrassed her, but since she saw in Alexander's demonically done-up wife with the wrestler's figure a kind of monumental bitch that she couldn't escape, a vile and violent woman, the epic grotesque monument to femininity, Emilia always found herself intimidated by her, and encountered this monument almost like a little girl, curtseying, and casting shy glances up to the height of the monument, which only further inflamed Messalina to dizzy admiration and exquisite courtliness. Messalina thought: She's so cute, what's she doing living with Philipp? she must love him, that's the only way, curious, it took me a long time to understand that, maybe he took her virginity, there are relationships like that, her first man, I don't dare ask her, wretched, everything about her is knackered, a fine figure and a fine head, she always looks good, and then that ratty squirrel jacket, a proper rag princess she is, wonder if she's any good in bed? I think she may be, I know Jack fancies her, gamine body, what about her and Alexander? but she never comes to see me, or if she does it's only together with Philipp, she's wasted on him, I ought to rescue her, he just exploits her, useless, Alexander asked him if he'd like to write a film for him one day, and what did he write? nothing, sheepish supercilious laugh, and ran off, can't make him out, obscure genius, café poet, Romanisches Café in Berlin, the Dome in Paris, and so serious all the time, what a scarecrow, a shame for her, pretty curved mouth she has.— And Emilia thought: What awful luck running into her, whenever I'm on selling trips I run into someone, I feel so ashamed, the silly plaid, of course she's spotted that I'm selling something, that I'm going to the pawnshop, to the antique dealer, she can tell just from looking at me, a blind man can tell, those nasty questions about Philipp always, any moment she'll ask how he's getting on with his book, those empty white pages lying around at home, I feel so ashamed, I know he could write a book and he can't, *Attack Means World War III*, what does she know about anything? To her, Edwin's just a name in a newspaper, she hasn't read a line of his, she collects celebrities, that society quack Gröning was at her salon, I wonder if it's true what they say, that she beats Alexander when he's unfaithful to her, what does she know? I'd better hurry to catch the green light.—

The green light. On they went, Bahama Joe. Josef looked across at the old pub, the Glocke; it had burned down to its foundations and come back to life as a wooden shanty. Josef tugged at his black master's sleeve: "Mister like to drink beer, maybe. Beer here very good." He looked optimistically up at him. "*Oh, beer,*" said Odysseus. He laughed, Bahama Joe, the laughter caused his broad chest to rise and fall: the waves of the Mississippi. He slapped Josef on the back, causing him to fall to his knees. *"Beer!"*—"Beer!" They went in, went into the famous old wrecked now newly resurrected Glocke arm in arm, Bahama Joe, and drank: the beer foamed on their lips like snow.

In front of the typewriter shop, Philipp hesitated. He looked at the window display. He shouldn't have done. He didn't dare to step inside. Skinny Countess Anne—she was a terribly efficient, conscienceless, heartless, and universally known scion of a politically supportive family who had helped Hitler to the Reichskanzler's chair, in return for which, once in power, Hitler exterminated the whole family, with the single exception of skinny Anne, a Nazi with a victim-of-Fascism pass, the one was by nature, the pass was *de jure*—skinny Countess Anne had met Philipp, the author of a book banned in the Third Reich, and forgotten after the Third Reich, sitting sadly in a sad café, and since she was always enterprising and up for a chat, she had got into conversation with Philipp. One-sided, very one-sided: My God, what can she want with me?— "You mustn't just let yourself drift!" she had said, "Philipp, take a look at yourself! A man with your talents! You mustn't let your wife feed you and keep you. You must get a grip on yourself, Philipp. Why don't you write a filmscript? You know Alexander. You've got connections. Messalina thinks you're terribly promising!" But Philipp thought: What film am I supposed to write? What's she talking about? Films for Alexander? Films for Messalina? *Passions of a Down-and-Out Archduke*, I can't do that, she'll never understand, but I can't do it, I don't know how it's done, *Passions of an Archduke*, what does that say to me? bogus sentiment, but real bogus sentiment, I don't have it, who wants to watch stuff like that? everyone, they say, I don't believe it, I don't

49

know, but I don't want to do it anyway!— "Well if you don't want to do that," said the Countess, "then do something else, Philipp, why don't you do some selling, I've got the rights to a new adhesive, businesses are crying out for it, why don't you try a spot of selling? There's no packaging anything nowadays without my adhesive, it saves time and material, just drop into the very next stationer's, and you'll make a couple of marks. You'll surely be able to sell twenty or thirty packs of it a day—you do the sums!" Thus the conversation with the bony and efficient Anne, a helpful opening, and now he was stuck, holding the pot of glue—he opened the door. An alarm yowled and he jumped. He shrank back as though he'd come in as a robber. His left hand clutched the container of the Countess's patented sticky substance in his coat pocket. The typewriters sparkled in the neon, and Philipp had an impression of their keyboards grinning up at him: the letters made a common front against him, a mocking maw-jaw, in which the alphabet gnashed its teeth at him. Was Philipp not a writer? The overlord of the typewriters? A browbeaten gentleman. If he opened his mouth to speak the magic word, they would start to jabber back: his willing servants. Philipp did not know the magic word. He had forgotten it. He had nothing to say. He had nothing to say to all the people going by outside. The people were sentenced. He was sentenced in a different way from the people outside. But he was certainly sentenced. Time had passed sentence on this place. It had sentenced it to noise and silence. What was it people said? *How Emmy Met Hermann Göring*, shouted the obnoxious posters from all sides. Enough noise for a hundred years. What was Philipp doing here? He was superfluous. He was timid. He didn't have the courage to approach the man in his elegant suit, which was much newer than Philipp's suit, and offer him the Countess's patented glue, which, as it now seemed to Philipp, was a completely absurd and useless product. I don't have a very strong sense of reality, I'm not a serious man I suppose that means, this man here is a serious man, I simply can't take this thing they all do seriously, the idea of selling something to this man is a joke, and at the same time I'm too cowardly to do it, let him seal his parcels with whatever he likes, what do I care? what does he have to seal parcels for? to send his machines, why does he send them? to earn money, so that he can eat well, and have good clothes, and sleep well, Emilia should have married him, and what do people do with the machines they've bought here? they use them to earn money and live well, and so they employ secretaries, and they stare at their calves, and they dictate letters that go, "Sirs, in response to yours of the –th inst., ours of the –th inst.," I could laugh in their faces, but the laugh's on me, I'm the mug, it's a crime against Emilia, I'm incompetent, cowardly, superfluous: a German writer.— "Has the gentleman come about anything in particular?" The elegantly clothed businessman bowed slightly to Philipp, clearly he wasn't having the easiest time of it either. Philipp's glance swept over the displays of shiny oiled machinery, the impish inventions ready for all sorts of mischief, to which a man might entrust his thoughts, his communications, his messages, his declarations of war. And then he saw the dictating machine. It was a tape recorder, as he had seen at a couple of radio readings he'd given, readings recorded on tape, and on the machine was the word *Reporter*. Is that what I am, wondered Philipp, a reporter? I could use that gadget to report, to tell people that I'm too scared and incompetent to sell glue, that I feel too proud to write a filmscript for Alexander to suit the taste of the people going by outside, that's why, I'm superfluous and a bit ridiculous, I myself think I'm superfluous and a bit ridiculous, but then I see the others, as for instance this salesman here, who imagines he can sell me something, whereas I don't back myself to sell him a pot of glue, and I don't think he's any less superfluous or ridiculous than I am!— The salesman looked expectantly at Philipp. "I'm interested in the Dictaphone over there," said Philipp. "That one, that's the best design on the market," replied the elegant salesman. He was very keen. "A first-class piece of equipment. Absolutely pays for itself. You can dictate your letters into it any time, on travels, in the car, in bed. Why don't you try it out—" He turned a switch on the box, and handed Philipp a little microphone. The tape ran from one reel to another. Philipp spoke into the microphone: "The *Neues Blatt* has asked me to do an interview with Edwin. I could take along this gadget and record our conversation. I will certainly feel awkward, coming to Edwin in the guise of a reporter. I expect he's nervous of journalists. He will feel obliged to speak platitudinously and encouragingly. I will be offended. I will be embarrassed. Of course he won't know me. On the other hand, I'm looking forward to meeting him. I admire him. Maybe it'll be a good meeting. I could take Edwin for a walk in the park. Or perhaps it would be better if I stuck to selling glue—" He stopped in alarm. The salesman smiled encouragingly. "The gentleman is a journalist? We've sold many of these Reporters to journalists—" He rewound the tape, and Philipp heard his own voice giving his thoughts on the upcoming interview with Edwin. The voice dismayed him. What it said humiliated him. It was a display, a piece of intellectual display. He could as well have taken off all his clothes. His own voice, the words it said frightened Philipp, and he melted out of the shop.

—like snow on their lips. They wiped them dry, and then plunged back into the earthenware tankards, the bock flowed into them, dribbled down their throats sweet bitter sticky aromatic. "*Beer*"— "Beer": Odysseus and Josef drank to one another. The little radiogram was sitting on the chair next to Josef. It was playing "Candy" now. *Candy-I-call-my-sugar-candy*. Somewhere, miles off, the record was being played, silent and invisible soundwaves were transmitted through the air, and here on the pub stool an oily voice, the voice of a fat man who did well for himself and his oily voice, was singing the words *Candy-I-call-my-sugar-candy*. The Glocke was well attended. People dressed in loden from the country, come to town to buy something, and businesspeople, whose premises were nearby and who wanted to sell the country people something, were eating white veal bratwursts. Klett the hairdresser peeled the skin off the whitish filling with his fingers and popped it in his mouth. *Candy-I-call-my-sugar-candy*. Klett smacked his lips and grunted contentedly. Only a moment ago, his hands had been in Messalina's hair. Messalina, wife of the actor. Alexander's shooting *Passion of an Archduke*, I bet it'll be wonderful.— "Your hair's a little dry this week, Madam, perhaps an oil massage. Your husband in uniform, that's something I'm looking forward to seeing already, *Passion of an Archduke*, there's nothing like a German film, you can say what you like." And now Messalina was sitting under the dryer. Five more minutes. Time for another sausage? The soft flesh, the juice dribbling down his fingers. *Candy-I-call-my-sugar-candy*. There were Greeks dicing at one table. They looked as though they were about to leap at each other's throats. Drama! "Hey, Joe, you wanna play? five times the stake if you win?"—"Those are bad men, mister, have knife." Josef pulled his face out of the beer tankard and looked loyally up at his master Odysseus. Odysseus's chest was convulsed with laughter, Mississippi waves, who could do anything to him? "*Beer*"—"Beer." The Glocke was gemütlich. Italian traders measured out bales of cloth, cut tags off the cloth with nimble scissors: Cellona wool, made in England. A couple of religious Jews were in breach of Moses's Law. They were eating unkosher, but they weren't eating pork, forgiven, forgiven on their travels, forgiven on their wanderings, forever wandering, forever on their way to Israel, forever in the dirt. *Fighting around Lake Nazareth, Arab League Claims Jordan.* One man was telling another about the landing in Narvik under Dietl "we were in the Arctic Circle," the other man talked about Cyrenaika in the Libyan desert, "Rommel's sun," they had got around, both of them, triumphantly, old comrades, one had been with the SS "in Tarnopol, Christ when the Scharführer whistled, they jumped."—"Just shut the fuck up and drink." They laid their arms over each other's shoulders and sang: *That-was-an-edelweiss.* "*Beer*"—"Beer." Girls prowled around, plump girls, stately girls, rough-looking girls *Candy-I-*

—*call-the-States!* In a padded phone cell in the big post room of the Central Exchange stood Washington Price. He was sweating in the closed box. He wiped the sweat off his forehead, and his handkerchief fluttered under the dim electric bulb in the cell like an agitated white bird in a cage. Washington was calling Baton Rouge, his hometown in the state of Louisiana. It was four in the morning in Baton Rouge, and it was still dark. The telephone had shrilled them out of their sleep so early, it couldn't bode well, it had to be bad news, they stood fearfully in the passage of the tidy little house, the trees rustled on the avenue outside, the wind rustled in the tops of the elms, trains were running down to the grain silos, wheat barges slid to the quays, a tug shrilled, Washington could see them, the old folks, the man in his striped pajamas, the woman hurriedly throwing an apron over her nightdress, he could see them in his mind's eye, hesitant, afraid, he reaching out his hand to the receiver, she reaching out her hand to hold it back, early morning news, calamity in the familiar house, such a strain to keep safe, Uncle Tom's cabin, stone house, house of a colored citizen, a respectable family, but the telephone carrying his voice from far away, a call from the white world, the hostile world, terrifying voice, voice longed for, they knew it, even before the crackle in the receiver and they heard his voice, the voice of their son, why was he staying away? the prodigal son, there was no fatted calf to be slaughtered, he himself had been slaughtered, he stayed past the end of the war, past the call of duty, stayed with the army, what was it to him? Germany, Europe, what distant squabble, the Russians, why not the Russians? our son the sergeant, his uniformed photograph on the sideboard next to the jug in white metal, next to the radiogram, *Commie Onslaught, Children Love Ludens Drops*, what is it? oh, they can sense it, and he knows they sense it: some entanglement. The old man picks up the receiver and answers, his father, chief inspector in the grain silo, Washington played in the grain, almost asphyxiated, a little boy in red and white striped dungarees, a black imp in the overspill, in a sea of yellow grain: bread. "Hello!" Now he was telling them: Carla, the white woman, the baby, he's not coming home, he wants to marry the white woman, he needs money, money to get married, money to save the baby, he can't tell them that, Carla threatening to go to the doctor, Washington needs money from the old people's savings, he announces the wedding, the baby, what do they know? They know. Entanglement, their son in trouble. No good news: sin. Or at least not a sin before God, but before man. They can see their alien daughter-in-law in the black quarter of Baton Rouge, see her pale skin, the woman from across the ocean, from across the pond, they see the section for colored people, the street of apartheid, how is he going to live with her? how be happy while she's crying? the house is too small, the house in the ghetto, Uncle Tom's trim cabin and the rustling of the trees on the avenue, the calm drift of the river, wide and deep, and in the depths peace, music from the neighbors' house, the hum of voices, dark voices in the evening, too much for her, too many voices, and only one voice, too close too near too present too dark, blackness and night and air and bodies and voices all together like a heavy velvet curtain, falling over the end of day with its thousand pleats. When evening comes—will he take her out dancing in Napoleon's dive bar? Washington knows, he knows as well as they do, the old folks, the good old people in the passage of the house under the rustling trees on the whispering river in the velvet pleats of night, that there's a board outside Napoleon's tavern on the night of the dance, for the enemywife, the enemygirlfriend the enemylover, who wasn't booty, who was earned, as Jacob wooed Rachel, no one will see the sign but everyone will be able to read it, in every eye there will be a sign WHITES NOT WELCOME. Washington telephones, he speaks across the ocean, his voice rushes ahead of the dawn, and the voice of his father solemnly flees the night, and the sign that once hung on the door of the cell that Washington shuts behind him read NO JEWS. President Roosevelt then got to hear of the sign, diplomats and journalists told him about it, and he talked about the Star of David by the fireside, and his fireside chat rushed through the ether and was broadcast from the sound box next to the white metal jug in Uncle Tom's cabin, and it unfurled in the hearts of his listeners. Washington joined up and went to war, *onward, Christian soldiers*, and in Germany the infamous laws disappeared, and the tablets of the vile law that embarrassed every human being were torn down and burned. Washington was decorated for valor, but in the fatherland that gave out the medals and the little ribbons, in the fatherland still stood the signs of arrogance, the thoughts of the subhumans, whether advertised or not, NO BLACKS. Entanglement, Washington has gotten entangled. He dreams, while telling his parents of his beloved (oh so lovable! is she lovable? is it arrogance? his arrogance? Washington *contra omnes*? Sir Washington doing battle against prejudice and ostracism?) he dreams, and in his dream he has a little hotel, a cozy little bar, and NONE UNWELCOME it will say in a wreath of colored fairy lights on the door—and that would be Washington's Bar. How can he make it clear to them? he is far away in Germany, they are far away on the banks of the Mississippi, and the world is wide and the world is free, and the world is bad and there is hatred in the world, and the world is full of violence, why? because everyone is afraid. Washington mops his sweating face. The white handkerchief bird flutters in its cage. They will send money, the good old folks, wedding money, crib money for the baby: it's toil and sweat, it's heavy full shovelfuls, shovelfuls of corn, it's our bread, and new entanglement, and trouble is our companion—

But as the baby stirred in her womb, she began to fear visible and invisible signs, Nebuchadnezzar dreams, Belshazzar writing, that could evict her from the paradise of automatic kitchens and dispel the pharmacopoeia of security, WHITES UNWELCOME, BLACKS UNWELCOME, either way they were affected, and it was over JEWS UNWELCOME that the father of her child, without especially knowing it or meaning to, had gone out to fight. Her baby was unwelcome to her, the black one, the brindled one, in its cavern still unknowing that it was a wild shoot, rejected by the gardener, heaped with accusation and recrimination, before it was even there to attract accusation and recrimination, and she stood in the examining room, what was there for him to examine? she knew it wasn't necessary to sit down on the chair, she wanted the intervention, the curettage, she wanted him to get rid of it, and wasn't he under obligation to her? what had he had from her? Coffee, cigarettes, expensive whisky at a time when coffee, cigarettes, and spirits were all completely unobtainable, you couldn't get the nastiest moonshine, what did he think he was doing, accepting such things? for rinsings, palpings, remedies, I've let him fondle my tits for long enough, now it's time he did something for me.— And he,

Dr. Frahm, specialist in gynecology and surgery, knew what was expected of him, he knew it without a word from her, he saw the significance of the protruding belly, and he thought: Hippocratic oath, take no life, the way they all swank about with that now, wonder who thought of it? a hangover after so much euthanasia, murder of mental patients, murder of the unborn, and I've got it in Gothic script, hanging in the corridor outside the consulting room, it's a bit dark there, and it looks really good, what is life? quants and life, the physicists have moved in on biology now, I can't read their stuff, there's too much mathematics in it, formulae, abstract knowledge, mental gymnastics, a body's not a body anymore, end of representation in the new painting, doesn't tell me anything, I'm a doctor, maybe I'm not cultivated enough, anyway I've got no time, barely enough for the specialist press, there's always more, I'm tired in the evenings, my wife wants to go to the cinema, a new film with Alexander, I think he's a jerk, but women? is sperm life? is an egg life? we're going to end up protecting gonococci, of course the priests talk about the soul, I should like to see one of those on the slab, wonder if Hippocrates had a city center practice, or did he take private patients? the Spartans threw children with abnormalities in the gorges of the Taygetos, military dictatorship, totalitarian system, clearly wicked, so Athens is better with philosophers and pederasts, but to get back to Hippocrates, he'd get such an earful if he ever turned up in my practice, "I'm going to end it all"—"If you don't agree to do it, Doctor"—"I want to be rid of it," and then to know where they go, the backstreets, the botched jobs, dying by the thousands, shopgirls, secretaries, they can barely feed themselves, what sort of future is there for a kid in those circumstances anyway? Welfare soup kitchens care home foster family unemployment prison war, I was a field doctor, all the red meat on the operating table, like rebirths, no limbs, born to die, eighteen-year-olds, they'd have been better off not being born, what lies ahead of that black baby? they shouldn't be allowed to copulate, but what's the chance of that, I wouldn't mind population control, Malthus, if you see what comes in during the surgery hours, I should look for another job, panel idiot, palatial insurance buildings, pennies for us, kind doctor, my father went into the countryside in a horse and trap, in summer the horse wore a straw hat over its ears, and what did my father give out? tapped them on their bellies and prescribed lime blossom tea, today they prescribe chemicals no one can even pronounce, medicine men is all they are, just another form of juju, and as for alternative medicine, psychotherapists are just another set of rascals, the wife gets amenorrhea because her husband has the hots for the office boy and doesn't dare say, the old I've-got-this-wart consultation, patients always want the newest of the new, ultrasound today, tomorrow it'll be something involving atomic fission, it's all driven by the magazines, I've got that stuff in my waiting room, all that spanking-new machinery, all-singing all-dancing, treatments like some kind of assembly line, who's going to pay for it? doctor doctor tribute to industry, the installments on their car, she'll have had a good time with her Negro, in Paris they're supposed to be quite besotted with them, *negroidization*, *racial treason*, the war propaganda in the *Völkischer Beobachter*, where did that get them, their racial purity? a race of bunker dwellers, the social indications promise difficulties, eugenic indication inadmissible, you get some pretty kids with mixed parentage, wonder what my wife would say if I wanted to adopt one? medical indication—"let's have a look then"—healthy, we need a name, breach of medical confidentiality—"morning sickness?"—almost too late for the syringe, take her to Schulte's clinic with all mod cons, proper nurses, don't mind working with them, have to talk to her about the fee, only-monkeys-work-for-peanuts, as Goethe never said.— "Frau Carla, I would suggest transferring you to the clinic right away."

The best for Carla. Washington was in the big sales hall of Central Exchange. He crossed to the ladies' department. What did he want? The best for Carla. The German salesgirls were friendly. Two women were choosing nightgowns. They were officers' wives, and the nightgowns were crêpe de chine in pink and eau-de-Nil. The women would lie in bed like ample Greek goddesses. The salesgirl left the women over their nightgowns. She turned to Washington and smiled. What did he want? There was a whirring in the air. He still had a sense of having the receiver pressed to his ear, hearing words coming over the ocean. Some technical wizardry left him back home in Baton Rouge. What wizardry placed him in the Central Exchange of some German city? What did he want? It was both good and scandalous: he wanted to marry. Whom did he want to make miserable, to whom did he want to bring grief? Was every step fraught with danger? Even here? In Baton Rouge they would have clubbed him to death. The salesgirl thought: He's shy, these huge men are always terribly shy, they're looking for undergarments for their girlfriends, and are too scared to ask.— She laid before him an array of things she considered appropriate to his case, little knickers and chemises, light delicate webs, proper whores' tackle, Just the thing for a girl, shadow-light, more to reveal excitingly than to mask. The salesgirl herself wore things like that. I could let him see them on me, she thought. Washington didn't want the garments. He said, "baby clothes." The salesgirl thought: Oh dear, he's already got her knocked up. They say they're supposed to make good fathers, she thought, but I wouldn't like to be carrying a child of one of them.— He thought: We should think about getting some kids' things ahead of time, so we're prepared, but Carla ought to pick them herself, she'll be furious if I choose them and take them back to her.— "No. Not baby clothes," he said. What did he want, then? He gestured vaguely back at the spindrift of erotic seduction. The officers' wives had chosen their nightgowns and looked angrily in Washington's direction. They called for the salesgirl. He's leaving her with the baby, thought the salesgirl, he's got someone else lined up, and he's buying the sexy undergarments for her, that's the way men are, white and black alike.— She left Washington for a moment and made out the bill for the officers' wives. Washington put his big brown hand on a scrap of yellow silk. The silk vanished under his hand like a trapped butterfly.

The black hand of the Negro and the dirty yellow hands of the Greeks picked up the dice, and rolled them on the cloth, let them bounce and spin and turn. Odysseus won. Josef tugged at his jacket: "Mister, we go, bad men." The Greeks pushed him aside. Josef clutched the radio tighter. He was afraid they might try and steal the little box. The music stopped for a while. A man's voice read news. Josef didn't understand what the man said, but he did pick out a few words, the words *Truman Stalin Tito Korea*. The voice in Josef's hand was talking about war, talking about conflict, talking about fear. The dice were thrown another time. Odysseus lost. He looked in perplexity at the hands of the Greeks, jugglers' hands pocketing his money. The brass band in the Glocke launched into their lunchtime concert. They played a tinny popular march. "No One Does It Like Us." People hummed along. A few banged their tankards in time. The people had forgotten their sirens, forgotten their bunkers, their collapsing houses, the men were no longer thinking of the yell of their sergeants, pitching them into the dirt in the barracks yard, the trenches, the field dressing-stations, drum fire, encirclement, retreat, they were thinking of parades and banners. Paris if the war had been over then, it was unfair that it wasn't over then. They had been cheated of their victory. Odysseus lost again. The dice were against him. The jugglers' hands performed their wonders. There was a trick. Odysseus wanted to find out what the trick was. He refused to be taken in. *No Upsurge of Militarism, Purely Defensive Posture.* In the din of the brass band, Josef raised Odysseus's music box to his ear. Did the voice in the box have a message for Josef the serviceman? The voice sounded very intense now, an intense whisper. Josef only picked out the occasional word, names of places, distant names of distant places, said in strange accents, *Moscow, Berlin, Tokyo, Paris—*

In Paris the sun was shining. Paris had not been destroyed. To go by the evidence of one's eyes, it was as though World War II had never been. Christopher Gallagher had a line to Paris. He was standing in the callbox from which Washington Price had just called Baton Rouge. Christopher too was holding a handkerchief in his hand. He wiped his nose with it. His nose was coarse-pored and reddish. His skin was rough. He had red hair. He looked like a sailor; in fact, he was a tax accountant. He was talking to Henriette. Henriette was his wife. They lived in Santa Ana, California. They had a house on the Pacific. Looking out of the windows, you could think you were looking at China. Now Henriette was in Paris. Christopher was in Germany. Christopher missed Henriette. He hadn't thought he would miss her so much, but he was missing her badly. He would have liked to have her with him. Especially, he would have liked to have her with him in Germany. He thought: We are so formal with each other, I wonder why that is? after all, I do love her.— Henriette was sitting in her room in a hotel on the Quai Voltaire. The Seine flowed past outside the window. On the opposite bank was the Jardin des Tuileries, often painted, still more often photographed, but always an entrancing scene. Christopher had a loud voice. In the earpiece, his voice sounded like a yell. He kept yelling out the same sentences: "I understand what you're saying; but believe me, you'd like it here. I'm sure you'd like it here. You'd like it a lot. I like it a lot." And she kept saying the same words back: "No, I can't do it. You know I can't." He knew it, but he couldn't understand it. Or he did understand, but in the same way as you understand someone's dream, and at the end you say: "Oh, never mind!" While she was talking to Christopher, she was looking down at the Seine, she saw the Tuileries in the sun, she saw the lovely spring Parisian day, the scene outside her window was like a Renoir, but she had the feeling that, through the priming, another, darker painting was showing. The Seine was turning into the Spree, and Henriette was standing at the window of a house on the Kupfergraben, and over there was the Museumsinsel, the Prusso-Hellenic temples, forever under construction, and she saw her father walking to work in the morning, as terribly upright as an Adolf Menzel figure, impeccable, not a speck of dust on him, his stiff black hat straight over his golden pince-nez, crossing the bridge to his museum. He wasn't an art historian, he had no immediate connection to the pictures, even though of course he knew them all, he was a senior government councilor on the board of the museum, an administrator who was responsible for the organization of the building, but for him it was his museum that he never let out of his sight even on holidays and whose respective art-historical directors he would view as incompetents, as clowns engaged for the amusement of the public, their performance beneath notice. He declined to move out to the residential quarters in the west of the city, out of sight of the museum, he remained in the apartment on the Kupfergraben, where conditions were spartan and Prussian (and where he remained even after his dismissal, till the day they came for him, him and his shy wife, Henriette's mother, who, from living in the shade of so much Prussianism had withered into a dependent with nothing to say for herself). As a little girl, Henriette had played on the steps of the Kaiser Friedrich Museum beneath the equestrian statue of the three-month Emperor, with the dirty, noisy, and magnificent rabble on the Oranienburger Strasse, the dress circle of the Monbijou Platz, and later on, following the Lyzeum period, as a trainee actress of Reinhardt's in the Deutsches Theater, walking over the bridge to the Karlstrasse, her former playmates, now teenagers, who now met under the hooves of the imperial horse to exchange furtive embraces, called "Henri" to her tenderly, and she waved back in ravishment, "Fritz" or "Paule," and the impeccable, the dust-free Councilor said: "Henriette, you can't do that." But what could she do, and what not? On the one hand, she could graduate with the Reinhardt Prize for being the best in her year; on the other, she couldn't play the female lead in Eichendorff's *Freier* in a production in Southern Germany, for which she had been contracted. She was abused and vilified, but she was never allowed to keep an engagement. It was all right for her to lead a vagrant life, and play in Zurich, Prague, Amsterdam, and New York nightclubs with a bunch of émigrés. It wasn't possible for her to be granted unlimited permission to stay anywhere, a work permit, or a long-stay visa for any country. It was all right for her to be expatriated along with other members of the ensemble from the German Reich. It was not possible for the impeccable Councilor to carry on working in the museum. It was possible that he was refused access to a telephone and his own bank account. It was possible for her to be washing dishes in a diner in Los Angeles. It was not possible to send money to his daughter from Berlin, while she waited for a film role. It was possible that, on losing her dishwashing job, and standing on the street, a very strange street, that she hungrily accepted an invitation from a stranger, who happened to be a Christian. He, Christopher Gallagher, married her. It was not possible for her father to keep the name of Friedrich Wilhelm Cohen; it was possible for him to be renamed Israel

Cohen. Did Christopher regret marrying her? He did not. It was not possible for the Menzelian figure, the Prussian official and his shy wife, to remain any longer in their native Berlin. It was possible that they were among the first Jews to be transported away: they left the Kupfergraben house for the last time at dusk, they climbed into a police van, and Israel Friedrich Wilhelm, upright, without a speck of dust, calm in his Frederician uprightness, helped her up, Sarah Gretchen, who was weeping, and then the door of the police van shut behind them, and nothing more was heard of them, until after the war everything came out, not about them in particular, but about them in general, the facelessness of their fate, the epidemic of their death—that was sufficient. Christopher's loud voice yelled: "So you're staying in Paris, are you?" And she said: "Please understand." And he yelled back: "I do understand. But you'd like it. You'd like it a lot. Everything's different now. I like it a lot." And she said: "Go to the Bräuhaus. There's a café opposite, called the Café Schön. That's where I used to sit and learn my lines." And he shouted: "Sure. I'll go there. But you'd like it." He was livid with her for staying in Paris. He was missing her. Did she like Paris? She could see the Renoirs again, the Seine, the Tuileries, the blithe light. Of course, she loved to look over so much that was intact, but in Europe destruction forced itself against intactness, it loomed like a noonday ghost: the Prusso-Hellenic temples on the Museumsinsel in Berlin lay looted and in rubble. She had loved them more than she ever had the Tuileries. She felt no satisfaction. She no longer hated. She was just afraid. She was afraid to go back to Germany even for three days. She longed to be out of Europe. She longed to be back in Santa Ana. By the shores of the Pacific there was peace, there was oblivion, there was peace and oblivion for her. The waves were the emblem of eternal return. The breath of Asia was on the wind, *Asia, World Problem Number One*, but the Pacific gave her something of the calm and security of the creature living for the moment, her grief was transmuted into a melancholy that swung out into the open expanse in front of her, her ambition to be admired as an actress died, it wasn't contentment, it was making do that filled her, almost a form of sleep, making do with the house, the terrace, the beach, this one point attained by chance, good fortune, or destiny in the vast whole of infinity. "Give Ezra my love," she said. "He's great," he roared back. "He gets by everywhere with his German. He translates for me. You'd have so much fun. You'd really like it here."—"I know," she said. "I understand. I'm waiting for you. I'll wait for you here in Paris. Then we can all go home together. It will be wonderful. It'll be wonderful to be home again. Tell Ezra! Tell him I'm waiting for you. Tell him to go and see everything. Tell Ezra—"

Ezra was sitting in Christopher's spacious, mahogany-paneled automobile. The car looked like an early model of a sports plane relegated to ground use. Ezra was flying all round the square. He was letting them have it with all he'd got. He was peppering away at the street. Panic set in among the crowd, that teeming mass of pedestrians and murderers, that strange bunch of hunters and prey. They sagged to their knees, they prayed and whined for mercy. They rolled about on the ground. They cradled their heads in their arms for protection. They fled like frightened deer into the buildings. The shop windows of the big stores were smashed to smithereens. Streaks of tracer flew into the shops. Ezra dived down at the statue, which was the centerpiece of the square in front of the Central Exchange. On the steps to the statue sat boys and girls of Ezra's age. They were chatting, laughing, playing heads and tails; they were selling, swapping, and arguing over a small collection of American goods; they teased a shaggy little dog; they fought and made up. Ezra spilled a sheaf of his luminous ammunition over the children. The children lay dead or wounded on the steps to the monument. The young dog crawled into a gutter to die. A boy yelled: "That was Ezra!" Ezra flew over the roof of the Central Exchange and banked steeply up. Once he was high above the city, he dropped his bomb. *Scientists warn against use*.

A little girl was wiping the dust off a sky-blue limousine. The little girl was working enthusiastically; one might have supposed she was cleaning the heavenly conveyance of one of the angels. Heinz had gone into hiding. He had climbed up onto the pedestal of the monument and was crouched under the Elector's horse. Historians had given the Elector the cognomen "the Pious." In the wars of religion, he had gone into battle for the true faith. His enemies, equally, were fighting for the true faith. In the question of faith, therefore, there was no clear winner. Perhaps the real loser was faith for allowing people to fight and die on its behalf. But in the course of the war, the pious Elector had become a powerful man. He had become so powerful that it was no joke where his subjects were concerned. Heinz did not concern himself with the wars of religion and the power of the Elector. He observed the square.

It was a nation of drivers that was spreading out below him. Cars were parked in long lines. When they ran out of petrol, they would become pumpkins, huts for shepherds, in the event that people could still breed sheep after the next war, hiding places for lovers, if, following death, people still sought covert places for their love. Just now the cars were nimble and shiny, a proud automobile exhibition, a triumph of a technical century, a saga of the victory of men over the forces of nature, a symbol of the apparent conquest of inertia and resistance in space and time. Maybe one day the cars would become obsolete. They would remain on the square like tin corpses. No one would be able to drive them. People would strip out of them whatever was useful, a seat for their behinds. The rest would rust. Women, women dressed fashionably and indifferently, women boyish and ladylike, women in olive-green uniform, female lieutenants and female majors, coquettishly made-up teenagers, an awful lot of women, because civilian employees, officers, soldiers, Negroes and Negresses, all formed part of the army of occupation, they inhabited the square, they called, laughed, waved, they steered the automobiles humming the song of wealth to themselves deftly between other parking cars. The Germans admired and hated the wheeled display. A few thought: At least ours used to march.— By their lights, it was better to march into a foreign land than to drive into it; it accorded better with the familiar laws and conditions to be supervised by landsers than by gentlemen motorists. The gentlemen motorists might be kindlier, and the landsers rougher; but that wasn't at issue; this was to do with the rules, sticking to the habits handed down over the centuries to do with the conduct of war, victory, and defeat. German officers who got by as traveling salesmen, waiting at the streetcar stop with their little case of samples, were angry when they saw ordinary American privates driving coolly past their superior officers like rich tourists in comfortable seats, without so much as a salute. That was democracy and disorder. The luxurious vehicles gave the occupation a whiff of excess, of profanation, of sybaritism.

Washington walked up to his sky-blue limousine. He was the angel for whom the little girl had polished the heavenly conveyance. The little girl curtseyed. She curtseyed and passed her cloth across the door. Washington gave her chocolate and bananas. He had bought the chocolate and the bananas specially for the little girl. He was a regular client of hers. Under the horse of the pious Elector, Heinz scowled. He waited till Washington drove off, and then he climbed down from the plinth.

He spat against the plaque with the list of the Elector's victories. He said: "That was my ma's nigger."

The children looked respectfully at Heinz. He impressed them, the way he stood there, spitting, and saying, "That was my ma's nigger." The hard-working little girl had gone over to the monument and was contemplatively eating one of the bananas his-mother's-nigger had given her. The young dog sniffed at the peel she dropped. The little girl didn't notice the dog. The dog wore no collar. He had a string round his neck. He seemed tame enough, but ownerless. Heinz was bragging: he had already driven that Yankee car, he could do that any time he liked: "My mother's going out with a Negro." The dark friend, the black feeder of the family, the generous and yet alien and disruptive presence in the apartment preoccupied him. Some days he would deny the Negro even existed. "What's your Negro doing?" the boys would ask him. "No idea. Don't know what you're talking about," he replied. On other occasions, he would make a sort of cult figure of Washington, describe his incredible physical strength, his wealth, his importance as a sportsman, and save the trump card for last, putting all these other attributes into perspective, when he concluded by saying that Washington and his mother were living together. His friends knew the story, which they had heard many times, they went on telling it to each other in their own homes, but just like in the cinema, they would always be sitting on the edge of their seats, waiting for the killer punch: he's going out with my mother, he eats with us at our table, he sleeps in our bed, they want me to call him Pa. All that came up from the depths of pleasure and woe. Heinz couldn't remember his father, who had disappeared on the Volga. A photograph of his father in a gray uniform did nothing for him. Washington might well be a good father. He was friendly, he was generous, he didn't punish, he was a well-known sporting figure, he wore a uniform, he was one of the conquerors, by Heinz's standards he was rich, and he drove a sky-blue automobile. Whereas what spoke against Washington was his black skin, the striking, unignorable mark of otherness. Heinz didn't want to be unlike the others. He wanted to be just like the other boys, and they all had white-skinned, German, familiar fathers. Washington was not universally familiar. People sometimes talked about him with disrespect. Some poked fun at him. Sometimes, Heinz wanted to come to Washington's defense, but then he didn't dare put forward a different opinion to the majority, the grown-ups, the Germans, people who knew what they were talking about, so he too said: "The nigger!" People spoke in an ugly way about Carla's relationship with Washington; they didn't scruple to use bad words in the boy's presence; but what Heinz hated most of all was when they patted his head with a false show of pity, and wailed: "poor kid, after all you're a German boy." So, Washington, without guessing it (but perhaps he did guess, perhaps he even knew it, and he kept out of Heinz's way, shyly, and looking off elsewhere), was a worry to Heinz, an irritation, a source of grief and pain and continual conflict, and it happened that Heinz avoided Washington, accepted presents from him unwillingly, and only rarely and sullenly went for drives in his magnificent and greatly admired car. He hung around, he persuaded himself that he loathed the blacks and the Yanks, all of them, and to punish himself for a position that was basically cowardly, and to prove to himself that he could say the thing with which the others thought they could persecute him, he incessantly went around crowing his "she's going out with a nigger." When he felt himself come under observation from Ezra in the airplane-esque car, he yelled out in his pretty fluent English (which he had picked up from Washington, purely so as to be able to follow the conversations between his mother and the Negro, to hear what they were planning, seeing as it concerned him too, the trip to America, their emigration-cum-homecoming, in which he, Heinz, wasn't sure whether he wanted to participate or not, on the one hand he might insist on being taken, then again he might go into hiding once all the things were packed): "*Yes, she goes with a nigger.*" Heinz was holding the dog by his string. The boy and the dog were tied together. They were like a couple of poor condemned wretches tied together. The dog pulled to get away from Heinz. Ezra watched Heinz and the dog. It was all like a dream to him. The boy shouting out, "*Yes, she goes with a nigger,*" the dog tied on a string, the equestrian statue of greenish bronze, they were all unreal, they were not a real boy, a real dog, a real monument; they were ideas; they had the light, giddy-making shimmer of figures in dreams; there was an intimate and an evil common cause between them and him, and the best thing he could do would be to wake up with a scream. Ezra had foxy-red hair, cropped short. His little brow creased under his foxy-red cap. He thought he might be lying in bed at home in Santa Ana. The Pacific was beating against the shore with monotonous wash. Ezra was sick. There was war in Europe. Europe was a distant continent. It was the land of the poor old people. It was the land of vicious myths. There was an evil country there, and in the evil country there was an evil giant, *Hitler the aggressor*. America was at war as well. America was fighting against the evil giant. America was idealistic. It was fighting for human rights. What rights were those? did Ezra have them? did he have the right not to eat his soup, to kill his enemies, the kids on North Beach, to talk back to his father? His mother sat at his bedside. Henriette spoke German with him. He didn't understand the language, and he did understand the language. German, quite literally, was his mother tongue, it was an older and more mysterious language than the American that was the language they spoke at home and outside, and his mother was crying, she was in the nursery crying, crying for strange people, disappeared, stolen, kidnapped, slaughtered, and the Jewish-Prussian senior civil servant and his soft, still Sarah/ Gretchen, led off *in the course of the liquidation,* they were told at the bedside of a sick child in Santa Ana, California, became characters in Grimm's German fairytales, just as real, just as dear, just as sad as King Thrushbeard, as Tom Thumb and Little Red Riding

Hood, just as strange as the story of the juniper tree. Henriette taught her son his mother tongue by reading him German fairy-tales, but once she thought he was asleep, then she would tell stories to herself, watching over his feverish sleep, worrying about him, the tale of his grandparents, and just like the hum of the newest language-teaching gramophone records, which taught you foreign sounds while you slept, the vocabulary of German pain, murmurs of grief and tears, etched themselves into Ezra's soul. Now he was in the forest, in the eerie magic thicket of dream and Märchen—the parking lot was the thicket, the city was the forest, his air attack hadn't helped, Ezra had to fight his way out on the ground. Heinz had a tousled head of long blond hair. He looked with displeasure at the other's newfangled American crew-cut hair. He thought: Here's a stuck-up kid, I'm going to take him.— Ezra asked: "Do you think you might part with the dog?" In his uncertainty regarding the language, he addressed him as "Sie" instead of "Du." To Heinz, this was one more indication of the stuck-upness of the strange boy, who sat as of right in the interesting-looking car (not like Heinz, with his doubtful place in Washington's), it was a rebuke, an assertion of distance (perhaps the "Sie" really was intended as a sort of barrier, as protection for Ezra, and not linguistic confusion), and he, Heinz, now followed suit, and the two eleven-year-olds, both bred in fear of war, conversed stiffly like a couple of well-bred adults. No, he did not think he would part with the dog. Nor was it his dog. The dog belonged to all the children. But it might be possible to sell him. It was worth staying in communication about. Heinz got the sense that something might be possible here. He didn't know what, but something. Ezra didn't even particularly want to buy the dog. But for a time he had the sense that he was duty bound to try and rescue it. But then the rescue receded in his mind, it wasn't important, what was important was the conversation, and something that had yet to emerge. It wasn't clear yet. The dream wasn't yet far enough along. The dream was just in its early stages. Ezra said: "I'm Jewish." He was Catholic. Like Christopher, he had received a Catholic baptism and teaching in the Catholic faith. But it belonged to the style of the Märchen that he was Jewish. He looked expectantly at Heinz. Heinz didn't know what to do with Ezra's confession. It perplexed him, it was as if he had pulled out a chess move he didn't see the point of. It would have perplexed him just as much if Ezra had explained he was a Red Indian. Was he trying to make himself interesting? Jews? Jews were traders, spectral businessmen, and they didn't like the Germans. Was that what he was? What did Ezra trade in? There weren't any wares in the airplane car. Maybe he wanted to buy the dog cheaply, and then sell him at a vast profit. Well, let him try! Just in case, Heinz repeated his own confession: "I would have you know, my mother lives with a Negro." Was Heinz threatening him with his Negro? Ezra had no associations with Negroes. But he knew there were black and white children who fought each other in gangs. So Heinz belonged to a black gang, well, that was a little surprising. Ezra had better be careful. "How much would you like for the dog?" he asked. Heinz said: "Ten dollars." That was all right. Ten dollars was all right. If the chump shelled out ten dollars, more fool him. The dog wasn't worth ten marks. "OK," said Ezra. He didn't know how he was going to do it yet. But he would do it. It would be all right. He would have to lie to Christopher. Christopher wouldn't understand that it was only a dream, and not something real. He said: "I'll get hold of ten dollars from somewhere." Heinz thought: Little tyke, think I'm going to fall for that one.— He said: "I'm not giving you the dog till I've got the money." The dog, unconcerned by the dickering, pulled at his string. The little girl had tossed him a piece of chocolate from Heinz's-mother's-black-man. The chocolate lay in a puddle, where it was slowly dissolving. The dog couldn't reach it. Ezra said: "I'll have to ask my father. He'll give me the money."—"Now?" asked Heinz. Ezra thought. Once again, his little brow creased below the foxy-red cap of stubbly hair. He thought: We can't do it here.— He said: "No, tonight. Come to the Bräuhaus. My dad and I are going to be at the Bräuhaus tonight." Heinz nodded. He said: "OK!" He knew the Bräuhaus area. The Negro Soldiers' Club was on the Bräuhaus Square. Heinz often stood outside and watched as his mother and Washington got out of the sky-blue limousine and walked past the black MPs into the club. He knew all the whores who prowled around the square. Occasionally, the whores would give him chocolate they had got from their black customers. Heinz didn't need their chocolate. But he was happy to take it from the whores. Then he could go up to Washington and say: "I don't want any chocolate." He thought: You'll get your dog, I'll give you the slip.

Odysseus gave them the slip. He gave the Greeks the slip, gave the nimble hands the slip, darting like nimble yellow lizards over the beer table. The throw came out for them. They plucked up the dice, and handed them to Odysseus; Odysseus lost; they scraped them up in their hand, threw them down, with luck on their side; they were dicing for marks and dollars, for the marks of manhood and girlie dollars, what was at stake was what they called life, the filling of bellies, intoxication, pleasure, spending money, because what it took to make the day tolerable for them cost money, eating, drinking, fucking, it all cost money, marks or dollars, and here they were at stake: what did the Greeks amount to, what was King Odysseus without money? He had deerslayer eyes. The band in the Glocke were chasing the white hind of their wishes and illusions. The beer had set them on imaginary chasers; they were proud huntsmen on steeds. Their impulses were hunting the white hind of self-deception. The mountain fusilier sang along to the band's tune, the Africa veteran, the Eastern Front soldier joined in. Josef, separated from his day's black master by the wiles of the Greeks, was listening to an account of the situation in Persia from Odysseus's music box *Paratroopers Dispatched to Malta*, but it was only noise to Josef's ears, the crashing of a sort of historical surf, a surf from the ether that came washing around him, the lived and incomprehensible ferment of history, a yeasty dough that was rising. Names were stirred into it, names and always more names, oft-heard names, the names of the hour in world history, the names of the major players, the names of the managers, the names of the locations, the scenes of the conferences, the scenes of the battles, the scenes of the crimes, how will the dough rise? what sort of bread shall we eat tomorrow? "We were the first in Crete," cried the Rommel veteran, "Crete was our first assignment. We kicked ass." There was the hind! Now he'd figured it out, deer-slayer eyes! The black hand was quicker than the yellow lizards with their conjuring trick. Odysseus reached in. He had the dice. This time, they were the real ones, the crooked ones, the cunning ones that brought luck, the cunningly substituted ones. He rapped them down on the wood: Victory! He threw them again, and again he had a lucky throw. He thrust out his elbows. The Greeks reeled backward. Odysseus's back shielded the table. The table was the front. He laid down a barrage on the wood, a veritable bombardment of good fortune: Chief Odysseus King Odysseus General Odysseus Managing Director Mister Odysseus Cotton Esquire. "We cleaned up the White Hills. When we went down to the valleys, we used concentric charges, and then in the brush we used tommy guns and knives and the odd pineapple. We were awarded the Crete medal." — "Bollocks!" — "Are you saying—" — "I'm saying bollocks to that. The real fighting was Russia. Everything else was kids' stuff. Comic books with four-color covers. True romance brochures. Jesus fuck! Colored covers. Here's your naked wench, and there's your paratrooper with death-bringing eyes. Same thing. I'd give my little'un a hiding if he ever came home with trash like that." The voice on the music box was saying: "Cyprus." Cyprus was strategically important. The voice was saying "Teheran." The voice did not say "Shiraz." The voice had nothing to say about the roses of Shiraz. The voice did not say "Hafiz." The voice was unacquainted with the poet Hafiz. As far as the voice was concerned, there had never been any Hafiz. The voice said: "*Oil*." And once again there was noise, unspecific-syllable noise, the stream of history noisily rushing past, Josef was sitting on the banks of the river, old, tired, defeated, still squinnying out for a little happiness before sundown, incomprehensible stream, incomprehensible babble of waters, the lulling rush of syllables. The Greeks didn't dare go for their knives. The white hind had got away from them. Black Odysseus had got away from them: wily, great Odysseus. He gave Josef some money to pay for their beers. "Too much, mister," said Josef. "Never too much money," said Odysseus. The waitress pocketed the bills: great grace of Odysseus. "Come on," said Odysseus. "Appeal to the Hague," said the voice. The voice was being carried by Josef, *Wilhelm II, Proposed to the Hague as Peace Emperor*, shaken by Josef, with his old man's walk he shook the trickle of great words. The river of history flowed. From time to time it burst its banks. It inundated the countryside. It left behind it the drowned, it left behind muck and mire, fertility, the stinking motherfield, a stew of fertility: where is the gardener? when will the fruits be ripe? Josef followed, small and twinkling-eyed, he too in muck and mire, still in muck and mire, once again in muck and mire, following his black master, the master he had chosen to follow for the day. When was blossom-time? When would the golden age come, the great age—

He had marriage on his mind. The sky-blue limousine drew

up in front of the tenement where Carla lived. Washington had bought flowers, yellow flowers. As he climbed out of the limousine, the sun broke through the cloudy sky. The light bounced off the metalwork of the limousine, and made the flowers burst into sulfurous blossom. Washington sensed himself being watched from the windows of the tenement. The little people who lived in many clusters, in every room three or four people, every room a cage, a zoo was more accommodating, the little people pressed up against the patched and starched curtains and jostled each other. "He's bringing her flowers. See that. He ought to be—" From some complex or other, it upset them to see Washington bringing flowers into the house. Washington himself came in for relatively little attention; he was just a man, albeit he was a black man. What came in for attention were the flowers, they counted the number of parcels he was carrying, and the car was eyed with bitterness. In Germany, a car like that cost more than a little house. It cost more than the little house in the suburbs that people yearned for all their lives. Max said so. Max ought to know. Max worked in a garage. The sky-blue limousine parked outside the door was a provocation.

A couple of old women had registered complaints about what was going on in the third-floor apartment. Frau Welz must have contacts with the police. The police refused to get involved, *cancer on democracy*. In actual fact, the police saw little reason to get involved. They couldn't get involved each time there was anything amiss in the city. Besides, the old women would have had cause to regret any intervention from the police. The police would have robbed them of the principal drama in their lives.

Washington walked up the stairs: jungles surrounded him. Behind every door they stood listening. They were domesticated; they could sniff the wild beast in him, but the times were not favorable, the times didn't allow the herd to throw themselves upon the alien creature that had forced its way into the territory of the herd. Frau Welz opened the door. She was coarse-haired, fat, baggy-assed, dirty. In her eyes, though, Washington was a tame animal: maybe not exactly a cow, but a goat, I'll milk that black billy— "She's not home," she said, and made to take the packages from him. He said, "Oh, that's too bad." He said it in the mild, distant way of blacks talking to whites, but his voice had an undertone of tension and impatience. He wanted to be rid of the woman. He loathed her. He walked down the gloomy corridor to Carla's rooms. From some of the doors, he was eyed by the girls, who took soldiers back to Frau Welz's. Washington suffered from where they had to live. But he was unable to do anything about it. Carla couldn't find them any other room. She said: "I can't get anywhere else with you." Carla suffered from it as well, but less than Washington, whom she was forever assuring of how much she was suffering, how unworthy all this was for her, which meant really how much she was abasing herself for him, how low she had to stoop, and he always had to try and make up for it with more love, more presents, more sacrifices, and it helped but only a very little. Carla despised and cursed Frau Welz and the girls, but when she was alone and bored, when Washington was at work in the barracks, she would fraternize with the girls, invite them round, gossip with them, girl talk, whore talk, or she would sit in Frau Welz's kitchen, drink cups of acorn coffee from the pot that was always bubbling on the stovetop, and tell Frau Welz (who would go on to tell the neighbors) anything she wanted to know. The girls in the corridor liked to show Washington what they had; they would pull open their pinafore dresses, adjust their garters, brush clouds of scent from their dyed hair. There was a competition among the girls to see which of them would get Washington into bed. Since they were only familiar with blacks in a state of arousal, their tiny brains concluded that they were always up for it. They didn't understand Washington. They didn't get it into their heads that he wasn't a john. Washington was born for a happy family life; but unhappy chances had thrown him off his path and into this apartment, to the jungle and the swamp. Washington hoped he might find a message from Carla in the living room. He thought Carla would be back soon. Maybe she had gone to get her hair done. He looked on the dressing table for a note that would say where she had gone. On the dressing table there were bottles of nail varnish, face lotion, pots of cream, and boxes of powder. There were photographs jammed inside the frame of the mirror. One of them showed Carla's disappeared husband, who was now on his way to his official death, his being declared missing presumed dead, and the taking off of the bond that tied him and Carla together in this world till-death-do-you-part. He was in field-gray uniform. His chest had on it the swastika against which Washington had gone to do battle. Washington looked at the man placidly. Placidly he took in the swastika on the man's chest. The swastika had become meaningless. Maybe the racist emblem had never meant anything to the man. Maybe Washington hadn't really been fighting against that. Maybe they'd both been cheated. He didn't hate the man. The man didn't unsettle him. He wasn't jealous of his predecessor. Occasionally, he would feel a little envious of him, for having done with everything. It was a dark feeling; Washington would repress it. Next to her husband in the mirror frame was Carla in her bridal outfit and white veil. She was eighteen when she married. Twelve years ago now. In those years the world that Carla and her husband had thought to live in long and securely had collapsed. Of course, that world hadn't been the world of her parents anyway. Carla had been pregnant when she had gone to the registry office, and the white veil on the photograph was a lie, or not really a lie, because no one was taken in, or could have been taken in by it, because the white veil was just a piece of ornamentation, and became a painful source of ridicule if it was taken to be the indication of an unbro-ken hymen, and it was by no means frivolous to think like that, because the times were if anything inclined to mock the idea that the bridegroom, the public celebration and compact over, would fling himself upon his bride, on his white sacrificial lamb, to find that idea shameless and frivolous, and yet marriage was de rigueur, the official and orderly business of matrimony, the blessing from the state, all for the sake of the children, the children who were to be born into the state, and were even solicited for, *visit beautiful Germany*, and Carla and her husband, then just married, believed in a Reich to whom one could and should give children, trust-ingly, dutifully, and responsibly, *children true wealth of the nation, marriage loans for young couples*. Carla's parents were also stuck in the mirror frame. Frau Behrend had got herself photographed with a bouquet of flowers, the music master was in uniform, but instead of his conductor's baton his left hand gripped the neck of a violin, which he held pressed against his seated thigh. And so Herr and Frau Behrend were peacefully united as a couple with poetic and musical inclinations. Heinz had been photographed as an infant, standing upright in his baby carriage, waving. He had forgotten whom he was waving to, presumably some grown-up; the person had been his father, who had stood behind the camera, taking the picture, and who shortly after had gone to war. Another picture, of larger format than the others, showed himself, Wash-ington Price: he was in his baseball uniform, with the white cap, bat, and fielding mitt. His expression was grave and dignified. And that was Carla's family. Washington belonged to Carla's family. For a while he stared stupidly at the photographs. Where was Carla? What was he doing here? He saw himself in the mirror, with his flowers and packages. It was funny, him standing in this room with the family snaps, the toiletries, and the mirror. For a moment, Washington was overcome by the feeling that his life was absurd.

He reeled in front of his reflection. From the room of one of the girls he could hear a radio playing music. The American station was playing the sad and majestic Ellington tune, "Negro Heaven." Washington felt like crying. As he listened to the music, a song of home from a whore's room in an alien land (and what land wasn't alien to him?), he felt the whole ugliness of existence. Earth was no heaven. Least of all a Negro heaven. But straightaway, his courage set off in pursuit of a new fata morgana, he got the idea that before long there would be a new picture stuck in this frame, the picture of a little brown baby, the baby that he and Carla were going to bring into the world.

He stepped into the kitchen, to Frau Welz's kitchen, to the bubbling cauldrons, and she gave him to understand, a witch in swathes of smoke, steam, and fumes, that she knew exactly where Carla was, he should set his mind at rest, there was something the matter with Carla, something had cropped up, he would understand, sometimes if people loved each other they got a little careless, she knew all about that, she probably didn't look as though she did, but she knew about these things, and the girls here, they all knew, yes, the thing with Carla, it wasn't too bad (he didn't understand, he, Washington, didn't understand, didn't understand this German witch's spells, an evil woman, what was she saying? what was the matter with Carla? why didn't she say she was at the hairdresser's, at the cinema? why these riddles? so many bad words), it really wasn't bad as she had such a good doctor, and had always been careful to look after the doctor even during the bad times, "I always said to Carla, Carla, I said, it's too much, but Carla always wanted to take him the best of everything, well, now we know what it's good for, Carla always giving him the best," there was absolutely no need to worry, "Dr. Frahm, Washington, Dr. Frahm will take care of it." That he understood. He understood the name, Dr. Frahm. What was the matter? Was Carla sick? Washington got a fright. Or had she gone to the doctor on account of the baby? But that couldn't be, that couldn't be. She couldn't do that, that of all things she couldn't, she mustn't do—

It was a joke. Someone had thought it might be amusing to tie Emilia to a load of property. But maybe it wasn't even a joke at that, maybe Emilia was so indifferent to every power, every plan, every consideration, every good or bad fairy, the spirit of chance, that there wasn't even enough there for a joke, and she had been thrown out into the trash along with her property, without anyone meaning to throw her out there, it had all happened by chance, accidentally, but it was a peculiarly stupid, mean, and mindless accident that had tethered her to goods, which others' and then her own wishes had continually prescribed as the means to a wonderful life, whereas the inheritance in fact only made possible a Bohemian existence, with disorder, uncertainty, begging trips, and days of hunger, a Bohemian existence that was grotesquely coupled with estate management and tax liabilities. The times had had no particular design on Emilia, neither for good nor ill, but Emilia's inheritance had fallen prey to the times and their plans, the capital was scattered, in some countries it had already been scattered, in others it was still about to be, and in Germany the hour loosened the hold on property like aqua fortis, it ate and corroded what had collected by way of wealth, and it was foolish of Emilia to take a few splashes of acid, inasmuch as any of them hit her, for any personal ill will to her on the part of destiny. No one intended any of it. The life that Emilia couldn't master was a turning point, it was a fateful time, but that was on the macroscale, whereas in one's own small world one might continue to have good or ill luck, and Emilia was unfortunate enough to cling stubbornly and fearfully to things as they disappeared, which gave rise to a distorted, disorderly, disreputable, and slightly absurd agony; but the birth of the new age was just as much beset with grotesquerie, disorder, disrepute, and absurdity. One might live on one side of things or the other, and one might die on this side or that of time's trench. "Great wars of faith are coming," said Philipp. Emilia got all that muddled up, she saw herself relegated to Bohemia because of her money worries, saw herself classed with people who enjoyed free meals and a license to clown, but were not respected, while her grandparents, who had done so much to multiply the family's wealth, would not even have given the time of day to such wastrels. Emilia hated and despised Bohemia, the impoverished intellectuals, the babbling incompetents, wearers of frayed trousers and their cheap girlfriends in their second time round Parisian taboo basement fashions with whom she lay in one gutter, whereas Philipp simply avoided this caste that Emilia so detested because he did not even recognize them as Bohemians, Bohemia was long gone, and the people who pretended there were still young intellectuals, revolutionaries, and aestheticians in cafés, they to him were just slumming it for the evening, enjoying themselves in to them a traditional way, whereas by day they were by no means such incompetents as Emilia thought them, working as graphic designers, writing advertising slogans, earning money for the film and broadcast, and the taboo girls were parked behind typewriters, Bohemia was dead, had died already before the Romanisches Café was bombed, it was dead before the first SA man stepped inside, in fact it had been garroted by politics even before Hitler arrived on the scene. When Lenin, the Zurich Bohemian, left for Russia, he left the door of the literary café shut behind him for the next several centuries. Anything left behind after Lenin was basically conservative, it was conservative puberty, conservative love of Mimi, conservative *épater les bourgeois* (though bear in mind also that the Mimi who was to be loved, and the bourgeois

who was to be *épater*'d, had both themselves died and been turned
into fairy-tale figures), until Bohemia eventually found its en-
tombment in certain bars, and changed from being a conservative
affair to a preserved affair, a museum piece, something to put in
your Baedeker. These places, these *boîtes*, these mausoleums of
the *Scènes-de-la-vie-de-bohème* were then in turn, and grotesquely
enough, haunted by Emilia, who needed to raise money to be able
to afford to go, whereas to Philipp they were quite simply an or-
deal, with their dance-creatures, and the why-don't-you-let-me-
treat-you-to-a-glass-of-wine patronage of the small businessmen
who favored them. "We never go anywhere," Emilia would then
protest, "you seem to forget I'm young, and want to have fun."
And he thought: Is your youth such a desiccated affair that it needs
this shower, this shower of drunkenness, alcohol, and syncopa-
tion, does your feeling require the air of unfeeling, your hair the
riffling breeze of will-you-sleep-with-me-tonight "but it'll have to
be quick because I have to go to work in the morning"?— Emilia
stood in no man's land, threatened from all sides. She was rich, but
disbarred from pleasure in her wealth, she had not been accepted
by Dives, she was not his child, but nor was she accepted and made
welcome by the working world, and the idea of having to be quick
because I have to go to work in the morning was one she confronted with blind, cold, and utterly innocent rejection. Now she
had made progress, she had taken some steps, she had put a bit of
the Scottish plaid walk behind her. Emilia had been to the pawn-
brokers. She had stood among the poor in the hall of the municipal
pawnshop. The hall was clad in marble, and it resembled a swimming pool that had had the water let out of it. The poor were not
swimming. They had gone under. They were not bobbing along.
They were on the bottom. Above was life, oh, the gleam and the
fullness of life were all safely on the other side of the marble walls,
beyond the glass roof that covered the hall, the milky panes of

glass, like a foggy sky that hung over the pond of the drowned. They were on the bottom of existence and leading a ghostly life. They stood in front of the counters, clutching their erstwhile possessions, the things of another life that had nothing whatever to do with their current life, the life they had led prior to drowning, and the goods they brought up to the counter seemed to them to be other people's, like stolen property they were trying to fence, and they behaved as timidly as thieves caught in the act. Was it all up with them? It was coming to an end, but it wasn't quite finished. Their property still connected them to life, just as ghosts cling on to buried treasures; they belonged to the limbo of the Styx, but there was a period of grace, the counter they bellied up to gave them six marks on the price of a coat, three for their shoes, eight for their featherbed, the drowned were gasping for air, they were released back into life once more, for hours or days at a time, the fortunate ones for weeks, *expiry time four months*. Emilia had passed a silver fish service over the counter. The Renaissance design of the service was not taken into consideration, the art of the silversmith was not considered, they looked for the silver mark, and then the service was tossed on the scales. The fish course of the rich Commercial Councilor's dinner lay on the pawnshop scales. "Your Excellency, the salmon!" The Kaiser's general asked for a second helping. *Full steam ahead, the Kaiser's motto for the century ahead.* The service didn't weigh much. The silver handles were hollow. The hands of Commercial Councilors, bankers, and ministers had held these handles, had helped themselves to salmon, to sturgeon, to trout: plump hands, ring-bedecked hands, fateful hands. "His Majesty mentioned Africa in his speech. If I might suggest, colonial bonds—" Fools! They should have invested in gold, and buried the lot, the fools, in gold it would have been safe, and I wouldn't be standing here now!— The pawnshop advances three pfennigs per gram of silver cutlery. Emilia was handed eighteen marks and a receipt from the counter. The drowned in the Stygian pool envied her. Emilia was among the elite shades, in her glad rags she was still a princess.

And then on, on in her Calvary procession, in her ragged princess fur, with her bundle of goods in the funny Scotch plaid: she stood outside the arch of Herr Unverlacht, which was another entry to the underworld, slippery steps led down, and behind dirty glass in the light of alabaster lamps, heavy pear-shaped opalescent light drops that he had once bought from the estate of a suicide and hadn't managed to sell off yet, she saw Unverlacht's great gleaming pate. He was broad shouldered and squat; he looked like a mover who one day had made the discovery that it was easier to make money by selling off old goods than humping them around, or like a stout man who plays the villain in wrestling bouts, but surely he had never been a mover or a wrestler, perhaps a frog, a fat and cunning frog, waiting in his vault for flies. Emilia went down, opened the door, and already she was full of revulsion. Her skin shrank back. This wasn't a frog prince looking out toward the door with cold, watery eyes, Unverlacht was what he was, unmetamorphosed, and no change back was to be expected, no prince would ever leap from out of the frogskin. A musical mechanism set in motion by Emilia's entry played *Ein-feste-Burg-ist-unser-Gott*. But there was no significance in that, it wasn't a declaration of any sort. Unverlacht had simply acquired the mechanism cheaply, as he had acquired the lamps, and now he was waiting for a buyer for these treasures. So far as the lamps were concerned, it was stupid of him to want to sell them: with their alabaster glow, they bestowed a real shimmer of Hades to his vault. "Well, Sissy, what have you got for me?" he said, and the froggy flipper hand (it was true, the fingers had grown together as with horny webbing) gripped Emilia by the chin, her little chin slid into the hollow of the froggy hand as into a maw, while Unverlacht's other hand was busy groping her young and taut behind. For a not quite ascertain-able reason, Unverlacht always called Emilia Sissy; perhaps she reminded him of someone who had once borne that name, and Emilia and the unknown, perhaps long since buried Sissy melted together in that vault into one being, which the owner met with lustful tenderness. Emilia shoved him away. "I've come to talk business with you," she said. All at once, she felt sick. The fug in the vault was unbreathable. She dropped her plaid on the floor and flung herself into a chair. The chair was a rocking chair, and the impetus she gave it set it rocking violently. Emilia felt she was in a boat at sea; the boat was swaying in the seaswell; a monster poked its head out of the waves; shipwreck loomed; Emilia was afraid she might be seasick. "Oh, stop it, Sissy," cried Unverlacht. "I've got no money. What do you imagine? Business is rotten." He looked at Emilia bouncing up and down; he saw her in front of him, be-neath him, stretched out in the rocking chair, her skirts had slid up, he saw her bare thighs over her stockings; little girl thighs, he thought; he had a fat and jealous wife. He was in an ill humor. Emilia excited him, her little girl thighs aroused him, her tired naughty face of a tired naughty little girl could have driven him wild if he'd been endowed with another drive than the one to make money. For Unverlacht Emilia was classy, a good family, he thought, he desired her, but he desired her with no more reality than one might desire an erotic picture in a magazine, and he didn't want to do more than fondle her, but even fondling her might get in the way of business: and he wanted to buy from Emilia, he only pretended not to have any money, that was part of his trade, the things Emilia brought him were good quality, from such a fine family, such a good house, and she let him have them cheap, she had no idea of what they were worth, what tiny panties she's wearing, it's almost as though she's not wearing any, but any second Frau Unverlacht might come barging into the vault, an angry, fat, armored toad. "Stop that rocking! What have you got for me, Sissy?" He always called Emilia "Du"; it pleased him to use the intimate form as if she really were just a little whorish street girl, and once again he thought of her "fine family, such a fine family." Emilia pulled herself together. She opened her plaid. Out came a little prayer rug; it was ripped, but it could be patched. Emilia spread it out. Philipp loved this rug, loved its delicate pattern, its vibrant blue on red, and Emilia had taken it quite deliberately, she had taken the rug because Philipp loved it and because she wanted to punish him, because he didn't have any money, and because she had to go to the pawnshop and to Unverlacht, and because he didn't seem to care that he didn't have any money and she had to take out her things and try to sell them with beggarly humility, sometimes Emilia saw Philipp as an ogre, but then at others he was her appointed savior, who was capable of anything, surprise, pain, but also happiness, fame, and fortune, and she was sorry she tormented him, and ideally she would now have knelt down on the prayer rug and prayed, prayed to God and Philipp for forgiveness for being so bad (she used the childish expression), but where was God, and which way was Mecca, where was she to turn with her prayer? Unverlacht, meanwhile, free of compunction, not tormented by any religious scruples, had avidly thrown himself upon the tears in the rug. They were such as to elicit from him shouts of triumph: "What a rag! Nothing but holes! These tears and rips! Worthless, Sissy, I tell you, rotten, threadbare, worthless!" He scrunched up the wool, held it against his bald head, pressed his ear to the rug, and exclaimed: "It's singing!"— "What's that?" asked Emilia, briefly baffled. "It's singing!" said Unverlacht, "it's creaking because it's so threadbare, listen, Sissy, I'll give you five marks for it, for your trouble, and because it's you."— "You're insane," said Emilia. She tried to assume an expression of icy detachment. Unverlacht thought: It's worth a hundred, at the most he would pay twenty for it. He said: "Ten on commission; and I'm digging my own grave, Sissy." Emilia thought: I know he's going to sell it for a hundred— She said: "Thirty, cash down." Her voice sounded set and determined, but in her heart she was tired. She had learned some of the tricks of the trade from Unverlacht. Sometimes she thought if she was able to sell a house (but she would never be able to, it would never happen: who buys houses? ropy old walls? who digs a pit for themselves? who puts themselves under the purview of officialdom, gets tangled up with tax authorities and building inspectors? who creates trouble for themselves? offers themselves up to the bailiff? who wants continual squabbles with tenants insisting on expensive improvements, tenants whose rent one would end up taking to the tax office, instead of living off it, as the old property owners of fairy-tales used to do, sitting there comfortably, with their hands in their laps?) if only she could!—it was one of her great dreams, at last to be able to get rid of one of her properties, but it seemed there was no one in the market for real estate today, a bad investment, open to perpetual meddling from the state—then maybe Emilia could open a secondhand shop of her own, and, like Unverlacht, live off the riches of the past and the estates of the dead. Was that the transformation, the de-metamorphosis? Not Unverlacht leaping out of his frogskin as a prince, but she, the charming Emilia, the beautiful young inheritrix of the Commercial Councilor's fortune, the rag princess, proposing to travel down to the underworld of awful dicker, the basement of trivial miserliness, from sheer fear of the future don the mask of the frog, the clammy thing waiting for poor flies. Was that her true nature, sluggish pondlife, the lurking, snapping mouth? But it was a long way yet to a secondhand dealership, there was no buyer in sight, and by then Philipp would have written his book, and the world would have changed.

Philipp had long been afraid of her, and his fear had perhaps helped to attract misunderstandings, the way carrion attracts flies, or, in the country they say that looking up at the clouds attracts storms. He had gotten into a whirlpool of ridiculous confusions of the sort that only ever happened to him, they seemed to lie in wait for him like traps, when (willingly enough, but inhibited by shyness, partly produced by the fact of the assignment, which others would have found encouraging) he had agreed to visit Edwin on behalf of the *Neues Blatt*. The *Evening Echo*, which only mentioned writers in its pages when, by virtue of having been awarded some prize or other, they had become public figures and could no longer be ignored, or, better yet, had died, assuring them of a mention in its *faits divers* columns, along with other little tittle-tattle *Argentine Consul's cat goes missing, Author André Gide died yesterday*, this literature-loving organ had dispatched an editorial trainee to Mr. Edwin's hotel to interview the famous writer, to ask him on behalf of the *Echo*'s readers whether he believed the Third World War would happen this summer, what he thought of the new line in ladies' swimwear, and whether in his view the atom bomb would return the human species to the level of monkeys. From some sort of misapprehension, perhaps because Philipp looked preoccupied, and because the young enthusiast, the trainee newshound, had been told that the award-winning beast that was her designated prey was a serious man, she took the unfamous and rather younger Philipp for Edwin, and launched herself upon him with her school English, enriched by some bar slang she had picked up from an American fling at last year's Carnival, while two pert and self-assured young men who accompanied her, representatives, like her, of the fourth estate, came in lugging dangerous-looking pieces of equipment, and bathed Philipp in flashlight.

The resulting commotion of lights and hoo-ha, so embarrassing and in some ways also shaming for Philipp (his shame escaped the notice of those looking on, it was an affair internal to Philipp), was attended by the consequence that other parties in the hotel lobby became curious, and learned that a case of mistaken identity had taken place, involving the famous Mr. Edwin, a still somewhat obscure confusion, and people were inclined to take Philipp for Edwin's secretary, and, full of sudden interest in the life of the poet, to besiege him with questions as to when the master might be available to be spoken to, questioned, seen, and photographed. A man in a many-belted raincoat, who seemed just to have flown round the globe on an important mission, but had experienced nothing on the flight and merely solved a crossword puzzle, this fellow so well protected against bad weather and intellectual suspicion inquired of Philipp whether the renowned Mr. Edwin might be willing to affirm, in connection with a certain widely circulated photograph of him, that he was unable to live, or indeed write, without the help of a certain brand of cigarettes, whose representative the weatherproofed one happened to be. Philipp took refuge in silence and passed hurriedly on, but he was unable to rescue himself as easily from the group of schoolteachers from Massachusetts. Miss Wescott grabbed hold of Philipp, fixed him like a kindly, well-kept owl through her wide horn-rims, and asked him whether he couldn't ask Edwin to give a little impromptu private reading to this traveling group of schoolmistresses, and, as she was sure she could safely say, Edwin-admirers, an introduction to what was after all a difficult, often obscure body of work, that could use a little explanation. At which point, before Philipp could get a word out, to explain his inability to intercede for them, Miss Burnett interrupted Miss Wescott. Be it as it might with impromptu private reading and society of admirers, Miss Burnett declared that Edwin would surely have better, more entertaining things to do with his time than mingle with a bunch of traveling schoolmarms, but Kay, the youngest, as it were the Benjamin of the little group, the young and pretty one, Miss Burnett would almost have called out, "the one with the green eyes," truly was an admirer of all poetry, in honest, straightforward, and disciple-like manner, in particular of Edwin's, and perhaps—and Philipp as his secretary would surely see this—it might refresh the celebrated bard, refresh him from his travels and in the alien land, to find at his feet an example of such youthful sweetness, and, in a word, Philipp was encouraged to take Kay to Edwin, so that he might write her a dedication, a remembrance of this day of their meeting in Germany in her copy of his poems, a volume of which she happened to have with her in a light India paper edition. Miss Burnett pushed Kay forward into the light, and Philipp saw her with emotion. He thought: I would feel the way that energetic woman thinks Edwin would feel if this young worshiper came along to see me— Kay seemed so uncomplicated, so fresh, she had the sort of youth that didn't seem to exist yet in Germany, she was unhindered, that was probably it, she came from a different atmosphere, from clear and bitter air, Philipp thought, from a different country, with breadth and freshness and youth, and she worshiped poets. Admittedly, Edwin had fled the country from which Kay had come: it was not known whether he had fled its breadth or its youth, but surely he hadn't fled from the prospect of Kay, maybe Miss Wescott, the friendly owl with the spectacles, but she probably wasn't as terrible as that, it was hard to know why Edwin had fled if you didn't know the country, as far as he, Philipp, was concerned, the New World, as manifested by Kay, seemed an attractive enough proposition. He envied Edwin. The more awkward was it for him now that he couldn't do anything for the delightful poetry buff who had come from the remote and youthful land of America, and that it would be all too absurd and difficult to tell her about himself, and to explain all the confusions and misunderstandings that were doing their fiendish work here. He tried to explain to the older ladies that he was by no means Edwin's secretary, and in fact was only here himself in order to speak to Edwin, and already the next misconception was born, because everyone took Philipp's words to mean that he was Edwin's friend, a dear associate, Edwin's German friend, his German colleague, every bit as famous in Germany as Edwin was worldwide, and the school-mistresses, they were polite and mannerly (far more polite and mannerly than their German counterparts), immediately apologized for not knowing Philipp, they inquired after his name, and Miss Burnett even pushed Kay a little nearer to Philipp, saying, "he's another poet, a German poet." Kay gave Philipp her hand and expressed her regret that she didn't happen to have a book of his on her person, so that she could ask him to sign it for her. Kay wore mignonette. Philipp didn't care for flowery scents, the perfumes he liked were blended from unidentifiable artificial ingredients, but mignonette suited Kay, it was an expression of her youth, an aura of her green eyes, and it reminded Philipp of something as well. Mignonette had grown in the Rector's garden, scented mignonette, and that sweet scent had been a part of the summer days when the boy Philipp had lain on the lawn with Eva, the Rector's daughter. Mignonette was light green. And Kay was light green too. She was a light green spring. Kay thought: He's looking at me, he likes me, he's not young but I bet he's terribly famous, I've only been here for a few hours and already I've met my first German poet, the Germans have terribly expressive faces, they look as distinguished as our bad character actors, I expect it must be because they're an old people and have suffered a lot, perhaps this poet was buried alive in his cellar during a bombing raid, it's supposed to have been awful, my brother says it was awful, and he was with the air force, he dropped bombs here, I couldn't stand it if people dropped bombs on me, or could I? perhaps you just think you won't be able to stand it, the poets in Dr. Kaiser's book of German literary history all look so terribly romantic, like criminals on

Wanted posters, admittedly those ones usually have beards, I expect he works all night, that's why he's so pale, or is he sad because
his country's been through such a bad time? maybe he drinks as
well, a lot of poets drink, I expect he drinks Rhine wine, I'd like to
drink Rhine wine too, Katharine won't let me, why am I here? he
goes for walks in forests of oak and composes poetry, a poet's a
weird thing to be really, I don't think Hemingway's weird like that,
Hemingway fishes, fishing isn't as weird as walking in forests, but
I would walk in an oak forest with a German poet if he asked me
to, I would walk with him if only so that I could tell Dr. Kaiser
about it. Dr. Kaiser would be pleased if I told him I'd been for a
walk in an oak forest with a German poet, but the poet won't ask
me to go with him, I'm too young, he might ask Katharine to go
with him, or Mildred, but he would love me if he trusted himself
to love an American girl, he'd love me much more than he could
love Katharine or Mildred.— Katharine Wescott said: "You must
know Mr. Edwin very well."— "From his books," Philipp replied.
But apparently they couldn't understand his English. Mildred Burnett said: "It would be nice if we could meet up again later. Perhaps we can see you in Mr. Edwin's company. Perhaps we wouldn't
annoy Mr. Edwin then." They seemed still to believe that Philipp
was going to Edwin as his old and trusty friend. Philipp said: "I
don't know whether I will go to Edwin; it's by no means certain
that you will find me in his company." But once again the schoolteachers seemed not to understand. They nodded at him in
friendly fashion, and chorused: "later on with Edwin, later on with
Edwin." Kay mentioned she was studying German with Dr. Kaiser,
German literature. "Perhaps I've read something by you," she said.
"Isn't it funny to have read something of yours, and then meet
you?" Philipp bowed. He was sheepish and felt offended. He was
being offended by a stranger who had no intention of offending
him. It was as though some prompter had given the sentences to

the strangers, who said them out loud with the intentions of flattering and respecting him, and only Philipp and the malign, invisible prompter understood what offense had been given. Philipp was livid. But he was also attracted. He was attracted by the girl, her fresh, honest, and uncomplicated respect for values that Philipp also respected, qualities he had once had, and had lost. A bitter delight lay in every misunderstanding he had with Kay. Kay also reminded him a little of Emilia, except that Kay was an uncomplicated and unburdened Emilia, and that, refreshingly, she didn't know him, or anything about him. But it remained painful that respect was being offered to him in such a discreditable, subtle, mocking way, that a Philipp was being held up to admiration who didn't exist, though he might easily have existed, a Philipp he had wanted to become, an important writer whose works were read even in Massachusetts. And straightaway he understood that his "even in Massachusetts" was a foolish thought, because Massachusetts was just as far and also just as near as Germany, from the point of view of a writer, naturally, to the writer standing in the middle the world around him was all equally near and equally far, or the writer was on the outside, and the world was the middle, was the task around which he was orbiting, something never to be accomplished, never to be achieved, and there was no near and no far; perhaps there was a foolish writer in Massachusetts who wanted to be read "even in Germany," for foolish people geographical distance was always a desert, a wasteland, the ends of the earth, the places where, as the phrase went, foxes bade one another goodnight, and the only place that was light was where oneself was fumbling around in the dark. But unfortunately Philipp hadn't become a significant author, he was just someone who called himself an author because that was the way he was listed in the population records: he was weak, he had remained on the battlefield where insanity and crime and scummy politics and the meanest war had all had it out, and Philipp's slender reputation, his first attempt, his first book had been overwhelmed by the loud-speaker shrieks and the noise of weapons, had been drowned out by the screams of the murderers and their victims, and Philipp was as though lamed, and his voice was as though choked, and already he saw with dread how the accursed battlefield that he was unable to leave, perhaps didn't care to leave, was being readied for a fresh bloody drama.

Following the misunderstandings in the hotel lobby, following the conversation with the traveling group of schoolmistresses, Philipp couldn't possibly go through with his intention of going to see Edwin. He would have to turn down the assignment to speak to Edwin for the *Neues Blatt*. Another failure. He was too ashamed, though, having been subject to all this attention, to walk out under everyone's eyes, to creep off like a beaten dog. Above all, he was ashamed in front of Kay's green eyes. He walked up the stairs that led to the hotel bedrooms, hoping to find some back stairs, some side exit that he could leave by. And then, on the principal stair-case he walked into Messalina. "I've been watching you for ages," said the vast one, plonking herself in Philipp's path. "Are you vis-iting Edwin?" she asked. "Who's the little girl with the green eyes? She's cute!"—"I'm not visiting anyone," said Philipp. "Then what are you doing here?"—"Just climbing some stairs."—"You can't fool me." Messalina made a gesture of tapping him coquettishly on the shoulder. "Listen, we're having a party tonight, and I'd like it if Edwin came. It'll be a gas. It'll be nice for Edwin too. Jack and Hänschen are coming. You know what I mean, you writers are all so—" Her freshly permed hair wobbled like a raspberry jelly. "I don't know Mr. Edwin," Philipp countered irritably. "I don't know what's got into you. You all seem to think I'm something to do with Edwin. I don't get it. I'm just in the hotel by chance. I've got something to do here."—"Just now you were saying you were

Edwin's friend. Were you trying to seduce that green-eyed looker? She reminds me of Emilia. They would make a fetching pair, her and Emilia." Messalina gazed down into the lobby. "Look, this is a complete misunderstanding," said Philipp. "I don't know that girl either. I'll never see her again." He thought: Shame, I wouldn't mind seeing you again, but I wonder if you'd like me?— Messalina remained implacable: "All right, so what are you actually doing here, Philipp?"—"I'm looking for Emilia," he said, in desperation. "Oh! Does she come here? Do you keep a room here?" She moved a little nearer to him. I shouldn't have said that, saying that was a mistake, thought Philipp. "No," he said, "I'm just looking for her. But I'm sure she never comes here." He tried to sidle past the bulk, but the raspberry jelly trembled menacingly, any second it might start to slip, turn into a cloud, a red cloud dissolving in red mist, in whose fumes Philipp would certainly die. "Let me go, won't you," he cried despairingly. But now, with her broad, drink-ravaged face pressed against his ear, she was whispering, as though in confidence: "How's the film coming along? The film for Alexander. He's always asking me when you'll bring him the script. He's so looking forward to it. We could all meet at Edwin's talk. You bring Emilia and the little green girl. Before the party, we'll all go to Edwin's talk, and afterward I hope—" – "Don't hope," Philipp rudely interrupted her. "There is nothing to hope for. There is no hope. Least of all for you." He dashed up the steps, on the landing he regretted his outspokenness, wanted to turn around, felt too scared, and opened a door that led past laundry rooms to a passage down, and finally to the celebrated hotel kitchen starred in so many guides.

Had Edwin lost all pleasure in the joys of the table? He was off his food. Not merely without appetite, no, frankly with disgust, he scorned the products of the famous hearth, the delectable specialties of the house that were brought up to his room in silver chafing dishes and porcelain bowls. He drank a little wine, Franconian wine, of which he had read, heard, and felt a little curiosity about, but the light fizzing drink from the stout-bellied bottle seemed to him too dry for lunchtime on a dark day. It was a sunshine wine, and Edwin saw no sunshine, the wine tasted of graves, it tasted the way old cemeteries smelled in bad weather, it was a wine that adapted itself to your mood, that made you laugh if you felt cheerful and cry if you were miserable. Certainly, Edwin was having a rotten day. He had no notion of the fact that downstairs in the lobby, an involuntary stand-in had received and suffered the irritating banalities and trivial adoration associated with the degree of his public fame, approaches and flatteries that were just as repugnant to Edwin as they had embarrassed and tormented Philipp, who had had to suffer them and who was not even their intended recipient. Philipp's mishap would only have deepened Edwin's grumpiness; Edwin would not have seen Philipp as having lightened his load, he would only have seen once again the comedy and questionableness of his own existence, but—as by a shadow—exaggerated, marked, and betrayed by Philipp's appearance in it. But Edwin never got to hear about Philipp. In purple leather slippers, in the Buddhist monk's robe in which he worked, he stalked around the frail table, on which the rejected dishes steamed and spread their aromas. The untouched repast angered him; he did not want to offend the cook, for whose arts Edwin would normally have shown rather more appreciation. With a guilty conscience, he left the dining table, and strode round the edge of the carpet, in whose weave gods and princes, flowers and mythical beasts had been depicted, so that the weaver's art resembled the illustration for a framing story in the Arabian Nights. So splendidly oriental, so floridly polymythic, was the floor covering that the poet was unwilling to tread directly on it, and, in spite of the fact that he was in slippers and in the garb of an Indian sage, he stayed respectfully on its edge. The good carpets and the fine kitchen were the pride of the old establishment, which had largely been spared the wreckage of the war. Edwin loved old-fashioned lodgings, staging posts on the caravan route of cultured Europe, beds in which Goethe or Laurence Sterne might have slept, nice, slightly rickety desks that might have been used by Platen, Humboldt, Herman Bang, or Hofmannsthal. He greatly preferred such veteran establishments to the new palaces, the machines for living of a Corbusier-type architecture, the sparkling tubular steel and revealing glass walls, and so it happened that occasionally on his travels he suffered from heating that didn't work, or bathwater that wasn't properly hot, inconveniences he tried to disregard, but to which his large and highly sensitive nose generally responded with a catarrh. Mr. Edwin's nose would have preferred warmth and technical comfort to the woodworm smell of old desks, the whiff of mothballs, human sweat, unchastity, and tears that rose from the weave of the old wall hangings. But then Edwin didn't live to suit his nose and his personal comfort (he loved his comforts, but could never completely surrender to them), he lived in discipline, in the stern discipline of the mind and in harness to an active humanistic tradition, a quite sublime tradition, of course, part of the sense of which was provided by the old inns, the Elephant, the Unicorn, and the Four Seasons, only part, of course, but in general he was eaten up by unrest, because the poet born in the New World accounted himself (and he was indisputably right to do so) part of the European elite, the late, and, one had increasingly to wonder, perhaps the last on the beloved Western continent, and nothing outraged and hurt Edwin more than the barbaric clamor, the terrifying prophesy—all the more so because it was not entirely devoid of greatness and genius—the jeer of that Russian, that holy mage, that obsessive, the great fool, fool in the sense in which the enlightened Greeks used the word, as Edwin insisted, but also the seer and the ur-poet, as Edwin had to admit (a poet he revered and avoided, for he was not personally drawn to the demonic, but to Hellenic-Christian reason, which did not exclude—within reason—the supernatural; but already the evicted specters of the cruel and the absurd seemed to be returning), the label of the West Asian promontory, which, following three thousand years of independence, of precociousness, of naughtiness, of the orderly-disorderly, of megalomania, was returning or falling back into the lap of its Asian motherland. Was it time for that, then? Was the hour come? Tired out by his journey, Edwin had wanted to lie down, but rest and sleep would not come, and the meal, scorned and viewed with revulsion, had not picked up his strength either. The city terrified him, the city disagreed with him, it had been through too much, it had experienced dread, seen the Medusa's severed head, a great profanation, a parade of barbarians risen from its own lower depths, the city had been punished with fire and with the destruction of its walls, it had been afflicted, it had brushed chaos, the plunge into unhistory, now it was hanging on the brink of the historical precipice, hanging at an angle and flowering, was it a false flowering? what held it there? the strength of its own roots (how eerie this gourmet repast on the teetering table in this place)? or did a thin strand link it to various interests, with the transient and mutually contradictory interests of the victors, the loose connection to the plans of the strategists and the moneymen, the credo, the belief, the superstition in the spheres of influence of diplomacy and the positions of power? it wasn't history but economics, not dazed Clio but Mercury with his bag of coin who governed the scene. Edwin saw the drama and the exemplary status of the city, it hung, hung over the abyss, it was in the balance, it hung in dangerous, strenuous balance, it might teeter back into the old and tested, or into the new and unknown, it could be true to its traditional culture, or sink into possibly temporary unculturedness, it might even disappear as a city, turn into a mass prison, embodying in steel, concrete, and technology the vision of the imaginary prisons, the *carceri d'invenzione* of the curious engraver, Piranesi, whose Roman ruins Edwin so greatly admired. The stage set was dressed for tragedy, but what happened at the front of the stage, in front of the ramp, the personal contacts with the world, they remained for now rather farcical. In the hotel all sorts of people were waiting for Edwin. They had been announced to him, journalists, photographers, one questioner had sent her request up to him, ridiculous questions, a moronic exchange. Edwin did not always avoid publicity and its representatives, they tired him out, admittedly, and it cost him something to speak to strangers, but on occasion, yes, in fact quite often, he had done it, had managed it, had sent folly away with a little joke or pleasantry, and won the sympathies of the opinion-makers, but here in this town he feared the journalists, he feared them because this was a place where world and time had been shaken and might at any time collapse into nothing, or into the new, the other, the unknown future, of which nothing was known, here he couldn't joke, here he couldn't find the easy, gracious, flip pleasantry that was expected of him. And what if he told them the truth? Did he know the truth? O oldest of questions: what was true? He could only have spoken to them of his apprehensions, his possibly absurd fears, given free rein to the melancholy that had come over him here, but fear and sorrow seemed to him to have been banished into the cellar here, into the cellars over which the houses had collapsed, and there for the time being they remained. The smell of these buried cellars hung over the city. No one seemed to be aware of it. Perhaps people had forgotten all about these tombs. Should Edwin remind them?

The city attracted him. Attracted him in spite of everything. He took off the silk monk's robes, and dressed conformably to the world, in the contemporary manner. Perhaps it was a disguise.

Perhaps he was no human being. He hurried down the steps, his light black hat from London's Bond Street drawn down over his brow at a slight angle. He looked utterly formal and also a little like an old pimp. On the lobby landing he spotted Messalina. She reminded him of an appalling woman, a ghost who worked as a society journalist in America, a professional gossip, and Edwin ran back up the stairs looking for another exit, went past laundry rooms, giggling girls who were swinging sheets covers shrouds, covers for cadavers and covers for love, for embraces, conception and dying breaths, he hurried through a world of women, through the margins of the mother Reich, and, thirsting for a different world, he opened a door and found himself in the spacious and celebrated hotel kitchens. The horror! The horror! The untouched repast in his room oppressed him again. How much Edwin would have liked otherwise to discuss the *Physiologie-du-gout* with the chef and watch the pretty kitchen boys shucking gentle gold-gleaming fish. And so he charged through the smells of bouillon and sharp vegetable steams, to a farther door that would hopefully open into the outside world—but then it didn't really do that. Edwin found himself standing in a courtyard of the hotel, in front of an iron structure that housed the bicycles of the staff, the cooks and waiters and lift-boys and room service personnel, and behind the bicycle rack stood a gentleman whom in his momentary confusion Edwin took to be himself, his mirror image, his doppelgänger, a bit of sympathetic/unsympathetic magic, but then he saw that of course it was a mistake, an absurd idea, it wasn't his own simulacrum standing there, but a younger gentleman who actually didn't even remotely resemble him, but who remained in some way sympathetic/unsympathetic, perhaps like a brother whom one didn't like. Edwin understood: the gentleman was a writer. What was he doing among the bicycles? Was he lying in wait for him? Philipp recognized Edwin, and after the initial moment of surprise, he thought, this is the chance to speak to him. We can have our talk, he thought. Edwin and I, we can talk together, we will understand one another; perhaps he will tell me what I am.— But already hope was evaporating, confusion triumphed, bewilderment at seeing Edwin here in the hotel courtyard, and Philipp thought, this is ridiculous, I can't take advantage of this to speak to him, and instead of taking a step toward him, he took a step back, and Edwin too took a step back, thinking, if this man were a little younger, I might take him for a young poet, an admirer of my work, and he wasn't aware of the absurdity of such an idea and its expression, Edwin would never have let it pass in writing, he would have blushed, but here, floating in the invisibility of the burgeoning idea it wasn't reflection that came out on top but the wish, yes, he would have liked to meet a young poet in this city, an acolyte, an imitator, he would have like to come across a disciple here, a poet from the land of Goethe and Platen, but this man here was no stripling, no beaming believer, his own doubt, his own sadness, his own worry were all plainly there in the man's face, and both thought in the hotel courtyard, having fled from other human society: I must keep out of his way.— Philipp had been in the courtyard for quite a while already. He couldn't get out. He hesitated about going through the staff entrance of the hotel, he was afraid of passing a time clock and a doorman. The porter would take him for a thief. How could he explain his wish to leave the building unobtrusively, by a back exit? What about Edwin? He too seemed uncertain. But standing in the front part of the courtyard, Edwin drew more attention than Philipp, and the porter stepped out of his little office, and called out: "Can I help the gentlemen?" Both poets now strode, keeping a shy distance between them, in the direction of the exit, they passed the time clock, the mechanical slaveowner, a measurer of hours and a counter of work, of which neither of them had had any experience, and the porter took them for men who on account of some romance had needed to use the staff exit, and he thought, so-and-sos, and he thought, layabouts.

Lying about gossiping and dreaming shallow, pleasant little dreams in a kind of perpetual doze, happy doze is here again, dreaming *stylish F, late 40s, seeks gentleman in secure position*, sat the women on state pensions, happy recipients of payments in the event of a spouse's death, alimony, and allowances, in the Domcafé. Frau Behrend also loved the venue, preferred venue of a like-minded community of ladies, where over coffee and cream one might give oneself over happily to the recollection of marital happiness, happily to the pain of abandonment, happily to the bitterness of disappointment. Carla had yet to secure pension and annuity, and Frau Behrend watched with fear and apprehension as her daughter stepped from the shadow of the Dom, into the bonbon-colored gleam of the traffic lights, into this cozy harbor of life, the softly plashing bay, the reservation of the delightfully cared for: a lost woman. Carla was lost, she was a victim, a victim of the war, she had been cast down in front of a Moloch, it was best to avoid contact with victims, she was lost to her mother, to the respectable circle of other mothers, lost to fatherland and morality, torn away from the parental hearth. But what difference did that make? There was no longer any parental hearth. By the time the house was destroyed by a bomb, the family had already dissolved. Its bonds were asunder. Perhaps the bomb only went to show that they had been loose bonds, the rope of habit, twisted out of chance, misjudgment, error, and folly. Carla was living with a Negro, Frau Behrend in an attic with the yellowing scores of public concerts, and the music master, besotted with his floozy, now serenaded harlots. When she spotted Carla, Frau Behrend looked around in alarm to see if any of her friends, her enemies, her friendly enemies, were sitting anywhere near. She did not like to show herself in public with Carla (who could say? maybe her Negro would show up as well, and then the ladies in the café would witness her disgrace), but still more Frau Behrend feared conversations with Carla in the solitary fastness of her attic. And Carla, who had come to the café looking for Frau Behrend, knowing it to be her mother's headquarters in the afternoons, with the feeling of having to see her before she went to the clinic to get rid of the undesired fruit of love, love? was it really love? was it not just having someone else, the despair of those thrown into the world, the warmth of body-lying-by-body? and the near/distant being in her body, was it not just the fruit of acquiescence, of familiarity with the man, his embrace, his penetration, the fruit of her little whoredom, the fruit of fear of not being able to make it on her own, which now had conceived a further fear, and wanted to bring that into the world? Carla saw her mother, fish-faced, flounder-headed, coldly and fishily dissuasive, her hand was stirring coffee and cream with a small spoon and it was like the fin of a fish, the slightly tremulous fin of a pitiable fish in a home aquarium, that was how Carla saw her, and was her vision a distortion? was that her mother's true face? another must have leaned down over Carla's crib, and only later, much later, when there was nothing to do with the little one or to worry about, only then had the fish emerged, the flounder-head, and the feeling that had brought Carla here to see her mother, to attempt a conversation, died as she reached Frau Behrend's place in the café. Frau Behrend had the momentary sensation that not her daughter but the cathedral tower stood crushingly before her.

Odysseus and Josef had climbed the tower. Josef was out of breath and drew in the lofty air when they had finally overcome the crumbling stone steps and steep ladders and reached the topmost level of the tower. The musical suitcase was silent. There was a break in transmission. All that could be heard was the gasping breath, and perhaps the tired, pumping heart of the old porter. They looked out over the city, over the old roofs, over the Romanesque, Gothic, and baroque churches, over the ruins of the churches, over the newly erected roof timbers, over the wounds of the city, the gaping holes of destroyed buildings. Josef thought about how old he had become, he had always lived in this city, never had he gone anywhere else, until the expedition to the Argonnes Forest and Chemin-des-Dames, he had always only carried bags for other people who were traveling somewhere, but in the Argonnes Forest he had carried a rifle, and at Chemin-des-Dames hand grenades, and perhaps, the thought had come to him in a foxhole, during a killing hour, to the music of drumfire, perhaps the people he was shooting at were travelers, perhaps he was throwing explosives at travelers, those people who were foreign visitors to him at home, had given him generous tips, so why didn't the police step in and prevent him from shooting them and killing them with bombs now? it would have been so simple, and he would have obeyed: war banned by law; but they were crazy, they were all crazy, even the police were crazy, they allowed murder, oh, but you weren't to think about it, Josef stuck to it, the drumfire passed, people grew tired of killing, life and travelers' suitcases had reasserted themselves, beer and snacks were back, till everyone went crazy a second time, it must be some sort of recurring illness, this time the plague affected his son, it took his son, and today it had given him a Negro, a Negro with a suitcase that spoke and that played music, and now the Negro had dragged him up the cathedral tower, never in his life had Josef been up the tower; it probably took a Negro to come up with the idea of climbing the tower. He is a very strange gentleman after all, thought Josef as he blinked into the distance. He was even a little afraid of Odysseus, and he thought, what will I do if the black devil suddenly takes it into his head to throw me off the tower?— He was giddy with so much thinking and so much distance. Odysseus gazed happily out across the city. He was on top. It was down below. He didn't know anything about the former history of the city, he didn't know anything about Europe, but he knew that this was a white folks' capital, a city from where they had gone on to found other cities like New York. The Black Boys all came from the forest. Had there never been a forest here, always just houses? Of course, there must once have been a forest here too, thick jungle, green growth, Odysseus saw huge jungles sprouting below, undergrowth, ferns, lianas spilled over the houses; what once had been might come around again. Odysseus smote Josef on the shoulder. The old porter was sent reeling by the blow. Odysseus laughed his wide King Odysseus laugh. Wind stirred up on the heights. Odysseus stroked a Gothic gargoyle up on the tower, a stone figure from the Middle Ages, which had banished devils to the tops of towers, and Odysseus pulled a red pen out of his tunic, and proudly signed his name across the gargoyle's belly: Odysseus Cotton, Memphis, Tennessee. USA.

What use were the Americans? It was disgraceful that Carla had gotten hooked up with a black man; it was terrible that she had got herself pregnant by a black man; it was a crime that she wanted to kill the child in her womb. Frau Behrend refused to think about it past that point. Things this terrible were simply inexpressible. If something happened that wasn't supposed to happen, you had to keep quiet about it. There wasn't love here, only abysses. This wasn't the love song that Frau Behrend listened to on the radio, this wasn't the film she liked to see, this wasn't the passion of a Count or a chief engineer as in the novelettes that were so elevating to read. Here there were only yawning abysses, disgrace, and perdition. If only she was safely in America, thought Frau Behrend, let America try and deal with the disgrace it's caused, we don't have any Negroes here, but Carla will never go to America, she will stay here with her little black bastard baby, she will come into this café with the black baby in her arms.— I can't do it, thought Carla, how does she know? has she got second sight in her fishy head? I wanted to tell her, but I didn't tell her, I can't even talk to her.— I know everything, thought Frau Behrend, I know what you'd like to say to me, you've made a mistake, now you want to do something bad, you want advice, well I can't give you any advice, just do your bad thing, run to the doctor, there's nothing else for it but to do the bad thing, I don't want you here with your Negro baby—

He wanted the baby. He saw the child of his loved one in danger. Carla was not happy. He hadn't made Carla happy. He had failed. They were both in danger. How could Washington express it? How could he say what he was afraid of? Reluctantly, Dr. Frahm had stepped out into the corridor. His surgery was just being cleaned. The door was open. A woman was passing a damp cloth over the linoleum. The damp cloth passed over the white legs of the large gynecological chair. Dr. Frahm had been disturbed during dinner. He had got up from table. He held a white napkin in his hand. There was a fresh red stain on the napkin: a wine stain. A smell of carbolic came out of the treatment room, an old wound-cleaning disinfectant smell sprayed into the air by the woman as she cleaned the room. What could Washington say to the doctor? Carla had been there. Dr. Frahm said so. He said everything was all right. What was the matter with Carla then? Why had she been here, if everything was all right? "A minor irregularity," said Frahm. Was there going to be some trouble here? So that was him, the black father. A good-looking man, once you got used to the skin color. "We're expecting a baby," said Washington. "A baby?" said Frahm. He looked at Washington in surprise. He thought, I'm playing the naïf here, Dr. Frahm had the strange impression that the Negro in the dark corridor, he was standing directly under the framed certificate, the so-called Hippocratic oath, had turned pale. "Didn't she tell you?" asked Washington. "No," said Frahm. What was the matter with this Negro? Frahm laid down his napkin. The red stain disappeared in the white pleats. It was as though a wound had closed. The thing couldn't be done. Carla would have to keep her baby. The little Negro wanted to live. There was a hint of disgrace in the air.

Frau Behrend kept silent, obstinately, offendedly, and flounder-headedly silent, and Carla continued to guess her thoughts. They were thoughts that Carla was capable of guessing and under-standing, her own thinking rarely moved that far from the moth-er-thoughts, maybe it was disgrace, maybe it was crime, the thing she did and wanted to do, Carla didn't think much of her own life, she was perfectly willing to deny it, she didn't live it, she thought she had to apologize for it, and she thought she had the times to plead in extenuation, the extenuation of the disorderly times, which had brought crimes and brought disgrace, and made its own children disgraced and criminal. Carla was no rebel. She believed. In God? In convention. Where was God? God might have agreed to a black bridegroom. An everyday sort of god. But even in her mother's time, God had only been a god for special days and holy days. Carla had not been brought to God. At communion she had only been brought as far as His table.

She wanted to bring her to God. Emmi, the nanny, wanted to bring the child in her care to God; she saw it as her God-appointed task to raise Hillegonda, the actors' child, the child of sin, the child neglected by its parents, in the fear of God. Emmi despised Alexander and Messalina; she had been hired by them, and was paid by them, paid very well, but she despised them. Emmi thought she loved the child. But one mustn't show Hillegonda love, one had to show her strictness to save her from the Hell into which she had fallen from her birth. Emmi talked to Hillegonda about death, to prove to her the vanity of her life, and she led her into tall, dark churches, to lead her thoughts to eternity, but little Hillegonda shuddered before death, and she shivered in the churches. They stood before the confessional in the side chapel of the cathedral. There was a crack in the pillar that Hillegonda was looking at, some bomb damage that had been patched with cheap plaster, that ran like a scab up to the stone spray of leaves at the top of the pillar. To take the child to God, the child had to be brought to God. Emmi saw how small and helpless the child looked, standing next to the mighty, plaster-daubed pillar. God would help Hillegonda. God would stand by her. He would look after the little helpless girl, so innocently/guiltily laden with sin. Hillegonda should make her confession. Even before the age of confession, she should confess to clear her soul of sin. What was she to confess? Hillegonda didn't know. She just felt afraid. She felt afraid of the silence, she felt afraid of the cold, of the size and loftiness of the church, she felt afraid of Emmi and of God. "Hold Emmi's hand." The sins of her parents? What sins were they? Hillegonda didn't know. All she knew was that her parents were sinners and rejected by God. Actors' child, thespian child, film child, thought Emmi. "Is God angry?" asked the child.

"Brilliant! Fantastic! Wonderful!" The Archduke was undressed, the Golden Fleece was taken off him. "Brilliant! Fantastic! Wonderful!" The head of production had seen the rushes: the day's takes were brilliant, fantastic, and wonderful. The head of production praised Alexander. He praised himself. A super film. The head of production felt himself to be the creator of a work of art. He was Michelangelo, talking to the press *Passion of an Archduke is coming out, top-notch German cast*. Alexander felt heartburn. The makeup had been wiped off his face. He was back to looking whey-faced. Where was Messalina? He would have liked to give her a call. He would have said: "I'm tired. Let's not have a party tonight, no people round. I'm tired. I need to sleep. I will sleep. Damnit, I'm going to sleep!" He would have said it on the telephone. He would have told Messalina how tired, empty, and wretched he felt. He wouldn't tell her tonight.

She sat in the hotel bar, drinking a Pernod. Pernod was wicked, it was a pick-you-up: Pernod Paris, Paris the city of love, *brothels shut down, damages view of France abroad*, Messalina flicked through her diary. She was looking for addresses. She needed women for tonight, girls, pretty girls for her party. It wasn't likely that Emilia would show. Philipp wouldn't let her come. And he wouldn't take the little green girl either, that delectable little American girl with the green eyes. But you had to have girls at a party. Who was going to strip? Just the ephebes? There were still some heterosexuals as well. Should she ask Susanne again? Always Susanne. She was boring. She didn't ignite passions. There weren't any girls any-more. Susanne was just a stupid tart.

There are so many tarts, thought Frau Behrend, and he has to go and light on Carla, and she has to say yes, she has to fall for him, how could she not have been disgusted, I know I would have been, why did she go to those barracks, what was she doing with the blacks? because she didn't want to stay at home with me, because she couldn't stand to hear me going on and on about her father all the time, back then I was still going on about his crime, and she had to go and speak up for him, had to defend him and his floozie, she's inherited that side of him, it's the musician's blood, they're gypsies basically, it was only the Wehrmacht that managed to restrain them for a time, him and her, what a man he used to be when he strode out at the head of his regiment, it was the war that turned him to the bad.—

It wasn't so bad. The newspapers had exaggerated. Here at any rate the war didn't seem to have raged quite so much, and it was this city that observers had written seemed to have been singled out by the fury of war. Richard, riding into the city on the air-port bus, was disappointed by the extent of the ravages he saw. He thought: I've flown such a long way, yesterday I was in America, today I'm in Europe, in the heart of Europe as good old Wilhelm would say, and what do I see? no heart, just a gray light, it's as well I don't have to stay here.— Richard had expected to see incred-ible devastation, streets choked with rubble, scenes of the kind that had been shown in the press in the immediate wake of the German capitulation, pictures that he had gazed at with the avid curiosity of a boy, while they had made his father cry. The piece of rag with which his father had wiped his eyes had been soaked in machine-oil, and he was left looking as though he'd got a couple of black eyes. Richard Kirsch drove through a city that wasn't all that different from Columbus, Ohio, and it had been in precisely Columbus, Ohio, that Wilhelm, his father, had mourned the destruction of this city. So what was it that had been destroyed here? A few old buildings had fallen down. Well, it was probably high time. The gaps would be closed. Richard thought he'd like to be mayor of this town, just for a time, an American-style mayor. The high-rises he would plant on their acres of scrap! The place would acquire a progressive aspect. He got off the bus and strolled through the streets. He was looking for the street where Frau Behrend lived. He looked in the shop windows, saw the imposing displays, *Consumer Index Figures Climb Again,* an abundance that surprised him, they could do with a few more advertisements here and there, but apart from that, the stores looked like the stores did at home, yes, they were often larger and more imposing than his father's gun shop in Columbus. So this shopping street was the frontier, the borderland that Richard was supposed to protect. From up in the air it all looked more straightforward and more logical, you thought in large areas, thought geographically, geopolitically, not in human terms, you drew lines across continents with a pencil over a map, but down there on the street, among the people, who all seemed to have something foolish and frightening about them, as it appeared to Richard, they were living in an unhealthy imbalance between idleness and frantic haste, in their totality they looked poor, but individuals seemed to have money, Richard had the feeling that there were several things not quite right about this picture, in this concept, that these people remained somehow inscrutable to him. Did he want to protect them? Let them dig themselves out of their European mess. He was here to defend America. If need be, he would defend America in Europe. The old Reichswehr man

Wilhelm Kirsch had left Germany after ten years in the service. He had been able to withdraw across the ocean in time, with his pension. Then came Hitler, and with Hitler came war. Wilhelm Kirsch would have become a dead hero or a general. Perhaps as a general he would have been hanged by Hitler or by the Allies after the end of the war for war crimes. Wilhelm had managed to slip the two extreme possibilities of honor and hanging by moving to America at the right time. But there was a further possibility he hadn't quite managed to elude, and that was humiliation. Richard, who from his very first unsteady footsteps in the store, had always seen his father handling weapons, their solid grips, their cold lethal muzzles, Richard had been surprised—as surprised as if he had been struck by a bullet from one of these things—that his father had not, like the fathers of his schoolmates, joined up, but rather, as an old gunsmith, opted for a factory job that would get him off active service. Richard was mistaken: his father was no coward, he hadn't wanted to save himself from the strains and sufferings and dangers of war, nor was it indifference to the new fatherland that kept him in the States, he felt a modest reluctance to attack his old fatherland, land of his birth, but the real reason that Wilhelm Kirsch did not go to war was his training in the Reichswehr, the sharp honing, the Seeckt training, the mastery of the rapid, easy way to kill an enemy, which had persuaded Wilhelm Kirsch that all force was repugnant and that any conflicts were better settled by talk, negotiation, compromise, and reconciliation than by gunpowder. For the emigrated Reichswehr soldier Wilhelm Kirsch, America was the promised land, the new state of peaceable men, the place of tolerance and the renunciation of force, Wilhelm Kirsch had traveled to the New World with the faith of the Pilgrim Fathers, and the war that America had conducted, whatever the rights and wrongs of it, had shaken the faith that Wilhelm Kirsch had acquired while in the German Reichswehr in sense, understanding, and peaceful coexistence, that faith had been shaken, and he was left wondering about the honesty of those old American ideals. The old German Reichswehr veteran had, in one of the strange turns encompassed by life, become a gun-dealing pacifist, while Richard, his American-born son, had quite different views on soldiering and war, and the father almost caught a resemblance between the son and that officers' generation of the 1920s, and anyway Richard volunteered, as soon as he was legally able to do so, for the US Air Force. Wilhelm Kirsch did not fight; Richard Kirsch was ready to fight for America.

Schnakenbach did not want to fight. He rejected war as a means of settling disputes, and he despised the profession of soldier, which he viewed as a throwback to a barbaric era, as an unworthy atavism in an advanced civilization. He had won and lost World War II quietly for himself. He had won his war, his just, dangerous, and tricky war against the recruiting commission, but he had returned from the fight an invalid. Schnakenbach had had an idea, a scientific idea, because with him everything followed scientific principles, and he would perhaps have been willing to fight a scientific war, a war without soldiers, a global war of brains, whose lonely possessors think up lethal formulas, sit behind switchboards, and by throwing a switch or button destroy the life in a remote part of the world. Schnakenbach had not been tempted to come forward and press a button in World War II, which hadn't been his sort of war at all, but he had taken pills. The pills he had taken had been staying awake pills, and he had taken them in sufficient quantities to keep him up for days, weeks, months almost without sleep, so that finally after this continual sleep deprivation his body had got into such a state that even an army doctor would have to send him home as unfit. Schnakenbach was not taken by the army, that dreadful atavism of human loss of dignity, but even when the war was over, he remained prey to drugs. His hypophysis and his suprarenal glands were malfunctioning, his organs went on strike against the chemical competition, and carried on with their protest even after the recruiting commissions had been wound up and the risk of becoming a soldier in Germany had gone away, at least for the time being. Schnakenbach had become addicted to sleep, sleep was getting its own back on him, a deep somnolence had come over him, so that he was asleep on his feet, and needed unusually large doses of Pervitin and Benzedrine to keep him at least half-conscious for a few hours of the day. These stimulants were only available by prescription, and since Schnakenbach was unable to get enough of them, he badgered Behude for prescriptions, or else, gifted chemist that he was, he tried to make the powders for himself. Thrown out of his job for habitual narcolepsy, having spent his small savings on scientific experiments, the impoverished Schnakenbach was living in the basement of a house belonging to a baroness, a patient of Behude's, who, since once years ago receiving a summons to present herself to the Labor Exchange, had suffered from the delusion that she had been called up to work on the streetcars, and who now left her beautiful house early every morning, and spent the next eight hours trundling back and forth across town on a certain line, which set her back three marks a day, and, even worse, left her "enervated," as she complained to Behude, from whom she requested a certificate that she was unfit for work, which he was unable to give her, since she had not been required to work in the first place. Behude tried to talk her out of riding on streetcars by an analysis of the patient's early childhood. He had identified an eight-year-long incestuous passion for her father, a commanding general, and seen this as projected on a streetcar conductor. But Behude's gradual revelation of this buried past had made the Baroness late for her imaginary job, which, as she went on to explain to Behude, had occasioned her grave unpleasantnesses at work. Behude didn't find Schnakenbach in his basement. He found an unmade, coal-dust-soiled bed, he found the trade school teacher's ripped jackets and trousers lying on the floor, he saw the glasses, retorts, and boilers of the home poison workshop on a garden table, and, scattered everywhere on bed, floor, and table, he found scraps of paper with chemical formulae on them, organic chemistry diagrams that resembled vastly blown up photographs of cancer tumors, they had something rapaciously growing, dangerously ill and continually expanding about them, points and circles seemed to throw off ever more new points and circles, carbon, hydrogen, and nitrogen split off, united, and multiplied in these pictures of ink spots and lines that, with the aid of phosphorus and sulfuric acid, were to banish sleep from Schnakenbach's skull, and make the desired consciousness drug. Behude thought as he gazed at the drawings: This is how Schnakenbach sees the world, the universe, this is how he sees himself, everything in his imagination is abstract, and grows from tiny particles into gigantic calculations.— Behude left a packet of Pervitin on the garden table. He had a bad conscience. He slunk out of the basement like a thief.

The waitress cleared the table. Frau Behrend's regular place in the café was now vacant. Mother and daughter had left. They had parted in front of the café, in the shadow of the cathedral. Whatever they might have wanted to say to one another had remained unsaid. Fleetingly, both had felt the desire to hug and be hugged, but then their hands had merely coldly brushed one another. Frau Behrend thought, you made your bed, you lie in it, leave me in peace, and that meant don't disturb my café, my peace and quiet, my contentment, my belief, and her belief was that decent women

117

like herself somehow had to be looked after, that the world would never go so awry that she wouldn't be left with her afternoon kaffeeklatsch with her ladies as a kind of consolation prize. And Carla thought: She doesn't know her world no longer exists.— But what world did exist? A dirty world. An utterly godforsaken one. The cathedral clock struck the hour. Carla would have to hurry. She wanted to pack her things and go to the clinic before Washington got back from the game. She had to get rid of the baby. Washington was crazy if he imagined he could talk her into having his child. The other world, the bright and beautiful world of the magazines, of the automatic kitchens, the television sets, and the Hollywood-style ranch apartment, all that didn't go with the child. But wasn't it already immaterial? Wasn't even this child, its birth or death, immaterial? Carla wondered whether she would ever make it to the beautiful dream world of the American magazines. It had been a mistake to get together with Washington. Carla had got on the wrong train. Washington was a decent guy, but unfortunately he was sitting on the wrong train. Carla couldn't do anything about that, she couldn't help the fact that he was sitting on the wrong train. All blacks were sitting on the wrong train. Even the leaders of jazz orchestras were sitting on the wrong train; only they were in the first-class compartments of the wrong train. It had been really stupid of Carla. She should have waited for a white American. I could have got myself a white guy, I would have been good enough for a white guy, are my tits sagging? no, they're not sagging, they're firm and round, what was it the guy called them? milk-apples. They're milk-apples still, my body's white, it's a little thick, but they like thighs with a bit of meat on them, plump, I'm plump, I'm always plump in bed, but that's good, shouldn't I have been allowed to enjoy myself? so what's the price I pay? a little tummy-ache, but I could have got myself a white guy.— Carla could have gotten on the right white train. It couldn't be helped now. Only the white American train was headed into the dream world of the magazine pictures, the world of affluence, security, and comfort. Washington's America was dark and dirty. It was a world as dark and dirty and dismal and godforsaken as this world here. Maybe I should die, thought Carla. Maybe dying would be the best thing.— Carla turned around, she looked back across the square, she looked to see if she could catch sight of her mother once more, but Frau Behrend had already left the cathedral square with rapid, cowardly steps, fleeing the catastrophe, and without another look back at her daughter. From the church, through its as yet unreplaced windows, the organ rumbled under the hands of the practicing organist, and the Stabat Mater filled the air.

Stormy weather: the music of the cinema Wurlitzer blew, stormed, surged, and rattled. It blew, stormed, surged, and rattled from all the loudspeakers. In time with the loudspeaker, the same notes blew, stormed, surged, and rattled from the music box that Josef had placed beside him on the bench. He was eating a sandwich. He was making heavy weather of the thick slices of bread. He had to open his mouth as wide as he could to be able to bite off a piece of sandwich. It had a duff taste. The ham had been smeared with a sweetish paste. The ham tasted off. Its sweetish taste bothered Josef. It was as if the ham had gone off, and then been sprayed with perfume. Also, the green lettuce leaves that had been put between the bread and the ham were not to Josef's liking. The sandwich was like the grave of a ham roll that was sprouting ivy. Josef choked down the sandwich reluctantly. He thought of his death. He ate the foreign-tasting, foreign food out of native politeness. He mustn't offend his master, Odysseus. Odysseus drank Coca-Cola. He set the bottle to his lips and emptied it. He sprayed the last gulp at the seat in front. He hit the bottom strut of the seat in front. Josef had got out of drinking the Coca-Cola. He didn't care for the newfangled stuff.

Washington was running. He heard the bat and the smack of the ball. He heard the blowing, storming, surging, and rattling of the Wurlitzer. He heard voices, the voices of the crowd, the voices of the fans, the calls, the whistles, the laughter. He ran around the field. He puffed and wheezed. He was drenched in sweat. The stadium with its grandstands looked like a gigantic striped clamshell. It was as if the shell wanted to close on him, to take the sky away from him forever, to press itself together, and crush him. Washington fought for breath. The Wurlitzer was silent. The loudspeakers spoke the words of the announcer. The announcer was speaking from Odysseus's suitcase. Washington's name filled the stadium. He had won his race. The name of the winner pressed itself against the shell and kept it from clapping shut. For the moment, Washington had defeated the shell. It wouldn't clap shut, it wouldn't crush him, it wouldn't eat him up for the moment. Washington had to keep on winning.

He's not on form, thought Heinz. He could tell from looking at Washington that he wasn't on form. He thought: He'll lose the next race, and if he loses the next race, they'll chew him out.— It annoyed Heinz that they would whistle at Washington, and laugh at him and boo him. Anyone could lose form. Were they all on form? Snotnoses. He felt ashamed. He didn't know quite why he felt ashamed. He said: "He won't make it next time."—"Who won't make it?" asked the boys. They had got tickets to the stadium from the German-American Youth Club. They had brought the little ownerless dog with his string up to the grandstand with them. "My mother's nigger, of course," said Heinz, "the nigger won't cut it next time."

Richard had found his way to Frau Behrend's house. He spoke

to the daughter of the janitor. The daughter of the janitor talked down to him, literally because she stood a couple of steps above Richard, but in a figurative sense as well. Richard was not the shining victor, the hero, that the ugly girl had been waiting for. Richard had come on foot; those the gods loved came on wheels. Richard, she could see, was a common soldier, albeit an airman. Airmen of course were a step up from ordinary soldiers, the fame of Icarus served to elevate them, but the daughter of the janitor didn't know about Icarus. If Richard had landed his plane on the steps and jumped out with a bouquet for her, then he might perhaps have been the long-awaited bridegroom of the charmless creature; but no, he couldn't have been her bridegroom: even then he would have been missing a knight's cross. The girl dwelt in a world of appalling prejudices. She had evolved a whole hierarchy of status, stiffer and sterner customs than in the Kaiser's times governed her outlook, and there were unbridgeable gulfs between one rank and the next. The idea of a social ladder with a top and a bottom enabled the janitor's daughter to tolerate her own low standing, as she thought, because she was all the more drawn by a social climb as promised her by the horoscope of the *Evening Echo*: she would succeed where very few succeeded, she might be at the bottom, but a prince would turn up or a factory manager and lead her up to the allocated rung of rank and respect. For reasons of destiny, this prince or factory manager might temporarily be found lurking in society's depths, perhaps in disguise, but without question he would come to conduct her to the shining heights. Fortunately, the janitor's daughter was certain she would immediately recognize the man in his disguise; there was no possibility of error. Richard was no disguised superior, she could tell, he belonged to the low-caste people, and needed to be treated as such. All Americans were low class. They only sometimes pretended they belonged to a better class. Even if they were rich, the janitor's daughter could see through them: they were people who stood on the bottom. Americans were no proper princes, no proper officers, no proper managers. They didn't believe in hierarchy: *democratic idea cemented in Germany*. With an offhand gesture the girl dispatched Richard in the direction of the grocery shop. Maybe Frau Behrend was at the grocer's. Richard thought: What's the matter with her? she's weird, doesn't she like us?— With glassy eyes the girl watched him go. She had the fixed expression and mechanical movements of a doll. Her mouth was open, and she had buckteeth. She resembled an ugly, cheap doll that someone had left on the stairs.

This time, Washington wasn't quick enough. He lost his race. He was puffing hard. His chest rose and sank like a bellows in a blacksmith's. He lost his race. The man on the mic was no longer Washington's friend. Out of every loudspeaker the announcer cursed. He was cursing agitatedly from the little box between Josef and Odysseus. Odysseus hurled a Coca-Cola bottle onto the field. Josef blinked anxiously around for approaching policemen. He didn't want Odysseus to be arrested. In the stands they were whistling and booing. Now they've got him, now they'll finish him off, thought Heinz. He struggled to keep them from booing him and finishing him off. But he too was whistling and booing. He howled with the wolves: "The nigger's finished. My mother's nigger's washed up." The children were laughing. Even the little ownerless dog was howling. A fat boy said: "That's right, they're sticking it to him!" Heinz thought: I'll stick it to you, snot-nosed wimp!— He howled, booed, and whistled. It was a game between the Red Stars and a visiting side. The spectators' sympathies were with the visitors.

Ezra wasn't supporting either side. Baseball bored him. One

side would win, or the other. That was always the way of it. One side won. Then after the game, they all shook hands, and trooped off to their separate dressing rooms. That was boring. People should fight real enemies. His little brow creased up. Even the cap of his stubbly red hair creased up. He had seen the boy with the dog again, the boy and the dog from the parking place outside the Central Exchange. The problem was preoccupying him. That wasn't a game, that was a fight. He still didn't know how he was going to go about it. Christopher asked: "What's the matter? You're not watching!" — "I don't like crummy baseball!" said Ezra. Christopher was angry. He liked watching baseball. He had been pleased that he could take in a game while he was in Germany. He had thought he would please Ezra by taking him to the stadium. He was annoyed. He said: "Well, if you don't like it, we can go." Ezra nodded. He thought: This is the way it has to be done.— He said: "Can you give me ten dollars?" Christopher was surprised that Ezra wanted ten dollars. "Ten dollars is a lot of money," he said, "is there something you want to buy?" — "I don't want to spend it," said Ezra. He looked across to where the children were sitting with the dog. Christopher didn't understand Ezra. He said: "If you don't want to spend the money, why should I give it to you?" Ezra was tormented by headaches behind his little creased brow. How slow Christopher was to understand anything! He just didn't get it! He said: "I need ten dollars in case I get lost. I could get separated from you." Christopher laughed. He said: "You and your worries. You're just like your mother." But then he thought Ezra's idea was quite a sensible one. He said: "OK. I'll give you ten dollars." They stood up and squeezed past the people in their row. Ezra quickly went up in a plane and dropped a bomb on the field. Both sides suffered horrendous casualties. Ezra took one last look back at Heinz and the dog and thought: I wonder if he'll come tonight? he's a shitass if he doesn't.

"Frau Behrend will be pleased," said the grocer. "If Frau Behrend came in now, she would be so pleased!" She pressed Richard back into a corner of the shop, where, hidden under some brown paper she kept the sack of sugar, which once more was in short supply. All at once Richard felt hungry and thirsty. Between himself and the grocery woman there was a ham on a platter, and next to his feet a case of beer. The air in Germany, or perhaps just the air in this shop smelling of traditional foods, seemed to make you hungry and thirsty. Richard would happily have asked the grocery woman to sell him a bottle of beer and a slice of the ham. But the woman was badgering him too much. He felt trapped in the corner of the shop. It seemed to him that she was keeping him next to the sugar so that she could keep her eye on them both and give them to whomever she saw fit. It annoyed him that he had followed his father's sentimental notion and looked up Frau Behrend, who from just after the war ended they had been sending food parcels to. The grocery woman had got on to the subject of the parcels now. She was describing the hunger of the time immediately after the war, and as she did so, she bent down over the ham, at which Richard was casting ever more covetous eyes. "They took everything from us, we didn't have anything," said the woman, "and then they sent us Negroes, you come from German stock yourself, you'll understand we had to start dealing with Negroes if we weren't to starve. That's the plight of Frau Behrend!" She looked expectantly up at Richard. Richard had an imperfect grasp of the German language. What was she saying about the Negroes? They had Negroes in the air force. The Negroes flew the same planes as the rest of them. Richard didn't have anything against Negroes. He didn't have an opinion of them either way. "The daughter," said the woman. She lowered her voice and leaned even farther forward in Richard's direction. The hem of her apron brushed the fatty rim of the ham. Richard didn't know anything about any daughter of Frau Behrend's. Frau Behrend hadn't mentioned this daughter in her letters to Wilhelm Kirsch. Richard wondered whether Frau Behrend might have got a daughter from a Negro to whom she had had to give herself out of hunger. But she was surely too old to have been able to sell herself for bread. Was Richard still hungry for a slice of ham? He thought of Frau Behrend's daughter and said: "I should have brought along some toys."—"Toys?" The woman didn't understand Richard. Was this young man, born in America, but sired by a German father, was he so Americanized that he had lost all sense of honor and decency? Was he making fun of German hunger and turmoil? She asked sternly: "Toys for whom exactly? We don't deal with that daughter anymore." She assumed that Richard would not deal with Frau Behrend's daughter either. Richard thought: What's all this to me? what's Frau Behrend's daughter to me? this feels like sinking into the swamp of origin, into Father's old home, into the constriction of the old family relationships.— He broke loose from the contemplation of the ham, and freed himself from the snares of this shop, which was a curious mixture of hunger and fatty foods, of mean-spiritedness, shortages, and illusions. His foot bumped against the beer. He said he would be spending the evening at the Bräuhaus, and Frau Behrend could find him there if she wanted. He didn't care whether he saw Frau Behrend or not—Frau Behrend and her Negro daughter.

"No bed has been reserved. We have no record of a bed reserved for you," said the sister. The sister had the monotonous voice of a recorded message on a telephone service. "We have no reservation. No record of anything in your name," said the voice. "But Dr. Frahm told me—" Carla was at a loss. "There must be a mistake, sister. Dr. Frahm told me he would phone ahead."—"We have no record of any call. Dr. Frahm hasn't telephoned." The sister had the face of a stone figure. She looked like a carved figure on a public fountain. Carla was standing with her little suitcase in the reception room of Dr. Schulte's clinic. In the suitcase, she had packed fresh clothes, a waterproof bag of cosmetics, the latest American magazines; illustrated color magazines depicting the domestic happiness of Hollywood actors. Kitted out with happiness from Hollywood, Carla was ready to have her baby taken away, to have the baby of her black boyfriend, the friendly enemy from dark America, killed. "You must have a bed for me. Dr. Frahm promised me. I am expecting an operation. It's urgent," she said. "Nothing has been reserved. We have no bed reserved for you." It would take an earthquake to move this stone figure; only on instructions from a doctor would she unblock the way to an abortion. "I'm going to wait here for Dr. Frahm," said Carla. "I promise you, Sister, it's just a mix-up." She felt like crying. She felt like telling the sister of the many presents she had given Dr. Frahm, at a time when there was nothing, no coffee, no brandy, no cigarettes. She sat down on a hard bench. The bench was as hard as a bench in court. The sister answered the telephone and spoke exactly like the recording at the post office: "I'm sorry, there are no vacancies. I'm sorry, we have no free beds." Monotonous, indifferent, mechanical, the nurse dealt with the invisible applicants. The beds in this clinic seemed to be very sought after.

Josef slept. He had fallen asleep in his seat. He had fallen asleep in his seat in the stadium, but he felt he was sleeping in a bed. He was used to hard beds, but this one here was a hospital bed, a bed in a paupers' hospital, an especially hard bed, his deathbed. He had reached the end of his life's journey. Fallen asleep in the stadium and on duty, on his porter's duty, on duty for a foreign gentleman traveled from a foreign land, surrounded by loudspeaker din of a senseless game played on turf, senselessly addressed by the same din and noise, which also came in the guise of a softer, personalized message addressed to him by the little box he had had to carry and to look after today, the sleeping Josef knew that this had been his final task, the transportation of the little case, the carriage of this little music case, a light, really an amusing little task for a great and generous, albeit, black master. Josef knew he would die. He knew he would die on this hospital bed. How could it be otherwise than that he would die in the paupers' hospital at the end of his life's journey? And was he ready to go, was he prepared to go on the long journey? He thought: God will forgive me, he will forgive me the little tricks and deceits of the tourist trade, after all the tourists come here in order to be cheated a little bit, they come here to be taken for a little bit of a ride. — They were strange nurses they had in this hospital. They went around in baseball clothes, and they carried clubs in their hands. Was God angry with Josef after all? Was Josef going to be beaten? At the portals of the hospital stood Odysseus. But this wasn't the friendly, generous Odysseus whom he had guided through the city. This was the Odysseus on the Cathedral tower, a fearsome and dangerous devil. He had become one with the gargoyle on the tower outcrop, the gargoyle on which he had signed his name and dwelling place; Odysseus was a black devil, truly, a bad black devil; he was nothing but a perfectly ordinary, terrible devil. What did the devil want with Josef? had Josef not always been good, but for the little tricks and deceits that formed part of the tourist trade? had he not carried suitcases for all and sundry? had he not gone to war? or perhaps it was the going to war that was a sin? had the performance of duty been a sin? was duty sin? duty, of which all spoke, which all wrote about, proclaimed, and celebrated? had his duty now been chalked up on the board, was it an item on God's reckoning, like an unpaid beer on a bar tab? It was true! It had always tormented

Josef. Secretly tormented him. He never liked to think about it: he had killed, killed people, killed his travelers; he had killed them at Chemin-des-Dames, and in the Argonnes Forest. Those two had been the only excursions of his life, Chemin-des-Dames and the Argonnes Forest, not pleasant places to visit, and they had gone there to kill and to be killed. Lord, what could I do? what else could I have done, Lord?— Was it just that for this chalked-up and never canceled debt of enforced killing he was being handed over to the devil, the black devil Odysseus? Hey! Hey! Hallo! Already the beating had begun. The devil had started to thrash him. Josef screamed. His scream merged with others' screams. He was being thumped on the shoulder. He started up. He came back to life. Odysseus the devil, Odysseus the friendly, King Odysseus the friendly devil was thumping Josef on the shoulder. Then Odysseus leaped up on to the seat in the stands. He was holding a Coca-Cola bottle like a grenade ready to be thrown. The loudspeakers were yelling. The stadium was shouting, yelling, whistling, stomping, and screaming. The voice of the announcer came hoarsely out of the little radio box. The Red Stars had won.

He had won. Washington had won. He had hit the greatest number of runs. He had pulled the victory for the Red Stars out of his own lungs. The shell would not clap shut. The shell would not clap shut yet. Maybe the shell would never clap shut on Washington, never steal the sky from him. The stadium had not gobbled him up. Washington was the hero of the stands. They called out his name. The radio commentator had made his peace with Washington. Washington was once again the commentator's friend. They all were cheering and applauding Washington. He wheezed and panted. He was free. He was a free citizen of the United States. There was no discrimination. How he was sweating! He would run on and on. He would run around the park faster and faster and more and more times. Running made you free, running took you into life. His running made room for Washington in the world. It made room for Carla. It made room for a baby. If only Washington could always run so well, run faster and faster, then they would all keep their room in the world.

"He was on form after all." — "Course he was on form." – "He was on form, the nigger." — "Don't say nigger." — "I was saying he was on form." — "He was on fantastic form." — "You said he wasn't." — "I said he was. Washington's always on form." — "You said your mother's nigger wasn't." — "Shut your mouth, creep." — "Wanna bet? You did say it." — "I said shut your mouth, creep." They fought leaving the stadium. Heinz was fighting for Washington. He had never said Washington wasn't on form. Washington was on fantastic form. He was fantastic, anyway. Schorschi, Bene, Kare, and Sepp stood around the kids who were fighting. They watched the kids hit each other in the face. "Sock him!" called Bene. Heinz stopped punching. "Not for you, creep." He spat out blood. He spat at Bene's feet. Bene raised his hand. "Leave him be," said Schorschi. "Cool it. Leave him to it, the idiot." — "Idiot yourself!" yelled Heinz. But he shrank back a little. "That was a boring game," said Sepp. He yawned. The boys had been given tickets by the German-American Youth Club. The tickets hadn't cost them anything. "What'll we do now?" asked Kare. "Dunno," said Schorschi. "Any ideas?" he asked Kare. "No. No idea." — "Cinema?" suggested Kare. "I've seen them all," said Schorschi. He meant all the current gangster and cowboy films. "Cinema's no good." — "If only it was evening," said Bene. "If only it was evening," the others chimed in. They seemed to set some hope in the evening. They drifted out of the stadium, hunched over, hands in their jacket pockets, elbows out, with slumped shoulders, as after a hard day's work. The golden horde. "Who's got the dog?" yelled Heinz. While he was fighting, Heinz had let go of the string. The ownerless little dog had run off. He had disappeared in the crowd.

"Damn," said Heinz, "I need that dog tonight." He turned furiously to his comrades. "You could have watched him, you snotnoses. That dog was worth ten dollars!" — "You should have watched him yourself, dirty Negro bastard." They fought some more.

Washington stood under the shower in the stadium's changing room. The cold spray sobered him up. His heart twitched. For a moment he couldn't breathe. Pungent sweat washed off him along with the water. He was still on form. His body was still on form. He stretched his muscles, thrust out his chest, his chest and muscles were still on form. He felt his genitals. They were fine too. But what about his heart? And his breathing? They worried him. There was something the matter there. And then his rheumatism! Maybe he didn't have that much in him. Maybe he didn't have that much more in him as an active sportsman. At home and in bed, he still had plenty. What could he do? What could he do for himself, for Carla, for the baby, and maybe for the kid, for Heinz? He had showered long enough. He toweled down. He could leave the service, sell the sky-blue limousine, have one more year as an athlete, and then maybe open a bar in Paris. In Paris people weren't prejudiced. He could open his bar in Paris: Washington's Bar. He had to talk with Carla. He could live with Carla in Paris, no trouble. They could open their bar in Paris, they could put up his sign, light it up with colored lights, his sign NONE UNWELCOME. In Paris they would be happy; they would all be happy. Washington whistled a tune. He was happy. He whistled as he left the shower room.

Dr. Frahm was washing up. He stood in the washroom of Schulte's clinic and washed his hands. In innocence old Pontius Pilate a fine feeling, he washed his hands with a good soap, and scrubbed his fingers with a stiff brush. He drove the bristles under his fingernails. He thought: Main thing is to avoid infection, he thought,

ought to cut my nails again, Semmelweis, they're filming him too, I read it in the paper, I wonder whether they'll show a case of metritis? that would be something, in close up, it could deter people, could deter people in all sorts of ways, no one will come along and film my life, well, I don't mind about that.— He said: "I can't do it. I'm sorry, Frau Carla, it can't be done." Carla stood next to him, stood next to the basin over which he was scrubbing his hands under the powerful flow of water from the nickel tap. Carla looked at the nickel tap, she looked at the water, she looked at the soap bubbles, at the hands of the doctor, which were lobster red from the soap, the brush, and the warm water. She thought: Butcher's hands, real butcher's hands.— She said: "You can't do this to me, doctor." Her voice sounded unsure and choked. The doctor said: "There's nothing the matter with you. You're pregnant. Probably third month. That's all." Carla felt sick. It was that disgusting, choking sickness of pregnancy. She thought: Why are we born like this?— She wanted to punch herself in the stomach, swelling again, growing plump like a melon. She thought: I've got to talk to him, I've got to talk to him, but I can't talk to him now.— She said: "But when we were in your practice, you said to come." The doctor said: "I didn't say anything. You see, the father wants the baby. I can't do anything." She thought: He's been here, the black bastard was here, he's queered the doctor, now Frahm doesn't want to help me, he doesn't want to do it, and all the stuff I've given him. She was sorry she had given the doctor so much coffee, so many cigarettes, so much brandy. She felt a little sicker. She had to grab on to the sink. She thought: I'm going to be sick, I'm going to vomit over his hands, over his disgusting red butcher's hands, think of everywhere those hands have been, those little trimmed fingernails reaching into your life.— She said: "But I don't want it! Will you understand, I don't want it!" She gulped and burst into tears. She's about to be sick, thought Frahm. She's gone very pale.

He pushed a chair behind her. "Sit down!" He thought: I hope she's not going to get hysterical, it could get me into so much trouble if I got rid of it for her.— Since he had picked up the chair, he had to lather his hands again. I'll try and talk to her, he thought, it always helps with women, they have a good cry, and later they're proud mothers.— He said: "Now please, be sensible about this. Your boyfriend is a good man. He looks to me like he'll make a good father. He'll take good care of you and the baby. You'll be surprised what a pretty baby you've got there. Remind me nearer the time, and I'll deliver it for you. I promise you, you'll have no pain. You won't feel a thing, and you'll have your baby!" I'll set it to her breast, he thought, and I hope she'll love it, doesn't look that way now, poor thing, not even born and already hated, but if the father insists, what else can I do about it? the father must have a sense of what's in store for the kid.— She thought: The pair of bastards have it all planned out, and it'll kill me, Washington bastard, bastard Frahm.— She said: "I'll take it to someone else." She thought: Who will I take it to? I expect Frau Welz knows someone, and the girls must know someone, I should have kept my coffee and cigarettes for the girls.— "No, you won't do that," said Frahm. "Enough now, Frau Carla. That's a much more dangerous course of action than you have any idea of. And then no one will be able to help you. Do you think I scrub my hands like this because I enjoy it? Or because I'm squeamish? I stopped being squeamish a long time ago." His mood was deteriorating. The woman was wasting his time; he could do nothing for her. She thought: I'd like to puke over his hands, that would be nice for him, my vomit all over his butcher's hands, that'd give him something to scrub at.— "It's not so awful," said Frahm. It's death, thought Carla.

It's terrible, thought Frau Behrend. What awful luck she had! She'd set out to have a nice cozy chat with the ladies in the Domcafé, and then her lost daughter had come bothering her, and got her all wrought up, no nice cozy chat at all, just disgrace and confusion, the disgrace of the times and confusion in disorder, error, and moral abysses, and, while she was going through so much unpleasantness, and disgrace was brushing her—couldn't she have stayed at home? it would have been more peaceful and cozy up in her attic, Carla wouldn't have come bothering her in her attic—a visitor had come for her all the way from America, a relative, the son of that Wilhelm who had sent her the parcels. What bad luck! The grocery woman told her about it. She had waved Frau Behrend into the shop, said she had some news for her. The young Kirsch boy had been there. He had talked about the parcels. And the woman, that poisonous, gossipy woman—oh, Frau Behrend could just tell, she didn't have any doubts—she of course had blabbed about everything, told him about Carla and her black boyfriend, she was certain to have passed on all the things that Frau Behrend had told her, and over in America they were so strict about Negroes, *racial shame, Aryan pass*, Negroes or Jews, it was much of a muchness, why did Carla have to go and do such a thing, never in the family history had there been anything like that, the Aryan certificate was without stain, and now this disgrace! "He'll be looking out for you in the Bräuhaus," said the grocery woman. In the Bräuhaus? That was a story, she should pull the other one! The young Kirsch boy comes here all the way from America to visit Frau Behrend, to see his German relative, and then he asks her to see him in the Bräuhaus. It wasn't possible! The woman must know it too! She hadn't wanted her to have her rich American relative. All Americans were rich. All white Americans were rich. The woman had begrudged her the food parcels too. Young Kirsch had probably left already, had gone home disappointed, back to the wealth and decency of America. Suddenly

Frau Behrend blamed Carla for young Kirsch's disappearance. Young Kirsch had fled because he couldn't stand so much immorality, he had fled the disgrace and the sordor. He had retreated in the face of Carla's sordor and disgrace. He and all his American wealth had washed his hands of the old German family, now sunk in sordor and disgrace. It was Carla's fault; all her fault. The grocery woman had done right in telling him. She was a decent woman. The grocery woman was a good and proper person. Frau Behrend herself would have told it too, had she known of someone's comparable disgrace. She leaned right across the counter. Her bosom brushed the cheese cloche, under which a caraway cheese was slowly melting. Frau Behrend whispered: "You told him then?"—"Told him what?" asked the grocer. She propped herself on her knuckles and looked directly at Frau Behrend. She thought: Watch it, you, or you won't get your sugar anymore.— Frau Behrend whispered: "About Carla, you know." The grocer directed her stern, reproving look at Frau Behrend, the look she had used to tame many customers already, poor customers, coupon customers, regular consumers. Don't think it couldn't happen again, *Farmers Unite against New Economic Laws, Unions Consider Rationing of Essential Foodstuffs*. The shopkeeper said: "What are you suggesting, Frau Behrend, how could I do such thing!" Frau Behrend straightened herself again. She thought: She did tell him, of course she told him.— The shopkeeper lifted the cheese cloche; the ripening process was already far advanced; the air filled with stench.

Philipp thought about the bridge over the Oder. It was a bridge under glass. The train crossed the bridge as through a glass tunnel. The passengers turned pale. The light fell into the tunnel as though filtered through milk; the sun became a pallid moon.

Philipp called out: "Now we're under the cheese cloche!" Philipp's mother sighed: "Oh dear, back in the East." The bridge over the Oder for Philipp's mother marked the transition between West and East. She hated the East. She sighed because she had to live in the East, away from the splendors of Berlin, or the Carnival celebrations in the Southwest. For Philipp, the East was the land of childhood; it meant the pleasures of winter, the cat by the hearth, apples baking in the oven; it meant peace, it meant snow, it meant beautiful, cold, quiet, gentle snow outside. Philipp loved winter. Dr. Behude tried hard to put up a cloche of optimism and summer over Philipp. He will never be able to take me back to childhood, he will not succeed in changing me. Philipp lay on the patient's couch in Behude's darkened treatment room. He kept crossing the Oder. He kept sitting in a train under the cloche of the bridge in a pale, transformed light. His mother was crying, but Philipp was going to the land of childhood, he was traveling toward cold, peace, snow. Behude said: "It's a beautiful summer's day. You've got a day off. You're lying in a meadow. You've got nothing to do. You're perfectly relaxed." Behude stood in his darkened room like a dream figure, leaning over the recumbent Philipp. The dream figure had gently placed its hand over Philipp's brow. Philipp lay on the doctor's couch in a rictus of suppressed laughter and irritation. Good old Behude was using all his strength to evoke summer vacation. Philipp didn't care about lovely summer vacation. He didn't have days off. He had never been on a vacation in his life. Life didn't give Philipp any time off. That was one way of looking at it. Alternatively, there was always something that Philipp wanted to do. He was always thinking of some great work that he was about to embark on, that would completely exhaust him. In his mind, he was readying himself for this great task, which both drew him and terrified him. He could truly claim that work never let go of him; it tormented and delighted him wherever he was, whatever he did, even in his sleep; he felt summoned to this task; but never or only very rarely did he actually do anything; he didn't even try. And, viewed in this way, his life had been one long vacation, a misspent vacation, vacation in bad weather, in bad lodgings, in bad company, vacation with too little spending money. "You're lying in a meadow—" He wasn't lying in a meadow. He was lying on Behude's couch. He wasn't mad. How many madmen, how many hysterics and neurotics had lain before him on this couch? And always Behude had tried to conjure up a beautiful vacation for his patients: vacation from dementia, vacation from fantasies, vacation from fear, vacation from addiction, vacation from conflicts. Philipp thought: You want me to dream? but I won't dream Behude's dream, Behude is looking for a regular civil servant at the bottom of everyone's psyche, I hate meadows, why should I lie in a meadow? I never lie in a meadow, nature freaks me out, nature disquiets me, a storm unsettles me with the change of electrical current on my skin and in my nerves, there's nothing worse than nature, only snow is good, quiet, kindly, softly falling snow.— Behude said: "You're completely relaxed. You're resting. You're happy. No worries can get to you. No bad thoughts are troubling you. You feel thoroughly well. You're dozing. You're dreaming. You dream only pleasant dreams." Behude tiptoed away from Philipp. He went into the next room, where the light was on, the room for the rougher psychiatric treatments that Behude preferred not to use. Switch panels and electrodes would have frightened Emilia, who was very much afraid of doctors and thought they were all sadists. Behude sat down at a desk and plucked Philipp's notes from a card index. He thought of Emilia. He thought: They're not a normal couple, but they are a couple, and actually I think their marriage is indissoluble, even though at first sight it appears to me more of a perversity than a marriage, it was perverse of Philipp and Emilia to enter a marriage, but the very fact that neither of them are marriage material keeps them together, I would like to influence them both psychotherapeutically, mutual healing of the one by the other, but what would be the point? what am I trying to heal them of? they're happy as they are, if I managed to heal them, Philipp would take a job on a newspaper and Emilia would sleep around, and is that what treatment is for? I ought to take more exercise, I spend too much time thinking of Emilia's infantile charms, she won't sleep with me, she'll only sleep with Philipp until she's cured, Emilia and Philipp give one another the perversity of a normal married couple with jealousy, bonding, and faithfulness.

Emilia recognized Edwin immediately. She knew that this man in the beautiful black hat, who had something about him of an old lord, something also of an old buzzard, and something of an old pimp, was one of Philipp's poets. Then she remembered a photo of Edwin that Philipp kept pinned to the wall over the stack of virgin white paper. Emilia thought: So that's Edwin, the famous poet, that's the kind of man Philipp wants to become, perhaps he will, I hope he does/I'm afraid he will, and then will Philipp look like Edwin? as old? as formal? I think he'll look less formal, less like a lord and less like a vulture, though he might look like the old pimp, poets didn't use to look like that, I don't want Philipp to be successful, if he was successful he might leave me, but in other ways I would like him to be successful, he should have so much success that we could go away together and always have money, but if we had money that way, then Philipp would be the one who had it, and I don't want Philipp to have the money, I want to have it.— Emilia knew herself pretty well. She knew that, if she did manage to sell one of her houses, she would give Philipp a generous spending allowance, but that she would always disturb him in his desperate efforts to write his long-planned book. I will stoop to anything, nothing would be too low for me, I would be worse than ever, I wouldn't leave him a single hour to himself, poor Philipp, he's so decent.— Often when she thought about Philipp, she would feel moved. She wondered whether she should make an effort to get to know Edwin. It was an opportunity that Messalina wouldn't have turned down. She would have tried to haul him off to her party, poor Edwin, Emilia wouldn't drag Edwin to any party. But she thought it might astonish Philipp if she could tell him that she'd got to know Edwin. Edwin was rummaging through the antiques in Frau de Voss's shop. He was examining the miniatures. He had fine, long-boned hands, strikingly hairy at the wrists. He was examining the miniatures through a magnifying glass, which gave him still more the appearance of a buzzard. Frau de Voss showed Edwin a rosewood Madonna. The Madonna had belonged to Philipp. Emilia had sold it to Frau de Voss. Edwin studied the Madonna through the magnifying glass. He asked how much the little Madonna cost. Frau de Voss whispered the price. She will have put a hefty markup on it, thought Emilia. Edwin set the beautiful figure back on the table. Emilia thought, he must be mean. Disappointed in Edwin, Frau de Voss turned to Emilia: "And what have you got for me, girly?" She always addressed Emilia as girly. Frau de Voss met customers who had something to sell with the hauteur of a former lady at court, and the strictness of a schoolmarm. Emilia stammered something. She was ashamed to open her ridiculous Scotch plaid in Edwin's presence. Then she thought: Why am I ashamed? if he has more money than Philipp, it's just luck.— She handed Frau de Voss a cup. It was a cup made in Berlin. The cup was gilded inside, and on the outside it had a miniature painting of Frederick the Great. Frau de Voss took the cup and set it down on her desk. Emilia thought: She's not going to deal with me now, because she wants to show her kindly face while

Edwin's there, and it won't be till he's gone that she'll show her true face.— Edwin didn't find anything among the antiques that interested him. Everything in the shop was second-rate. The little Madonna was too expensive. Edwin knew the prices. He wasn't a collector, but every so often he would buy a piece he liked. He had stepped into Frau de Voss's shop because he was bored. He had suddenly been overcome with boredom in this city. If you walked through its streets in the afternoon, the city was neither especially rich in history nor especially vertiginous. It was ordinary, an ordinary city with ordinary people. Maybe Edwin would write about his afternoon in the city in his journal. That wouldn't be published until after his death. It was to contain the truth. In the light of truth, the afternoon in this city would no longer be ordinary. Edwin picked up Emilia's cup. He looked at the picture of Frederick the Great. The cup pleased him. A good face, thought Edwin, full of intellect and pain, his poems and his wars were terrible, but he kept Voltaire on a retainer, and Voltaire wrote terrible things about him.— He inquired after the price of the cup. Frau de Voss gestured in some embarrassment to Emilia and tried to draw Edwin into a sort of alcove at the back of the store. Emilia thought: She's annoyed, because if I find out what Edwin paid, she'll hardly be able to fob me off with whatever she had in mind.— The awkwardness of the shop owner tickled Emilia. She thought: Funny that Edwin is interested in the same things that Philipp likes.— Edwin saw through Frau de Voss's little game. He wasn't interested. He didn't go into the alcove with her. He set the cup down on the desk and turned to go. Emilia wondered whether she should pick up the cup and offer it to Edwin on the street. But she thought: That's importuning, and it would turn Frau de Voss against me for good, even now she'll not give me much, just out of irritation, but Edwin hardly noticed me, he noticed me about as much as you notice an old ugly chair, that's all I was for Edwin, an old ugly chair,

I hate writers, they're such conceited so-and-sos.— Edwin, once outside, thought, she was poor, she was afraid of the antique seller, I could have helped the young woman, but I didn't, now why did I not help her out? that would be worth going into.— Edwin will mention the cup and Emilia in his journal. It will be in the light of truth. In the light of truth, Edwin will examine whether on that afternoon he was a good man or a bad man. In any case, the light of truth will be shed on Edwin, Emilia, and Frederick the Great.

No illumination, no revelation, no light of truth. Where was Philipp lying? In the darkened room. He's allowing me to dream, little dream doctor little psychotherapist, sits next door, and fills in my notes, my dream notes, little psycho-bureaucrat, sets down: Philipp is dreaming, he dreams of meadows, vacations, and sum-mer happiness, stuff your meadows will you, I'm a guest of Frau Holle's, she shakes out her featherbeds, down comes the snow cool gentle soft happy peaceful snow, the cozy tiled stove, a cat stretching and meowing, the apples sizzling away in the oven, I'm dressing puppets for the puppet theater, I'm dressing them for my little stage on the bench by the stove, it's fun playing at theater, but the most important thing is getting the dolls ready, one doll is going to be dressed like Emilia, one doll like the little Ameri-can girl with the green eyes, she could play Don Gil Don Gil with the green trousers, pert green trousers pert green eyes fresh and alert *Sanella always refreshing* a saber in her hand, my little lover, or are you the boy who set out to discover fear? you're short of something you need to be a boy, a grief to your girlfriends, but you can learn to discover fear, now how to dress Emilia? she is Ophelia the-poor-child-drawn-down-by-her-melodies-down-in-to-a-muddy-death, when I was fourteen I used to recite *Hamlet* to myself, to-die-to-sleep-perchance-to-dream pubescent pain, now I'm dreaming at little Dr. Behude's, shall I show him my Hamlet? he's always waiting for something indecent, erotic confessions, little surrogate father confessor, I still remember Hamlet, I've a good memory for everything that happened then, an excellent memory, the lake in front of our house was frozen over from October to Easter, the farmers drove across the lake on their wooden sleighs to haul the big trees out of the forest, felled giants, Eva, her pirouettes on the ice, the frost-jangling sun, Eva used to skate for me without tights, her mother was indignant, she was afraid she'd get an ovarian infection, didn't say so of course, thought we didn't know what that was, forgot about the encyclopedia though, she looked like a big mother hen chook-chook-chook, Emilia won't go skating, she thinks exercise is a waste of time, laughed herself silly when Behude said she ought to play tennis, Emilia runs around the city, Lene-Levi-drunk-at-night: heard that where? on the Kurfürstendamm in prehistoric times, later on the SA marched there, cats are supposed to see the world differently to us, all in brown or yellow, the city Emilia sees is a city of antiques with dirty dealers, she's out for money, her devil's on her back, she lugs her milord's travel plaid around the junkshops, goes down into their basements, the snakes, frogs, and amphibians, Hercules slew the Hydra, Emilia's Hydra's got more than nine heads, it has three hundred and sixty-five a year, three hundred and sixty-five sallies against the monster of impecuniousness, she sells anything in our apartment that's not nailed down, she lets the amphibians reach up her skirts, it disgusts her, but she gets money, and then she drinks it all up, stands at the bar like a lush, one more, "Cheers, neighbor," the other drinkers take her for a whore, "business bad today?"—"with this weather"—"with this weather"—"how's about it then?"—"how's about what?"—"well, us two"—"afraid not"—"are you?"—"I am"—"shitty life"—"here, have a drink," soon she'll look like Messalina, smaller, more delicate, but with Messalina's boozer's face, splotchy coarse-pored skin, Messalina tries to tempt Emilia to her parties, she wants to throw her to Alexander the housewife's dream of an archduke or to her ancient perverts, and she's surprised that Emilia doesn't show, Emilia doesn't like orgies, she doesn't like Messalina's desperados, Emilia has her own despair doesn't need anyone else's, she says she runs all over town on my behalf, so I can write my book, but then she hates me for it when she gets home, if I ever wrote anything she'd rip it up, Emilia my Ophelia: *o-pale-Ophelia-belle-comme-la-neige*, I love you but you'd do better to leave me, though you wouldn't make it on your own either, you will be squashed by your houses, you're already squashed by your houses, you're just a tender raging little boozed-up ghost of despair, my fault? sure, my fault, everyone's fault, old fault, forefathers' fault, historic fault, in her rage she screams at me that I'm a Communist, was I ever that? I was never that, I could have been a writer, I could have been a Communist, never was either, Kisch called me "Comrade" in the Romanisches Café, and I called him "Mr. Kisch," I was fond of him: Kisch roving reporter, roving whither? I detest violence, I detest oppression, does that make me a Communist? I don't know, social studies: Hegel Marx dialectics Marxist materialist dialectics—never understood it, call me an emotional Communist: always feeling futile indignation on behalf of the poor, Spartacus Jesus Thomas Münzer Max Holz, what did they all want? to be good, and what happened? they were killed, did I fight in Spain? the hour never struck for me, I kept my head down during the dictatorship, I hated but quietly, I hated but in my room at home, I spoke in whispers with the like-minded, Burckhardt said you couldn't make a state with people like him, I could appreciate that, but you can't destroy a state with people like that either, no hope, not for me, Behude claimed there was hope for me, Rilke poetry: somewhere in the East stands a church, swimmy, not practical, the East in me: landscape of childhood, my *recherche-du-temps-perdu*, seek-and-ye-shall-find, the smells, the baked apples, the sounds, the electric crackling fur of the cat, the grinding of the sleigh runners on the ice, Eva with her bare legs turning her pirouettes on the ice all alone: snow peace sleep—

Sleep but no return home to self, a falling, a felling. Like a heavy boulder in water, solid, insensate, Alexander in his apartment plummeted into sleep. No dream lived in the portrayer of the Archduke. Dressed as he was, he had thrown himself down on the sofa; this was where the tribade Alfredo had lain the night: Alexander felt no stirring of interest. He was just tired. He'd had it up to here. The part of the Archduke. The idiotic speech cylinder of the Archduke. The borrowed heroism. What had he done in the war? Acted. Exempted. Whom did he play? Heroic fighter pilots. He crash-landed four times and survived them all—his foes and rivals weren't so lucky. He had never even been up in a plane. The idea of flying anywhere terrified him. When the bombs came down, he was huddled in the diplomat bunker in the Adlon. That was the top people's bunker. Landsers on holiday were not admitted there. The bunker had two stories. Alexander sat in the lower one: the war kept its distance. After the attack, Hitler Youth boys cleared the rubble from the streets. The boys dug in the rubble for victims. They stopped Alexander for his autograph. They stopped Alexander the hero, the daredevil Alexander. They confused Alexander with his shadow. It made him dizzy. Who was he? An up-and-at'em-trusty-sentimental-brave-macho-hero? He had had enough. He was tired. He was all heroed out. He was like a drawn capon: fat and hollow. His face bore an expression of stupidity: it was unmade-up and empty. His mouth gaped open, and through the dazzling white of his capped teeth came a snore of dullness and sickness, of sluggish digestion and lethargic peristalsis. Two hundred pounds of human flesh lay on the sofa, at least they weren't dangling on the butcher's hook, but for the moment, with his wit switched off, the little stream of kidding and joking around that in this body did duty for a soul, Alexander was just meat, and two hundred pounds of it. Hillegonda came bouncing into the room. She had heard Alexander's car draw up outside, and briefly she mustered the courage to let go of Emmi's hand and go alone into the world full of sin. Hillegonda wanted to ask Alexander whether God was really angry, whether God was angry with Hillegonda and Alexander and Messalina. God wasn't angry with Emmi. But perhaps that was a lie of Emmi's. "Daddy, is Emmi allowed to lie, ever?" The child didn't receive an answer. Maybe God was just then angry with Emmi. Emmi was always standing at God's tribunal. Even very early, when it was just getting light, she had had to go into God's darkened halls of justice. Alexander had been summonsed too. He had been summonsed to appear before the tax authorities. He had been scared. He had shouted, "The accounts are all over the place!" Was Emmi's account perhaps also all over the place? The child was torturing herself. She would have liked to be on a better footing with God. It could be that God's anger was not directed at Hillegonda at all. But her father said nothing. He lay there, as if dead. Only the gurgling and snoring from his open mouth showed that he was still alive. There was Emmi calling Hillegonda. She had to go back to Emmi's hand. Emmi had been summonsed again. She had to go down on her knees again, on the tiles, on the cold hard stone tiles, she had to bow down before God in the dust.

The church of the Holy Spirit gave the square, the hospital, and the inn their name. The inn was a disreputable place. Where were they now? When Josef was little, the market stallholders had used to meet in that inn. The stallholders used to ride into the city with horse and cart, and Josef helped them yoke and unyoke the horses. At that time, the old quarter round the Heiliggeistplatz had been the heart of the city. Later, the center had moved. The old quarter died. The market died. The square, the houses, the hospital, and the church were all bombed in the War, but they had been dead long before. Never would anyone have enough money to pay for these ruins to be rebuilt. The quarter went to the bad. Thieves, pimps, and whores used to meet here. Where had they got to? It was Josef's old home, the quarter where he had played as a child and worked as a child, where he had taken his first communion. Where were they all? They were all sitting in the pub. The pub was full, noisy and full; a heavy warm atmosphere of smells and smoke filled the room, swelled out the room like gas in a flaccid balloon. Where were the market traders? The market traders were dead. They lay in their graves in their village cemeteries beside their white churches. Their horses, which Josef had harnessed, had gone to the knacker's. Josef and Odysseus were drinking schnapps. Odysseus said the schnapps was gin. It was Steinhäger. It was a cheap, fake Steinhäger. In the music box on Josef's lap, a chorus was singing *she-was-a-nice-girl*. How did they come to be here? What were they doing here? The little Josef had gone begging for milk. The farmer's wife had poured milk into his jug. Josef had run back across the square and tripped. The jug had smashed. The milk was spilled. Josef's mother beat Josef. She beat him hard, about the ears. Life is hard for the poor; they make it still harder for themselves. *She-was-a-nice-girl*. What were they doing here? They were settling up. Odysseus paid Josef. He pulled out his wallet. The Greeks had been unable to cheat him. Odysseus gave Josef fifty marks: magnificent great King Odysseus. Josef blinked as he looked at the note through his glasses. He folded it up and laid it carefully between the pages of his dirty notebook and put the book in the breast pocket of his porter's tunic. The tourism business had once again paid off. It was agreed that Josef would keep Odysseus company till the evening, till Odysseus found himself a girl, and disappeared with her into the night. *She-was-a-nice-girl.* Great Odysseus. He looked into the fog of sweat, uncleanness, bratwurst smoke, tobacco clouds, alcohol haze, piss reek, onion ooze, and stale human breath. He waved Susanne over. Susanne was a flower with Guerlain scent in a pit of filth. The pit was where she wanted to be. Tonight she really wanted to be in the pit of filth where she belonged. She was disappointed by classy people. Disgusting damned tight pigs. Alexander had invited her, famous Alexander. Who would ever believe her? No one. Had he come to her, choosing her from a whole host of girls, he, of whom every woman dreamed? Who would believe it? Had she slept with Alexander? A grunt, *Experience Passion of an Archduke for yourself*, the pigs had been drinking, they had drunk like pigs. And then? Not the revelation of a godhead. No Alexander taking her in his arms. No hero come to rescue her. Women. Susanne had been spanked. Spanked by women. And then? Kisses caresses touching hands on her thighs. Women had kissed caressed touched her, women's hands hot and dry lay on her thighs. And Alexander? Extinguished sluggardly swollen-lidded looks out of dead glazed eyes. Did he see anything through those eyes? did they take anything in? where did Alexander laugh and love? where did he woo women and raise them up to him? In the Thalia Palace, corner of Goethe- and Schillerstrasse, five performances a day. Where did Alexander snore? Where did he hang lifelessly over the edge of a sofa, and his flesh hang lifelessly? At home, when he had invited girls back. What was Susanne's recompense after such a night? They forgot to give her anything. Susanne thought: After that washout with Alexander why not a nigger, I'm not a dyke, I'm straight.— Cigarette in hand, she stalked over to Odysseus. The scent from Messalina's bottle kept her company in the heavy, smelly air of the pub like a separate separating atmosphere, differently heavy, differently fragrant. Susanne pushed Josef and the singing box aside on the bench worn smooth and shiny by many behinds. She pushed the box and the old man aside like two lifeless things, and the more worthless of the two was the old man. One might get money for the box. One could no longer get money for Josef. Susanne was Circe and the Sirens, at that moment she was them, she had just become them, and maybe she was also Nausicaa. No one in the pub noticed there were all these others in Susanne's skin, these antique beings; Susanne didn't know whom she had in her, Circe, the Sirens, and perhaps Nausicaa; the silly girl thought she was Susanne, and Odysseus had no idea of the ladies he was encountering in the person of this girl. Young skin framed Susanne's arm. Odysseus felt the pulse, felt the throb of blood in the arm on his neck. The arm was cool and freckled, a boy's arm, but the hand that, after the embrace, reached down to Odysseus's chest was warm, was feminine and sexual, *she-was-a-nice-girl*.

She loved jewels. The ruby is the fire the flame, the diamond the water the source the wave, the sapphire the air and the sky, and the green emerald is the earth, the green of the greening earth, the green of meadows and forests. Emilia loved the sparkling sheen, she loved the iridescent splendor of cold brilliants, the warmth of gold, the god's eyes and animal souls of colored stones, the fairy-tales of the orient, the diadem of the sacred elephant, *Aga Khan's Weight in Jewels, Tribute of the Faithful, Industrial Diamonds Essential for Defense Industry*. This was not Aladdin's cave. No magic lamp burned here. Herr Schellack, the jeweler, said: "No." His mighty chin was soothed with powder. He had a face like a sack of flour. If Emilia had had the magic lamp of the pretty Aladdin, the sack would have burst, and the evil spirit, the guardian of these treasures, would have gone up in a puff of smoke. What would Emilia have done? She would have filled the plaid with gold and jewels. But don't worry, you jewelers, there isn't really any magic; there are pistols and coshes, but Emilia won't avail herself of them, also, you have your alarm systems, though they won't save you from the devil when he comes for you. Herr Schellack looked graciously upon Kay, a customer who promised much, a young American, possibly a granddaughter of Rockefeller's. She was looking at corals and garnets. The old jewels were bedded on velvet. He told her of the families who had owned them, the women who had worn them, he reported on the dire circumstances that forced their sale, he told her a lot of little Maupassant stories, but Kay didn't listen to him, she gave no thought to jewel caskets hidden among undergarments in wardrobes, or greed, inheritances, and prodigality, nor to the throats of beautiful women, or their full arms, their delicate wrists, not on formerly manicured hands, the carefully shaped fingernails, nor to the hunger that gulps down the bread in the baker's window with its eyes, she thought merely: What a beautiful bracelet, look at that shining ring, how that ring glitters, how that brooch shines.— Moon-pale, of pearls, enamel, and diamanté roses, the necklace lay before Schellack the powder-faced, and once again he said, once again turning to her, the glow of benevolence that had shone for Kay, abruptly out, as though turned off by a switch, a bulb dimmed and switched off, and he said: "No." Herr Schellack didn't want to buy the jewels. That was grandmother's jewelry, he said. That was exactly what it was, grandmother's jewelry, Secret Commercial Councilor jewelry; grandmother cut, grandmother setting, the taste of the 1880s. What about the diamanté roses? "No, worthless! Worthless!" Herr Schellack raised his brief arms, his pudgy hands, hands like two plump quails; it was a gesture that made one afraid that Herr Schellack would try to take to the air, that in his regret and manifest disappointment, he would attempt to fly away. Was Emilia listening to him? She was not listening to him. She was not even looking at him. His gestures escaped her attention. She was thinking: How nice that girl is, how really nice, she's a really nice girl, she's that nice girl I might once have become, it makes her so happy how everything is so red, red as wine red as blood red as fresh young lips, that it glitters and sparkles, she doesn't yet know to think that she'll get nothing for her jewels if she ever has to sell them, but I know, I'm an old merchant man, I love those colored stones but I would never buy them for myself, they are an insecure investment, far too vulnerable to the vicissitudes of fashion, only diamonds offer a little security, the latest cut, the newest *nouveau riche* taste dominates, and gold of course, pure gold, that's a sensible acquisition, as long as I have gold and diamonds I don't need to work, I don't want to be woken by any alarm clock, I never want to have to say "sorry, Mr. Office Manager, sorry, Foreman, sir, I missed my streetcar," then I really would have missed the streetcar, if I ever had to say that, the streetcar of my life, never! never! never! and you my lovely, you with your corals and garnets, Herr Schellack will ask far too much of you for those little rings and crosses, those little chains and pendants, but try going to him, sweetheart, and offering him that same ring and chain, try it, offer them to him, and he'll tell you your pretty corals and garnets aren't worth anything, nothing at all, and then you'll have learned your lesson, then you'll know, my lambkin, my green girl from America.— Emilia picked her jewels back off the counter. Herr Schellack said with a sluggish smile, "I'm very sorry, Madam." And he thought with that she would go. He thought: Too bad, that's the way the clientele declines, her grandmother will have bought the necklace from my father, she will have paid two thousand marks for it at the time, two thousand in gold.— But Emilia didn't go. She was in search of freedom. She wanted to be free, if only for an instant. She wanted to perform a free act, an act that was not determined by any external force or necessity, and not driven by any motive either, except for the motive of being free; and that was no motive at all, that was a feeling, and the feeling was there, free of all motive. She went over to Kay and said: "Leave those corals and garnets. They're pretty and red. But these diamonds and pearls are prettier; even if Herr Schellack says they're old-fashioned. I'd like to give them to you. I'm giving them to you because you're nice." There. She was free. An extraordinary feeling of happiness swept through Emilia. She was free. Her happiness would not last. But for the moment she was free. At first, her voice had trembled. But now she was jubilant. She had dared, she was free. She put the necklace on Kay and fastened the lock at her neck. And Kay too was free, she was a free being, not as consciously as Emilia, and thereby perhaps even more unquestioningly free, she stepped over to the mirror, and looked at herself long with the necklace put on her, didn't notice Schellack who had his mouth open to protest but could find no words, and said: "Yes. It's beautiful! The pearls, the diamonds, the necklace. It's so lovely!" She turned to Emilia and looked at her with her green eyes. Kay was innocent, while Emilia was a little exultant. But both girls had the wonderful sensation of rebelling, they felt the great joy of rebelling against commonsense and custom. "You must have something of mine too," said Kay. "I don't have any jewels. But perhaps you'd take my hat." She took the hat off her head, it was a small pointed traveling hat, with a colored feather, and she set it on Emilia's head. Emilia laughed, looked at herself in the mirror, and cried out delightedly: "I look like Till Eulenspiegel. Just exactly like Till Eulenspiegel!" She pushed the hat farther back on her head, and thought, drunk,

I look drunk, but I swear I haven't touched a drop, though I'm sure Philipp wouldn't believe me.— She ran over to Kay. She embraced Kay, she kissed Kay, and when she felt Kay's lips, she thought, perfect, it's the taste of the prairie—

—just like a Western, thought Messalina. She hadn't found Susanne at home, but she had been told she would be in the pub on the Heiliggeistplatz. Just like a Western, but we've stopped making them, artless nonsense.— She strode confidently into the haze, into the coarse magical reek of the place, where in former times people drank their morning drams before going on to watch them burning witches in the marketplace. Messalina was shy. Her shyness was still visible in the photograph of her attending her first Communion in a white dress, holding a candle in her hand. But even when that picture was taken, in the atelier of one of the last photographers to work in a velvet jacket and a big floppy bow tie, and to say "bitte recht freundlich" (Messalina hadn't made a friendly face in her picture: shy, yes, but shy already fighting implacably and cruelly against her shyness), even then she hadn't wanted to be shy, not play that part, not be pressed back against the wall, and it was on the day of her first Communion, the start of her growth spurt, her period came, and she grew and grew in vice and cruelty and fleshliness, she turned into a monument of vice and cruelty, that, depending, terrified or ravished people: but who knew that inside, she had remained shy? Dr. Behude knew. But Dr. Behude was much shyer than Messalina, and as he did not compensate by projecting a wild brazenness, he didn't dare, out of shyness, to tell Messalina, and yet that, from Behude, would have been the magic word, a word of monumental destruction, and Messalina would have returned to her pure early state before

Communion. They all looked at Messalina, the little whores and the little pimps, all the little petty thieves, and even the little detective, who, identified by all, was sitting here in disguise: Messalina intimidated them all. Only Susanne was not intimidated. Susanne thought: That bitch, if she gets between me and my black hunk.— She wanted to think, then I'll scratch, bite, beat, and stamp on her, but she didn't think it, she wasn't intimidated, but she was frightened, she feared Messalina's blows, because she had felt them. Susanne stood up. She said: "Just a minute, Jimmy." Two clouds of identical perfume, Guerlain de Paris, made a common front and held firm against sweat, piss, onions, sausage water, beer breath, and smoke. Susanne was invited to come to Alexander's tonight, and she thought, it'd be pretty stupid of me if I did that, lousy business, but what if Alexander did sleep with me? sleeping's not a problem, he'll sleep, but not with me, he can't do it anymore, and if he could, who would believe me, and if no one believes me, I'd rather have some action from the black guy, even if I'm not really in the mood, but frustrated dykes? not for me, *First Legion Warns against Antiwar Sentiment, Justice Minister Declares Anyone Who Refuses to Stand Up for Wife and Child Is No Man*. But it seemed inappropriate to Susanne to turn down an invitation from a lady, a member of society, a grandam of a monumentality, furthermore, dimly sensed by Susanne. She said she'd come, of course, happy, delighted, only too glad, and she thought, don't hold your breath, you can kiss my ass, as long as you keep your distance, I want my peace and quiet, take yourself for something better than me, don't you? I wouldn't trade places with you, not for a long time. Messalina had taken a look around the pub. She had spotted Susanne's empty place beside Odysseus, and she said: "Bring the black guy, if you like." She thought: Maybe the queers would like that.— Susanne wanted to reply, wanted to come up with some excuse, wanted to claim that she was nothing to do with the black man, or again she could always accept on behalf of Jimmy or Joe or whoever he was, it hardly mattered, she wasn't going anyway, when there was sudden noise and violence. Odysseus had been robbed, his money was gone, his dollars and his German bills had disappeared, the music box was playing "Jimmy's Boogie-Woogie," King Odysseus was hurt, he was offended, he reached for the nearest man, he hauled out a pimp or a thief or the little detective, accused him, shook him, "look at the gorilla, King Kong, the fucker, get him out of here, the Negro fucker, out," the rabble leapt to their feet, the herd reestablished itself, comradeship prevailed, *Collective Good takes precedence over individual,* they threw themselves at him, picked up beer steins, chairs, blades, they threw themselves at the great Odysseus, the battle raged, surged, convulsed, Odysseus was in enemy country, his life was at stake here, the table went over, Josef clung on to the music box, he held it over his head, protectively he held "Jimmy's Boogie-Woogie" over his head, the notes rattled, the syncopations blared, it was like being back in the dugout, there was the drumfire again, it was Chemin-des-Dames, it was the Argonnes Forest again, but Josef did not participate in the battle, he was atoning, he did not kill, he floated on the waves of a distant river, he fled with Odysseus, who had fought his way out, with the music of the river from a distant continent, "Jimmy's Boogie-Woogie," washing around them. Messalina stood alone, innerly cowed, but a rock, a monument to look at, in the commotion. No one offered Messalina any violence. She stood in the center of the pub like a generally respected monument that belonged there. Susanne, however, followed her new man. It would have been wiser not to. It would have been wise to stay. It might even have been wise to leave with Messalina. But since Susanne was Circe and the Sirens and possibly also Nausicaa, she had to follow Odysseus. She had to follow him in the teeth of reason. She was tangled up with Odysseus. She hadn't really intended to be. She hadn't been able to resist, she had been stupid, and now she was being foolish. Odysseus and Josef ran across the Heiliggeistplatz. Susanne ran after them. She followed "Jimmy's Boogie-Woogie."

The bells of the Heiliggeist Church were ringing. Emmi and Hillegonda were kneeling on the flagstones. There was a smell in the church of old incense and fresh plaster. Hillegonda shivered. She shivered with her bare knees on the cold flagstones. Emmi crossed herself and prayed forgive-us-this-day-our-daily-trespasses. Hillegonda thought: What are my trespasses? if only someone would tell me, oh, Emmi, I'm scared.— And Emmi prayed: "Lord, who has destroyed this city, and will surely destroy it once more, for they are not obedient to Thy will, and they disregard Thy commandments, and their shouts are an abomination in Thine hearing." Hillegonda heard piercing shouts from outside, and it was as though stones were being thrown against the door of the church. "Emmi, can you hear? Emmi, what's that noise? Are they trying to hurt us, Emmi!"—"It's the devil, my child. The devil is about. You must pray! Oh Lord, deliver us!"

They lay behind rubble and stones from where the bomb had hit the church. The mob was attacking them, Susanne thought, what am I getting myself into? I'm crazy to get myself into this, but they drove me crazy yesterday at Alexander's, and now I'm getting myself into it.— "Jimmy's Boogie-Woogie."—"Money," said Odysseus. He needed capital. He was at war. He was back in the old war of white against black. There was that war going on too. He needed money to conduct war. "Money! Quick!" Odysseus grabbed hold of Josef. Josef thought: This is just like at Chemin-des-Dames, the black man isn't the devil, he's the traveler I killed, he's the Zouave or the Senegalese I killed on my trip to France.— Josef didn't put up any fight. He just froze. In front of his old eyes, the scene of his childhood turned into a European battlefield with non-European fighters, with foreign visitors, who wanted to kill or be killed. Josef clung on to the case as hard as he could. The case represented his duty. He had been paid for carrying the case. He had to keep hold of it. "Jimmy's Boogie-Woogie"—

They stood facing one another, friends? enemies? spouses? they stood facing one another in Carla's room, in Frau Welz's tarts' apartment, in a world of unchastity and despair, and, living in such a world, they were screaming at one another, and Frau Welz left her witch's kitchen, the stove with the bubbling vapors, slunk along the corridor, and hissed through the doors of the girls' rooms—open a crack—where they were getting ready, naked, in panties, in tacky robes, making their toilette, putting on their faces for the evening, not fully formed, only part-powdered faces, they heard the hiss of the madam, the lusty glee in the voice because bad things were happening: "Now he's beating her, the nigger. Now he's smacking her round. Now he's showing her. The only surprise is that it's taken him this long." Washington was not hitting her. Plates and cups were flying against his chest, at his feet were shards: the shards of happiness? He thought: I can go, if I take down my cap and go all this will be behind me, maybe I'll forget it, it'll be as though it never happened.— Carla screamed, her face puffy with tears: "You set the doctor against me. You dirty dog! You went to see Frahm. Do you think I want to keep your bastard? Do you think I do? They'd point at me with their fingers. I shit on your America. Your dirty black America. I'm staying here. I'm staying here without your bastard, even if it kills me, I'm staying!" What held him back? why didn't he take down his cap? why didn't he go? Maybe it was stubbornness. Maybe it was delusion. Maybe it was conviction, maybe faith in people. Washington heard what Carla was yelling at him, but he didn't believe her. He didn't want to break the bond that was threatening to tear, the bond between black and white, he wanted to tighten it by having a child together, he wanted to set an example, he believed in the possibility of an example, and maybe his faith demanded martyrs as well. For a moment it crossed his mind to hit Carla. It is always despair that wants to strike, but his faith overcame his despair. Washington took Carla in his arms. He held her tightly in his strong arms. Carla wriggled in his arms like a fish in the grip of the fisherman. Washington said: "We love each other, why shouldn't we get through this? Why shouldn't we make it? We just have to remember to love each other. When all the others are calling us names, we have to love each other. Even when we're very old, we have to love each other."

Odysseus lashed out with a rock, or else a rock flew out of the crowd, and struck Josef on the forehead. Odysseus tore the money, the banknote, out of the porter's notebook, the tattered logbook where Josef wrote down his errands and his earnings. Odysseus ran. He ran around the church. The mob followed him. They saw Josef lying on the ground and saw the blood on his forehead. "The nigger murdered old Josef!" Then the square was suddenly thronged with people who came up out of basements, out of hiding places and holes in the walls, everyone in the quarter had known Josef, old Josef, or little Josef, he had played here, he had worked here, he had gone to war, he had returned to work, and now he had been murdered: he had been murdered for his wage. They stood around him: a gray wall of old and poor people. From the music box next to Josef came the strains of a Negro spiritual. Marian Anderson was singing, a beautiful, soft, and full voice, a vox humana, a vox angelica, the voice of a dark angel; it was as though the voice wanted to soothe the dead man. I've got to get away from here, thought Susanne, I've got to get away from here quickly before the police come, before the MPs come, before the radio car comes.— She raised her right hand to her breast, where she felt the money she had taken from Odysseus's pocket. Why did I do that, she thought, I've never done anything like that before, I've been corrupted, those pigs at Alexander's have corrupted me, I wanted to get my own back, I wanted to get my own back on those pigs, but you only ever avenge yourself on the wrong people.— Susanne walked through the gray wall of the old and the poor, which parted to let her through. The old and the poor let Susanne pass. They gave her some of the blame for the events, there was always a woman involved in a tragedy, but they were no psychologists and no detectives, they didn't think, *cherchez la femme*, they thought, she's poor like us, she'll grow old like us, she's one of us.— Not until the wall had closed behind Susanne did a boy yell out: "Yankee whore!" A couple of women crossed themselves. A priest came along and bent down over Josef. The priest pressed his ear against Josef's chest. The priest was gray-haired, and he had a tired face. He said: "He's still breathing." From the hospital came four lay brethren with a stretcher. The lay brethren looked poor, like failed conspirators in a classical drama. They laid Josef on their stretcher. They carried Josef across into the Hei- liggeist Hospital. The priest followed the stretcher. Behind the priest came Emmi, dragging Hillegonda along behind her. People thought they were with Josef, and then the sirens were heard, the sirens from the radio car and the military police. From all sides, the sirens moved in on the square.

It was that moment, it was the evening hour when bicyclists rushed through the streets, careless of their lives. It was the hour of falling dusk, the hour of shift-change, of shutting up shop, the hour when the working population made their way home, and the nightworkers set off. Police sirens shrilled. The ambulances cleared a path through the traffic. Their flashing blue lights gave their speed a spectral quality: the St. Elmo's fires of the city, portending danger. Philipp loved this hour. In Paris, it was the *heure bleue*, the hour for dreaming, a space of relative freedom, a moment of liberty from day and night. The people were released from their factories and shops, and they weren't yet caught up in the demands of their ordinary lives and the expectations of family. The world hung in the balance. For a moment, everything seemed possible. But maybe that was just an illusion of Philipp's, the outsider, who had no job to leave and no family to return to. The illusion would be followed shortly by disappointment. Philipp was used enough to disappointments; he wasn't afraid of them. The evening light clarified. The heavens burned in southerly colors. It was an Etna sky, a sky as over the ancient theater in Taormina, a blaze as over the temples of Agrigentum. Antiquity had arisen and sent a smiling greeting across the city. The contours of the buildings were etched against the heavens and the sandstone façade of the Jesuit church as Philipp passed, it was of a dancing beauty, it was a piece of Italy, it was humanist, wise, and of carnivalesque exuberance. But where had humanism, wisdom, not to mention exuberance led? The *Evening Echo* called out the awfulness of the day *Pensioner Preferred Death, Soviets Get a Bloody Nose, Another Diplo-*

mat Defects, German Military Reorganization a Step Closer, Explosion Shows Glimpse of Hell. How fantastically earnest and stupid it all was! A diplomat had changed sides, he had gone over to the enemies of his government, and that was a *Cynical Betrayal.* The official world was still at pains to think in hollow phrases, in clichés long since devoid of any content. They saw fixed, immovable lines, countries, and continents, frontiers, allegiances all staked out, they seemed to view a man as a member of a football team who would play for the club of his birth all his life. But they were mistaken: the lines were not here and not there, and they didn't follow national boundaries. The front was everywhere, whether you could see it or not, and life was continually changing its orientation to the billions of points on the line. The line ran through the middle of countries, it divided families, yes, it ran right through individuals: two souls, yes, two souls dwelt in every breast, and sometimes the heart beat for the one, and sometimes the other. Philipp was no more inconstant than anyone else; on the contrary, he was an eccentric. But even he could change his views on the state of the world thousands of times a day, with every step he took. Can I see it all straight, he asked himself, do I really know what makes the politicians tick? am I privy to the secrets of the diplomats? I'm pleased whenever someone switches from one side to the other, and shuffles the pack a bit, then the powers will get something of the feeling we have, the feeling of helplessness, can I still keep up with science? do I know the latest formula for the cosmos, am I capable of reading it?— All those who were walking, cycling, or driving along the road, making plans, distracted by their anxieties or enjoying the evening, they were all continually being gulled and tricked, and the augurs who were swindling and tricking them were no less blind than the ordinary blind. Philipp had to laugh at the naiveté of political propaganda. He laughed about it, even though he knew it could end his life. What about the others on the street? Were they laughing too? Was it past a joke? Were they, unlike Philipp, too busy to laugh? They didn't notice what crumbs they were tossed, and what fools were being made of them. For some reason, I'm immune to their blandishments, thought Philipp, and yet when I hear a phrase I like, and then sometimes a call from the other side that I like even better, I keep playing ridiculous roles, I'm the old easygoing centrist, I'm in favor of listening to all views, if views have to be listened to at all, but then the earnest people on both sides get het up and yell at me, that my tolerance is a spur to intolerance, they are enemy brothers, each intolerant to the marrow, each dead set against the other, and only united in spewing bile at my feeble attempts to remain unprejudiced, and each of them hates me because I refuse to join them and bark against the others, I don't want to play in any team, not even in this hemispheric football game, I want to be me.— There was still hope in the world: *Cautious feelers put out, No war before autumn—*

The schoolmistresses from Massachusetts were walking through the city in a crocodile, like schoolgirls. The class was on their way to the Amerika Haus. They were quietly enjoying the evening. The teachers wanted to hear Edwin's lecture, and see a little of the life of the city first. They saw no more of the life of the city than the city saw of the lives of the schoolmistresses. Nothing. Miss Wescott had taken command. She strode along at the head of the class. She led her colleagues, following the map in the guidebook. She led them confidently, and without getting lost. Miss Wescott was in a bad mood. Kay had disappeared. She had left the hotel in the afternoon, to go window-shopping. Then at the agreed time, she wasn't back. Miss Wescott reproached herself. She should have prevented Kay from going off into the strange city all alone.

Did they know what the locals were like? Were they not enemies? Could they be trusted? Miss Wescott had left a message in the hotel that Kay was to get into a taxi and head straight for the Amerika Haus. Miss Wescott didn't understand Miss Burnett. Miss Burnett said Kay might have met someone. Could one place confidence in Kay? She was young and inexperienced. One could not. Miss Burnett said: "She will have met someone who's a bit more fun for her than we are." — "And you're so calm about that?" — "I'm not possessive." Miss Wescott bit her lips. That Burnett woman was immoral. And Kay was plain naughty. That was all. Kay had got lost, or lost track of time. The teachers were crossing the great square, a place designed by Hitler to be the memorial grove of National Socialism. Miss Wescott drew attention to the intended function of the square. There were birds sitting on the grass. Miss Burnett thought: That stuff that Miss Wescott keeps spouting, we don't understand any more than the birds do about it, the birds are here by chance, we are here by chance, and maybe the Nazis were here by chance, Hitler was a chance, his politics were a dreadful and stupid chance, maybe the world is a dreadful and stupid chance of God's, no one knows why we are here, the birds will fly off and we will walk on, I hope Kay hasn't gotten into trouble, it would be silly if she got herself into trouble, I can't say this to Miss Wescott, she'd go nuts, but Kay is a temptation to seducers, it's not her fault, she just draws them to her, the way the birds do the hunters and their dogs.— "What's the matter with you?" Miss Wescott asked Miss Burnett. Miss Wescott was in a huff; Miss Burnett hadn't been paying attention. Miss Wescott thought Miss Burnett had the face of an emaciated beagle. "I've been looking at the birds," said Miss Burnett. "Since when have you been interested in birds?" asked Miss Wescott. "I'm interested in us and our species," said Miss Burnett. "Those are sparrows," said Miss Wescott, "common or garden sparrows. You'd be better advised to take a little interest in world history." — "It's all the same thing," said Miss Burnett, "it's all a matter of sparrows. You're just a sparrow too, Miss Wescott, and our little fledgling Kay has just tumbled out of the nest." — "I don't know what you're talking about," said Miss Wescott primly, "I am not a bird."

Philipp walked into the hall of the Altes Schloss, where the state had set up a wine bar, to assist the turnover of domestic wine production. The hall was very full at this time. Officials from innumerable ministries and departments were tanking a little happiness before going home, home to their wives, their sullen children, and their lovelessly reheated suppers. It was a man's world. There were hardly any women there. Only a couple of woman editors. But they weren't really women. They were on the *Evening Echo*, and they were dousing the fire of their headlines in wine. Philipp thought he ought to go home, home to Emilia. But he wanted to go and hear Edwin as well, even though the encounter with him had been so embarrassing. If I don't go to Emilia now, I won't be able to go back tonight, thought Philipp. He knew that Emilia would get drunk if she didn't find him home in the evening. He thought: If I was in our apartment, alone with all those animals, I'd get drunk too, I'd get drunk if getting drunk was something I still did at all, but I gave up drinking like that a long time ago. — The wine they had in the Altes Schloss was very good. But Philipp didn't want any more wine. He was very good at enjoying himself, but he had lost his taste for most of the joys you could have. He was pretty determined that he would go back to Emilia. Emilia was Stevenson's Jekyll and Hyde. Philipp was in love with Dr. Jekyll, who was the charming and good-hearted Emilia, while he hated and feared the loathsome Mr. Hyde, the Emilia of the late evening and the night, a wild souse and a poisonous Xantippe. If Philipp went home now, he would still find dear Dr. Jekyll there, but if he went to Edwin's lecture, the frightful Mr. Hyde would be waiting for him. Philipp wondered if he couldn't arrange his life with Emilia in some way differently, completely differently. It's my fault if she's unhappy, why can't I make her happy?— He thought of moving out of the house on the Fuchsstrasse, the dilapidated villa he found so oppressive. He thought: We could move into one of her unsaleable houses in the country, the houses are full of tenants, we can't get the tenants out, so we just have to build ourselves a little hut in the garden, well, that's all right, other people have done that too.— He knew that he wouldn't build anything, no hut, no little house in the garden. He knew he couldn't get Emilia to leave the house on the Fuchsstrasse. She needed the atmosphere of family strife, the ever-present signs of financial catastrophe before her eyes. Nor could Philipp see himself ever moving out into the countryside. He needed the city, even if he had no money. He sometimes read gardening books and imagined he could find peace growing some plants or other. But really, he knew that was an illusion. He thought: If we were in the country, if we were in our little hut, or building it, we would tear each other to pieces, whereas in the city we still love each other, we just pretend not to.— He paid for his wine. Unfortunately, he had failed to notice the editor of the *Neues Blatt* at the table of the *Evening Echo* ladies. The editor was unhappy with Philipp about the interview he hadn't done. He expected that at the very least Philipp would go to Edwin's talk and review it for the *Neues Blatt*. "Why don't you go yourself," countered Philipp. "Oh no," said the editor, "we've got you for that kind of thing. Come on, you owe me."— "Will you pay for the taxi?" asked Philipp. "Put it on your expenses," said the editor. "No, I mean now, this minute," said Philipp. The editor fished a ten-mark note out of his pocket and gave it to Philipp. "We'll do the sums later," he said. That's how far gone I am, thought Philipp, selling myself and Edwin.

Frightened by the fight on the Heiliggeist Square, and confused and accompanied by the police sirens, Messalina rushed into the quiet bar in the hotel. Messalina felt so tense that she thought she would surely burst in the silence. Isn't anyone here? she wondered. Being alone was ghastly. Messalina had fled from the whores' bar, back in the direction of what she took to be proper society, the sort of proper society at the edge of which she liked to play her little games. Messalina never altogether cut adrift from the society of law-abiding people. She never gave anything up. She only wanted double helpings of everything. The company of well-mannered people gave her stay and purchase; from there, she could easily go and fraternize with the ill-mannered, conclude some temporary carnal compact with the class she thought was the proletariat. She had no idea! She should only have asked Philipp. Philipp would have complained eloquently about the puritanism of the proletariat. Philipp was not an especially excessive man. Messalina took him to be a monk. But that was something else again. Philipp often warned: "We are heading for a century of puritanism!" In a somewhat ill-defined way, he would appeal to Flaubert, who mourned the passing of the lady of pleasure. The lady of pleasure was no more. To Philipp the puritanism of the working classes was a disaster. Philipp would have been very much for a loosening of the bonds of private property, but he was very much against any restriction of the joys of life. Incidentally, he drew a distinction between ladies of pleasure and professional mourners, and in Philipp's taxonomy the entire local prostitution belonged to the latter. What wild and uncivilized people, thought Messalina, fighting like that.— Messalina's house witnessed only aesthetically conceived encounters, conducted with proper ceremony. Messalina looked around. The bar seemed to be quite empty. But no, in a very far corner sat two girls: it was Emilia and the little American with the green eyes. Messalina got up on tiptoe. The great monument was swaying dangerously. She wanted to sneak up on the little girls. They were drinking and laughing, they were hugging and kissing each other. What was going on here? What was that funny hat Emilia was wearing? She had never used to wear a hat. Like most other insecure people, Messalina was liable to think that other people were conspiring against her, and that they had secrets from which Messalina was excluded. The little American girl with the green eyes was unsettling to her. She had been talking with Philipp, and now here she was exchanging hugs and kisses, little girls'-boarding-school-crush-kisses, with Emilia. Who was the little charmer? Where had Philipp and Emilia dug her up? Maybe they will come to my party after all, then we'll see what she's made of, thought Messalina. But then she caught sight of Edwin, and she got back on her feet. Maybe she could secure Edwin. Edwin was the greater catch, though probably not quite as toothsome. Edwin came into the bar in rapid strides and hurried up to the counter. He whispered something to the barman. The barman poured Edwin a large cognac in a red wine glass. Edwin emptied the glass. He had stagefright, lecturefright. He drank the cognac to combat his agitation. Outside the hotel, the consular automobile was already waiting. Edwin was trapped by his acceptance. An awful evening! Why ever had he consented to it? Vanity! Vanity! The vanity of the wise. Why hadn't he stayed in his hermitage cell, his cozy apartment stuffed with books and antiques? Envy of the fame of actors, applause-envy of ovations and stars had driven him out. Edwin despised actors, stars, and the crowds off whom and with whom they lived. But it was seductive, the applause, the crowds, the young people, the camp followers, they were a temptation and a seduction if one had sat at one's desk as long as Edwin had and striven in solitude for understanding and beauty but also for recognition. There was that ghastly society columnist again, that woman on the stairs, that sex giantess, she was staring at him, he had to flee. And Kay called out to Emilia: "There's Edwin! Didn't you see him? Come with me! I have to go to his talk. Where's that note from Miss Wescott? Please come with me! I'd forgotten all about it!" Suddenly Emilia sent Kay a hate-filled look: "Oh, forget Edwin! I hate writers, they're all dummies! I'm not going anywhere!"—"But he's a poet," Kay exclaimed, "how can you say such a thing!"—"Philipp's a poet too," said Emilia. "Who's Philipp?" asked Kay. "He's my husband," said Emilia. She's mad, thought Kay, what's her game? she's mad, she's not married at all, she can't expect me to stay sitting here with her, I'm pretty drunk, God knows there are enough crazy women in my travel group, but she's delightful all the same, that crazy little German woman.— She called out: "Well, I'll see you!" She kissed her hand at Emilia, a last fleeting gesture, and spun off after Edwin. She had been drinking whiskey; now she would speak to Edwin; she would ask him for his autograph; she no longer had Edwin's book in her hand, what had she done with it? where had she left it? but if Edwin signed a chit at the bar for her that would do. But Edwin was hastening away. Kay ran after him. Emilia thought: Serves me right, now here's Messalina.— Messalina watched Edwin and Kay running out in annoyance. Now what was going on? Why were they running off like that? Had they formed some plot against Messalina? Emilia would have to explain it to her. But Emilia had vanished, she had disappeared through a tapestried door. There were just a couple of empty glasses on the table, and that funny hat that Emilia had been wearing. It lay there like a disappointment and a reproach. This is witchery, thought Messalina, it's witchery, and I'm all alone in the world.— She reeled brokenly to the bar. "A triple," she called out. "What would you like?" asked the barman. "Oh, anything. I'm tired." She really was tired. She hadn't been this tired in a long time. She felt terribly tired suddenly. But she mustn't feel tired. She had to go on to the talk, she had so much more planning to do for the party. She reached for the tall glass, brimming with clear schnapps. She yawned.

The day was tired. The evening light in the sky, the setting sun shone straight into the sky-blue limousine, and for a moment the light dazzled Carla and Washington. The light was dazzling, but it was also cleansing and purifying. Carla and Washington's faces were both lit up. Washington waited to pull down the visor. They drove slowly along the riverbank. Only yesterday, Carla had dreamed that they would go for a trip like this along Riverside Drive in New York, or on the Golden Gate in San Francisco. Now her heart was calm. She wasn't driving to any magazine dream apartment with recliners, televisions, and fully automatic kitchens. It had been a dream. A dream that had tormented Carla, because in her heart of hearts she had always been afraid she wouldn't get as far as Dreamland. Now the weight of her yearning had been taken from her. In her room, she had felt stunned. When Washington walked her to the car, she hadn't been more than a sack over his arm, a heavy sack full of something dead. Now she was released. She wasn't released from the child, but from the dream of a lazy bliss of existence, from the idea that you could turn a dial and deceive life. She believed again. She believed in Washington. They drove along the river, and Carla believed in the Seine. The Seine wasn't as wide as the Mississippi, or as distant as the

Colorado. But on the banks of the Seine they would both feel at home. They would both become French, if necessary, she, a German, would become a Frenchwoman, and Washington, a black American, would become a Frenchman. The French were pleased when people wanted to come and live with them. Carla and Washington would start the bar called Washington's Tavern, where no one is unwelcome. Another car overtook them. Christopher and Ezra were sitting in the car. Christopher was feeling good. He had bought a cup in an antique shop, a cup made in the Berlin porcelain factory, showing a picture of a great Prussian king. He would take the cup with him to the Seine. He would give it to Henriette in the hotel on the banks of the Seine. Henriette would be pleased with the cup with the picture of the Prussian king on it. Henriette was Prussian, even if she was now also an American. All these nationalities are silly, thought Christopher, we should put a stop to it, of course everyone feels some local pride in the place where they were born, I'm proud of Needles, Colorado, but that's not going to make me want to kill everyone that wasn't born there.— If there's no other way, I'm just going to have to kill him, thought Ezra, I'll pick up a rock and smash it against his head, and then I'll run to the car, the dog will have to be in the car already, and that kraut won't be getting any dollars, if Christopher puts his foot on the gas quickly enough.— Ezra's little forehead had been creased with worry for hours. Christopher had given Ezra the ten dollars. "So now you won't get lost," he had joked, "or if you do, the ten dollars will help you find me again."—"Yeah, yeah," Ezra had said. He seemed not to be interested in the thing with the money anymore. He had pocketed the ten dollars indifferently. "Will we get to the Bräuhaus on time?" asked Ezra. "What do you want with the Bräuhaus?" wondered Christopher. "You keep asking whether we're going to get there on time."—"Oh, just so," said Ezra. He mustn't give anything away. Christopher wouldn't like the idea.

"But when we get to the bridge, we're turning around," insisted Ezra. "Of course we'll turn around then, why shouldn't we turn around?" Christopher wanted to get a look at the bridge that the guidebook said afforded a romantic view over the valley. Christopher thought Germany was a beautiful country.

Behude had a choice of three bars. Seen from outside, they all looked the same. They were all the same temporary structures, they had the same bottles in the windows, the same prices on the board. One bar belonged to an Italian, the other to an old Nazi, and the third to an old prostitute. Behude chose the old Nazi bar. Emilia sometimes drank a glass or two in the old Nazi bar. It was masochism in her. Behude propped his bicycle against the crumbling, pressed-junk wall of the bar. The old Nazi had sagging cheeks, and dark glasses over his eyes. Emilia wasn't there. I should have gone to the old tart's after all, thought Behude, but now he was at the old Nazi's. Behude ordered a vodka. He thought: If the old Nazi doesn't keep vodka in his bar, I can go. The old Nazi had vodka. Really I'm more the type for mineral water, thought Behude, I should have been a sportsman, not a psychiatrist, it's terrible for your health.— He drank the vodka down and shuddered. Behude didn't like alcohol. But sometimes he drank in spite of that. He drank at the end of his consultation hours. He thought: And the empty sagging bag.— That was a student song. Behude had never sung it. He had never sung any student songs. But the bag was empty and sagging. He himself was empty and sagging, he, Dr. Behude, at the end of every consultation was empty and sagging. And he was the bag as well. Two of his patients had borrowed money off him today. Behude could hardly turn them away. After all, he was treating people for difficulties in adjusting to daily life. That Nazi's empty and sagging as well, he thought. He ordered another vodka. "It's all about to go off again," said the Nazi. "What is?" asked Behude. "Well, you know, dedum-dedah," said the Nazi, and he mimed hitting a big snare drum. They've got the wind in their sails, thought Behude, whatever happens next, they're on the way back.— He drank the second vodka and shuddered again. He paid. He thought, I wish I'd gone to the old tart's, but he didn't have enough money left to go on to the old tart.

Emilia stood in the old tart's bar. She had wanted to go home. She hadn't wanted to come home drunk, because then Philipp would be cross, or sometimes he would cry. Recently, Philipp had been behaving a little hysterically. It was crazy of him to worry about Emilia. "I can take my drink," said Emilia. She knew about the separation of Dr. Jekyll and Mr. Hyde that Philipp applied to her. She would have liked to come home to him as Dr. Jekyll, the dear, good doctor. Then she would have said to Philipp that there was a bit of money left over from the city pawnshop money, from the money for the king's cup, from the money for the prayer rug. They would be able to pay the electricity bill. She would have told Philipp about the necklace she had given away. Philipp would have understood. He would have understood too why once she'd hung the necklace around the neck of the green-eyed American girl, she'd felt so free afterward. But all in all, it had been annoying. Philipp would tell her right away, "You should have walked away. You should have put the necklace on her, and then you should have walked away." Philipp was a psychologist. That was a wonderful thing, and it was also annoying. It was impossible to keep secrets from Philipp. It was better to tell him everything. Why didn't I walk away? I suppose because her lips tasted so wonderful, of wild prairie, do I have a thing for girls? no, I don't think I do, but maybe

I would have flirted with her a little bit, like a pretty little sister, petting and kissing and won't-you-come-and-say-goodnight, that would have been good, silly old Edwin, any human relationship is silly, if I'd walked off right away, I would have felt good today, I should never have spoken to that American, I hate her now!— But it wasn't sorrow that had driven Emilia to the old tart. Emilia had withstood her desire to go and have a drink at the old tart's. But she had been led astray. Just behind the hotel she had run into the ownerless dog, trailing its string collar. "You poor thing," she had exclaimed, "you might get run over." She had beckoned the dog to her. The dog sniffed the scent of Emilia's other animals, and straightaway he showed that he was looking for a job; Emilia to him was a good person, and his nose didn't mislead him about that. Emilia saw that the dog was hungry. She had brought him into the old tart's bar and bought him a sausage. Since she happened to be waiting there, she drank a kirsch. She drank the sharp bitter-kernel distillation of the cherry. She drank it out of bitterness at her life, and the bitterness of the day, the bitterness of the thing with the necklace, the bitterness with Philipp, and the bitterness of living in the Fuchsstrasse. The old tart was friendly, but she was bitter also. Emilia drank with the old tart. Emilia invited the old tart to have a drink with her. The old tart was like a frozen jet of water. She was wearing a big hat, which was like the frozen extremity of the jet of water, and then she was wearing gloves ornamented with jet. The jet on her gloves clinked like ice, each time she moved her hands; it clinked like little pieces of ice in a glass that you shake. Emilia admired the old tart. When I'm as old as she is, I won't look anywhere near as good, I won't look half as good, nor will I run my own bar, I will have left my money in her bar, she has never drunk at her own expense, she has only ever drunk at the expense of men, I will never stop drinking at my own expense.— The dog wagged its tail. He was a very clever dog. He didn't look it, but he was clever. He sensed that he had the capacity to move the human being who had taken him up. He would be able to rule this woman. The prospects of ruling over her were much better than they were with the children, who were moody, unpredictable gods. This new goddess was a kind goddess. Like the psychiatrist Behude, the dog was of the opinion that Emilia was a good person. Emilia will not disappoint the dog. "You're staying with me," she said. "Yes, little fellow, I know, we're going to be inseparable."

Richard was at the Italian's, propped against the bar. Where had he got to? He had just sort of walked in. The door had stood open. He had thought this place might be a drugstore. He had thought: Maybe I'll meet a girl, it would be neat if I met a German girl on my first night in Germany.— Instead, he found himself on a battlefield. Bottles, glasses, and corkscrews became fortresses and tank divisions, cigarette packets and matchboxes became squadrons of airplanes. The Italian owner of the bar was a demented strategist. He showed the young American airman how Europe should be defended. Once successfully defended, he went over on the attack, and wiped out the East. "Take a couple of bombs!" he cried. "Take a couple of bombs, and you've won!" Richard drank a vermouth. He was surprised that the vermouth tasted bitter. It tasted like bitter sugar water. Maybe the fellow's right, thought Richard, maybe it really is as simple as that, a couple of bombs, maybe he's right, wonder why Truman didn't think of it? a couple of bombs, what's the Pentagon worrying about?— But then Richard remembered something; he remembered something from a history lesson some time, or from a newspaper he'd read, or from some speech that he'd heard. He said: "But that's what Hitler did, that's what the Japanese did as well: they just attacked, attacked overnight—"—"Hitler was right," said the Italian, "Hitler was a great man!"—"No," said Richard, "he was a monster." Richard turned pale, because he found it embarrassing to argue with someone, and because he was angry. He hadn't come here to argue. He couldn't argue; he didn't understand what was going on here. Perhaps the people here saw everything entirely differently. But nor had he come here to deny his American principles; the principles he was so proud of. "I've not come here to act like Hitler," he said. "You're going to have to," said the Italian. In a fury, he threw the fortresses, tank divisions, and air squadrons all of a heap. Richard ended the argument. "I've got to go to the Bräuhaus," he said. He thought: You lose all perspective here.

The warrior who hadn't wanted to be a warrior, the killer who hadn't wanted to kill, the murdered man who had dreamed of a gentler death, lay on the hard bed in the Heiliggeist Hospital, he lay in a whitewashed room, in a monk's cell, he lay under a cross with the crucified Christ, a candle burning by his head, a priest kneeling beside him, a woman kneeling behind the priest with a far sterner expression than the man of God, the representative of an implacable religion, which viewed even dying as a sin, so hard was her heart, a little girl was standing in front of him, staring at him, and more and more policemen were pressing into the little room like extras. On the street, police sirens were wailing. The quarter was being searched. The German police and the American military police were looking for great Odysseus. The Angel of Death had long since placed his hand on Josef's forehead. What did he care about the sirens? What did he mind about the police of two countries and two continents? When Josef was working, he had always kept out of the way of the police. Nothing good ever came from the police. Only warnings or orders to move along. Best was when no one was asking for Josef. If anyone called for him, they always wanted something; and then it was always something unpleasant that they wanted. Now he was throwing the whole city into confusion with his dying. It wasn't what the old porter meant to do at all. Briefly he regained consciousness. He said: "It was the traveler." He didn't say it to get the man in trouble. He was glad it had been the traveler. His debt was canceled. The priest absolved him of his sins. Emmi crossed herself and murmured her Lord's Prayer. She was an intent little prayer mill. Hillegonda was thinking: There was an old man; he looked dear; he was dead; death looked dear; death was not frightening; it was sweet and quiet; but Emmi reckoned the old man had died in a state of sin, and that his sins needed to be forgiven; Emmi didn't seem at all certain that his sins would be forgiven him; God was not yet resolved to forgive them; at best, he would be merciful and pardon them; God was very strict; there were no entitlements with God; you couldn't claim anything before God, everything was sin; but if everything was sin, then it didn't matter what you did; if Hillegonda was naughty, that was a sin, but if she was good, it was still a sin; and why had the man grown so old if he was a sinner; why had God not punished him any sooner, if he was a sinner; and why did the man look so sweet? so it was possible to hide the fact that you were a sinner; you couldn't tell just from looking at someone if they were or not; how could you trust anyone?— And once again, Hillegonda felt the stirrings of a suspicion of Emmi: could you trust Emmi, devout, praying Emmi, mightn't her devoutness be a mask, a disguise for the devil? If Hillegonda had been able to talk about it with her father, but her father was so stupid, he said there was no such thing as a devil, maybe he thought there was no God either: oh, but he didn't know Emmi, there was a devil. You were always in his power. All those policemen: were they God's policemen, or the devil's? They were getting the dead old man, to punish him; God wanted to punish him, and the devil wanted to punish him. In the end, it came to the same thing. There was no way out for the dead old man. He couldn't hide anywhere. He couldn't resist. He couldn't run away anymore. Hillegonda felt sorry for the old man. It wasn't his fault. Hillegonda went up to the dead Josef and kissed his hand. She kissed the hand that had carried so many suitcases, a wrinkled hand, with creases full of earth and dirt, full of war and life. The priest asked: "Are you his granddaughter?" Hillegonda burst out crying. She hid her head in the priest's robe and sobbed bitterly. Emmi broke off her prayer, and said irritably: "She's an actor's child, Your Reverend. Lies, pretense, and playacting are all in her blood. Punish the child, save her soul!" But before the priest, who suddenly stopped stroking Hillegonda, could make a reply to the nanny, a further voice spoke up from under Josef's hospital bed and funeral bier. Odysseus's music box, which had been placed under the bed, and had been quiet for a while, suddenly spoke up again. This time it spoke in English accents, soft, quiet, melodious, a beautiful, cultivated, ever so slightly pretentious Oxonian voice, the voice of a philologist, and it was pointing out Edwin's importance and drawing attention to his lecture in the Amerika Haus. The voice saw it as a boon for Germany that Mr. Edwin, a crusader of the intellect, had come to this city, to attest to the spirit, the tradition, the deathlessness of the intellect, for the old Europe, which, from the days of the French Revolution, said the voice, citing Jacob Burckhardt, had been shaken in its social and intellectual framework, and had been in a condition of perpetual agitation and quivering. Had Edwin come to lay the shaking to rest, to order the disorder, and to set up—of course, in a spirit of continuity—new tablets with new laws? The priest, thinking back over Josef's life, moved by the unrest that the death of the old porter had provoked in the diocese, and finding himself strangely affected by the grim devotion of the nanny, with her stone face that contained no warmth, no joy, and moved too by the sobbing of the little girl, whose tears ran into the folds of his priestly robes, the man of God was listening with half an ear to the English voice, the voice from the music box under the deathbed, and he had the sense that the voice was speaking of a false prophet.

Schnakenbach, the sleeper, the sacked trade schoolteacher, the insufficiently learned Einstein, had spent the afternoon in the reading room of the American Library. He had dragged himself to the Amerika Haus in a condition of half-sleep, and, as if watched by a guardian angel, had once more escaped death at the hands of streetcars, cars, and bicycles. In the library reading room, he had piled around him all the chemical and pharmacological publications he could find. He wanted to learn about the latest state of research in America; he wanted to see how close they were in the great America to the production of sleep-hindering preparations. There seemed to be many comatose people in America. The Americans were giving a great deal of attention to the problem of remaining awake. Schnakenbach could learn from them. He made notes. In his tiny handwriting he wrote and drew formulas and shapes; he calculated; he watched the level of the molecules; he bore in mind that there were both left- and right-handed combinations, and that he must find out whether his life, that portion of the general life, that combination of chemical energies that said Me, that for a while was Schnakenbach before it was returned to the great crucible, was left- or right-handed. And as he was pondering this, sleep, his enemy, his affliction, caught up with him. Schnakenbach was a well-known figure in the reading room. They did not disturb his sleep there; they did not tear him from his enemy's embrace. The librarian had an unusual clientele. The reading room exercised a great fascination on the homeless, heat-cheats, eccentrics, and nature freaks. The nature freaks came barefoot, draped in homespun linens, with long hair and tangled beards. They demanded works on witchcraft and the evil eye, cookbooks for raw diet, publications on life after death and on the exercises of Indian fakirs, or else they immersed themselves in the latest works in astrophysics. They were cosmological spirits, nibbling on nuts and roots. The librarian said: "I am always waiting for someone to wash their feet in the library, but no one ever does." The American Library was a wonderful institution. Its use was completely free. The library was open to everyone, it was almost a version of Washington's Tavern, the bar that the black American citizen Washington Price wanted to open in Paris, where no one would be unwelcome. Schnakenbach slept. While he slept, the great lecture hall in the building filled up. Many came to hear Edwin speak. Students came, young workers came, a few artists came, who, for existential reasons, wore beards, and would not take the berets off their heads, the philosophy class from the seminary school came, peasant faces who were turning to the spirit, to strict observance or simplicity, two streetcar conductors, one burgomaster, and one bailiff, who had writers among his customers, and so had been deflected from the straight and narrow, and otherwise many well-dressed and well-nourished people came. Edwin's lecture was a social event. The well-dressed people had jobs in film or broadcasting, or they worked in advertising, if, that is, they weren't fortunate enough to be members of parliament, senior civil servants, or even ministers or officers in the occupation or consular officials. They all of them were interested in the European mind. The commercial sector of the city seemed to have less interest in the European mind; they had dispatched no representatives. The ones who had turned out in force, though, were the designers, scented, feminine gentlemen who had brought their models with them, tall and lovely girls who had nothing to fear from them. Behude had sat down among the priests. It was a gesture of solidarity. He thought: We can offer psychiatric and spiritual support at any moment, nothing can go wrong.— Messalina and Alexander were holding court. They stood next to the stage and were lit with flashbulbs by the press photographers. With them was Jack. He was wearing a pair of AWOL American officers' regulation (summer) pants, and a striped sweater. He was unkempt and looked as if he had just that moment got out of bed to answer the door. At his side was Hänschen, his boyfriend, sixteen, wheat blond, in his navy confirmand's suit and his best behavior and the merest touch of makeup. He looked with cold, pale eyes at the designers and their models, Hänschen, Hänschen klein, was Hans in Luck: he knew how to get his bread buttered. And now Alfredo, the sculptress, appeared. Her tense, tired, disappointed face, the pointy face of a cat on an Egyptian hieroglyph, was reddened, as though she'd slapped it a few times to gain courage and color to face the evening. Against Messalina, Alfredo looked so small and delicate, you wanted her to pick her up so that she would at least be able to see something of what was going on. Alexander was being congratulated. A few pompous asses and a few lickspittles were congratulating him. They hoped they too might be caught in the flashlights and have their faces in the paper: *Alexander in conversation with Pepin the Short, Conservatives consider lottery for the arts, found academy.* They were talking (what else?) about *Passions of an Archduke, better films in the New Germany, it's down to the screenplays, poets recruited to the film front.* "It's supposed to be a marvelous film," swooned a lady whose husband edited the *Law Journal*, and so earned enough money to get his wife kitted out by the feminine designers, *Vampire in women's clothing.* "Piece of shit, actually," said Alexander. "Oh, you're so funny," tootled the lady. Of course, she thought, of course it is a piece of shit really, but how can he say so out loud? might it not be a piece of shit? then it could only be a slow and sanctimonious piece of shit, *Neorealism out of fashion*. The schoolmistresses from Massachusetts were sitting in the front row. They had their notebooks out, and to hand. They took those standing in the flashbulbs for coryphées of intellectual life in Europe. (They were fortunate enough never to have seen any of Alexander's films.) "This promises to be a very interesting evening," said Miss Wescott. "What a circus," said Miss Burnett. They were both eyeing the wide double doors at the back, to see if Kay might not finally appear. They were both very worried about her. Edwin was conducted onto the stage through a little door to the side. The photographers dropped on one knee like archers and fired off their flashbulbs. Edwin bowed. He had his eyes closed. He put off the moment when he would have to look out into the auditorium. He felt a little dizzy. He thought he wouldn't be able to get a word out, not a syllable. He was sweating. He was sweating with fear, but also with happiness. All these people had come to hear him! His name had established itself worldwide. He didn't want to exaggerate, but these people were here to listen to his words. Edwin had given his life to intellectual effort, he had worked at the intellectual coalface, he had become intellect, and now he could pass on the intellect: disciples came to him in every city, the intellect would not die. Edwin laid his manuscript on the lectern. He adjusted the lamp. He cleared his throat. And then the wide door at the back opened one more time, and Philipp and Kay ran down the steps that led to the lecture hall. Philipp had met Kay at the door. The doorkeeper hadn't wanted to admit anyone else, but Philipp had flourished the press pass of the *Neues Blatt* like a charm, and the man had allowed them to pass. Philipp and Kay sat down at the side of the auditorium, on a couple of folding chairs that were generally reserved during the-atrical performances for the fireman and the policeman. No fire-man and no policeman had turned out for Edwin's lecture. Miss Wescott nudged Miss Burnett. "Do you see that?" she whispered. "It's that German poet, I don't know his name," said Miss Burnett. "She's been hanging around with him." Miss Wescott was shocked. "So long as she's done nothing worse," said Miss Burnett pertly. "It's terrible," groaned Miss Wescott. She wanted to jump up and run over to Kay; she had the feeling she should call the police. But Edwin cleared his throat once more, and silence settled over the auditorium. Edwin wanted to begin with Greek and Latin antiq-uity, he wanted to bring in Christianity, the connection between the Biblical tradition and the Classics, he wanted to speak about the Renaissance and offer judicious praise and blame to the Ratio-nalism of the French eighteenth century, but unfortunately, in-stead of words, only sounds reached his listeners' ears, a gurgling and crackling and hissing as of some fairground entertainment. Edwin, at the lectern, did not immediately realize that the public address system in the auditorium was malfunctioning. He sensed restlessness in the hall, and a climate unfavorable to intellectual concentration. He spoke a few more words on the historical sig-nificance of the West Asian promontory, when he was interrupted by a scraping of chairs and calls to speak up. Edwin was in the position of a funambulist, who is halfway along his rope and real-izes he can go neither forward nor back. What did the people want? Had they come to mock him? He stopped and held tight to the lectern. There was a rebellion in progress. Technology was rebelling against the intellect, technology, the noisy, unnatural, troublesome, headstrong child of the intellect. A few eager volun-teers rushed forward to adjust the microphone. But the fault lay with the loudspeaker system. I am helpless, thought Edwin, we are helpless, I have put my trust in this stupid, wicked megaphone, could I have dared step before these people without this invention, which is now making me ridiculous? no, I could never have dared, we are not human anymore, not whole people, I could never have spoken directly to them as Demosthenes once did, I need tin and wire that press my voice and my thinking as through the mesh of a sieve.— Messalina asked: "Do you see Philipp?"— "Yes," said Alexander, "I need to talk to him about his script. He won't have had any ideas yet."—"Oh, come," said Messalina, "he'll never write anything. But that girl. The cute one, the American. He's seducing her. What do you say to that?"—"Nothing," said Alexander. He yawned. He was going to sleep. Why shouldn't Philipp seduce whomever he wanted. He must be pretty virile, thought Alexander. "You idiot," whispered Messalina. The crackling in the loudspeaker system had become audible in the reading room also, where it had woken Schnakenbach. He too had wanted to hear Edwin's lecture, he too was interested in the European mind. He saw it was already late, and that the talk had already started. He staggered upstairs and reeled into the hall. Someone thought Schnakenbach was the house electrician, who must have been asleep in the basement somewhere, and mistakenly handed him the microphone. Schnakenbach suddenly saw himself with an audience; sleep-numbed as he was, he thought he was standing in front of the class he had taught before he had been compelled to give up his job as trade schoolteacher, and so he yelled into the microphone the great worry that obsessed him: "Don't sleep! Wake up! It's time!"

It was time. Heinz watched the square between the Bräuhaus and the Negro soldiers' club. There were a lot of police in the square; there were too many police in the square. The detachment of MPs in front of the club had been reinforced. The MPs were especially tall, well-grown Negroes. They wore white puttees, white belts, and white gloves. They looked like the Nubian legionnaires of some Caesar. Heinz still didn't know how he was going to proceed. The best thing would be to grab the money and disappear into the ruins. The American boy would never be able to find him in the ruins. But what if he insists on seeing the dog? of course he'll want to see the dog, before he hands over his money.— It was a nuisance that the dog had run off like that. It could put the whole deal in jeopardy. But it was ridiculous to suppose that Heinz would pull out of the deal just because the dog wasn't there. Heinz had hidden himself well. He was standing at the entrance of the Broadway bar. The bar was closed. The entrance was dark. The owner of the bar had preferred to decamp to Broadway proper. In the New World there was security. In the Old World you might die. You might die in the New World too, but at least you would die in greater security. The owner of the Broadway Bar had left fears, debts, darkness, and girls behind in Europe. He had also left behind graves, a large grave in which his murdered relatives lay. Forgotten and discarded, photographs of the naked girls were stuck on the dirty wall in the dark passage. The girls were smiling and holding little veils in front of their cunts with teasing gestures. YANKEE WHORES—a protester had scribbled. The girls were smiling, they were still teasing, still teasingly holding their little veils in front of them. A Nationalist had scribbled GERMANY, AWAKEN on the wall. The girls were smiling. Heinz pissed against the wall. Susanne walked past the dark entrance to the bar. She thought: Those pigs, they'll piss anywhere.— Susanne was on her way to the Negro Soldiers' Club. The black MPs checked out Susanne's papers. They held the papers in their dazzling white-gloved hands. The papers were in order. A jeep full of white MPs drew up in front of the club, sirens wailing. The white MPs called out some information to their black colleagues. The white MPs didn't look as stylish as the black ones. Compared to the black MPs, they looked shabby. Susanne disappeared into the club. One of the white MPs thought: Somehow it's always the niggers that get the prettiest girls.

In the club, a German band was playing. The club was poor. An American band would have been too expensive. So a German band was playing, and the German band was pretty good too. It was the band of Trumpet Major Behrend. The band played a lot of jazz pieces, and in between they played things like "The Hohenfriedberger March," or Waldteufel's "Spanish Waltz." The black soldiers liked the march a lot. They weren't so keen on the Waldteufel. Trumpet Major Behrend was satisfied. He liked playing in American army clubs. He felt pretty well paid for his trouble. He was happy. Vlasta was making him happy. He looked across to Vlasta, who was sitting at a little table, next to the band. Vlasta was bent over some sewing. From time to time she looked up, and then Vlasta and Herr Behrend would exchange smiles. They had a secret: they had set up against the world, and won; they had set up, each of them, against his own background and views, and they had exploded the ring of prejudice that had wanted to confine each of them. The German Trumpet Major in the Wehrmacht had got to know and love the little Czech girl in the Protectorate of Bohemia and Moravia. A lot of men slept with local girls. But they despised the girls they slept with. Only a few loved the girls they slept with. The Trumpet Major loved his Vlasta. At first, he had fought against his love. He had thought: What am I doing with this little Czech girl?— But then he had ended up loving her, and his love had changed him. It hadn't changed just him, the girl too had become a new person. When German Wehrmacht officers were being hunted down in Prague, Vlasta hid Herr Behrend in her cupboard, and later she fled Czechoslovakia with him. Vlasta had cut all her ties; she had left her fatherland; and Herr Behrend had cut most of his ties as well; he had cut his ties to his whole former life: both of them felt liberated, they were free, they were happy. They hadn't thought it would be possible to be so free and so happy. The band was playing Dixieland. Under the Trumpet Major's baton, they were playing one of the earliest jazz compositions. It sounded as German and romantic as the *Freischütz*.

Susanne thought the band were boring. Those silly palefaces were much too staid. The band hardly corresponded to what Susanne would have thought of as swing. She wanted drama, she wanted thrills; she wanted to abandon herself to the drama and the thrills. It was too bad that all Negroes looked alike. How could you tell? She would end up going off with the wrong guy. Susanne was wearing a striped silk dress. She wore it over her bare skin, like a shirt. She could have had her pick of the whole room. There was no one who wouldn't have gone with her. Susanne was looking for Odysseus. She had stolen money from him, but since she was Circe and the Sirens and maybe also Nausicaa, she had to go back to him, and not leave him in peace. She had stolen his money, but she wouldn't give him away. She would never give him away; she would never tell anyone that he had murdered Josef. She didn't know whether Odysseus had murdered Josef with the rock, but she thought he had. Susanne wasn't sorry that Josef had died, we all have to die some time, she thought. But she was sorry that he hadn't murdered someone else. He should have murdered Alexander or Messalina. But no matter whom he killed, Susanne would stand by him. We need to stand together against the pigs.— Susanne hated the world, from which she felt excluded and exploited. Susanne loved everyone who turned against this hateful world, who knocked a hole in its cold and brutal order. Susanne was faithful. She was a reliable comrade. You could trust Susanne. There was no fear of her tipping off the police.

Heinz pressed himself against the wall with the naked girls. A

German policeman was strolling past the entrance to the bar. That night, the German and the American police were fizzing around like angry wasps knocked out of their nest. A Negro had murdered a porter or a taxi driver. Heinz wasn't quite sure. There was talk about it all over the Old Town. Some said it was a taxi driver, others that it was a porter. A porter doesn't have any money, thought Heinz. He peeped out of the passage and saw Washington's sky-blue limousine draw up to the Negro club. Washington and Carla got out. They went into the club. Heinz was surprised. It was a long time since Washington and Carla had last been to the club. Carla hadn't wanted to go anymore. She had refused to mingle with the whores who went there. If Washington and Carla were going to the club again, something must have happened. Heinz didn't know what had happened, but it had to have been pretty important. It unsettled him. Were the two of them going to America? was he going with them? was he not going with them? did he want to go at all? He didn't know. At the moment, he would have liked best to go home, and go to bed, and think about whether he should go to America. Maybe he would have cried in his bed. Maybe he would just have read about the adventures of Old Shatterhand and eaten chocolate. Could you believe what Karl May said? According to Washington, there were no Indians except in Hollywood pictures. Should he go home? should he go to bed? should he think about all these difficulties? Then along came the car that resembled an airplane. It drew up, and the parking superintendent waved it to a spot. Christopher and Ezra climbed out. Ezra looked around. So he had come. He wanted to do business. Heinz couldn't back out now. It would have been cowardly of him to back out at this stage. Christopher walked into the Bräuhaus. Slowly, Ezra followed him. He kept looking round. Heinz thought: Wonder if I should give him a signal? But he decided: No, it's too soon, his father, the old Yank, has to be sitting over a beer first.

He's so young, even for one of the young Yankees he's young, thought the girl, it's his first evening in Germany, and already I've met him.— The girl was pretty. She had dark curly hair and white teeth. The girl had made Richard speak to her on the street. She had noticed that Richard wanted to get in conversation with a girl, and that he was too shy to do it all himself. So the girl had made it easy for Richard. She had stood in his way. Richard understood that she was making it easy for him. He liked her, but he thought, what if she's diseased?— He had been warned about that in America. In America they warned soldiers about to go abroad about the dangers of young women. But he thought: I don't want anything from her, and maybe she isn't diseased at all.— She was not diseased. Richard was in luck. Nor was she a street girl either. The girl sold socks in the department store next to the station. The department store did well out of the socks. The girl didn't do so very well from selling them. What she did earn, she handed over to her parents. But then she didn't want to spend her evenings sitting around at home and listening to the music on her radio that her father demanded: glowworm-glimmer-glimmer, the endless, deadly boring request program, the longest-lived heritage of the German Reich. The glowworm glimmered and her father read the newspaper. He said: "Things were different, under Hitler! Things had some gusto then." Her mother nodded. She thought of the old, burned-out flat; there had been some gusto then; certainly, the flames had burned with gusto. She thought of her long-treasured and swiftly charred trousseau. She was unable to forget the linen fold and the trousseau, but she didn't dare to contradict her husband: he was the doorman at the Vereinsbank, a man who commanded respect. The girl wanted a bit of fun after the socks and the glowworm music. She wanted her own life. She didn't want to repeat the life of her parents. The life of her parents wasn't worth repeating. Her parents were failures. They were poor. They were cheerless, unhappy, embittered. They sat embittered in the bitter room with the bitter chirpy music. The girl was after another sort of life, another sort of joy, if need be, another sort of pain. The girl liked American boys better than she liked German boys. The American boys didn't remind the girl of the bitterness of home. They didn't remind her of all those things she had had it up to here with: the shortages, the pointing-up-at-the-ceiling hush, the pokiness of the flat, the nationalist ill feeling, the national unease, the moral dourness. American boys were a breath of fresh air, the air of the wide world. The magic of the distance from which they came glamorized them. American boys were friendly, silly, and easygoing. They weren't so weighed down by fate, fear, doubt, the past, and perspectivelessness as German boys. Also, the girl knew how much a clerk made in a department store; she knew the sacrifices he had to make to buy himself a suit, a shoddy, readymade suit in which he would look unhappy and ill at ease. The girl would one day marry an overworked, disappointed, badly dressed man. But today the girl wanted not to think about that. She would have liked to go dancing. But Richard wanted to go to the Bräuhaus. Well, she supposed the Bräuhaus could be fun as well. So they went to the Bräuhaus. Even though in the Bräuhaus they played the same glowworm music.

The rooms were overcrowded. The community of people and peoples of the Bräuhaus, much celebrated and often hymned, was seething. The beer was flowing and foaming out of big barrels; it flowed and foamed in an unbroken stream. The tapsters didn't bother to turn off the taps, they held the liter glasses under the flow, pulled them away from the beer, cut the foam, and already they held the next glass under the flow. Not a drop was wasted. The waitresses lugged eight, ten, a dozen liter glasses to the tables.

The feast of the god Gambrinus was being celebrated here. People clanked glasses, drank up, smacked the glasses down on the table, and waited for them to be refilled. The Oberländer band were playing. They were old gentlemen in short lederhosen, showing red hairy knees. The band were playing the glowworm music, they played *Sah-ein-Knab-ein-Röslein-stehn*, and everyone in the room sang along, they linked arms, they stood up, they jumped onto the benches, and they roared out a slow and flat and sentimental rendering of *Röslein-auf-der-Hei-hei-den*. They sat down again. They drank some more. Fathers drank, mothers drank, little children drank; oldsters stood around the washtubs, hunting for little ends of beer in the mugs waiting to be washed that they then greedily swilled down. There was talk of the murdered taxi driver. A black soldier had murdered a taxi driver. It was Josef's death that was being talked about; but Fama, the goddess of rumor, had changed the porter into a taxi driver. Fama thought a porter an insufficient victim of a murder. The mood was not favorable to the Americans. People scolded and tutted; they had something to complain about. Beer in Germany raises the national feeling. In other countries, it may be wine or whiskey. In Germany, it is beer that levers and animates patriotism: a dull, none too illuminating drink. Individual members of the occupying forces, who had lost their way in the windings of the Bräuhaus, were met with friendly and good-neighborly cheer. A lot of Americans loved the Bräuhaus. They thought it was great and gemütlich. They thought it was even greater and more gemütlich than they had been led to believe they might from what they had read or heard about it. The Oberländer Band played "The Badenweiler March," the favorite march of the late Führer. You just had to buy the band a round, and they would play the march to which Hitler had used to enter the assembly halls of National Socialists. The March was the tune of recent and fateful history. The room rose as one from their chairs, like a single bosom swelled with enthusiasm. These were not Nazis, mind, who were getting to their feet. They were just beer drinkers. It was the atmosphere that got them up onto their feet. It was a giggle. Why the long face? Why think of things past and buried and forgotten? The Americans too were swept along by the atmosphere. The Americans too got to their feet. The Americans too hummed along to the Führer's march, or beat out the rhythm with their fists and feet. American soldiers and German soldiers who had come through embraced one another. It was a warm, purely human fraternization, without political dimensions or diplomatic significance. *Fraternization Prohibited, Fraternization Allowed, The Week of Good Neighborliness.* Christopher thought it was fantastic. He thought: What can Henriette have against this? Why can she not forget? She should see it here, it's wonderful, what great people they are.— Ezra watched the band, and he watched the people. His brow had more creases than ever; it was very short, and very narrow now. He felt like screaming! He was in a dark forest. Every man here was a tree. Every tree was an oak. And every oak was a giant, a wicked fairytale giant with a club. Ezra sensed he couldn't stand being in this forest much longer. He wouldn't be able to suppress his fear much longer. If the boy with the dog didn't come soon, Ezra would scream. He would scream and run away. Frau Behrend pushed her way through the rows of drinkers. She was looking for Richard, the young American relative, the son of the sender of the parcels, you never knew, perhaps we were in for another bad time soon, *Conflict Heightened/Deepened,* relatives had to stick together. How foolish of the boy to have her come here to the Bräuhaus! There was an American at almost every table. They were sitting there like our men, almost like Wehrmacht soldiers; only they had bad posture, they sat sloppily, not smartly. Too much freedom makes them degenerates, thought Frau Behrend. She started speaking to some of the younger ones: "Are you Richard? I'm your Auntie

Behrend!" She was greeted with incomprehension or laughter. A few called out, "Sit down, Auntie," and pushed a beer mug in her direction. A fat fellow, almost a barrel himself, gave her a smack on the behind. Those soldiers. Of course, it was only really their tanks and airplanes that defeated us.— Frau Behrend hurried on. She had to find Richard! Richard mustn't tell them at home what that poisonous shopkeeper had told him. Frau Behrend had to find Richard. She saw him sitting with a girl, quite a pretty girl with curly black hair. The two of them were drinking out of a single mug. The girl had her left hand on the young man's right. Frau Behrend thought: Is that him? it could be, from his age it could be him, but it can't be him, it can't possibly be him, he wouldn't bring his floozie along when he's arranged to meet his aunt.— Richard noticed that the woman was watching him. He got a fright. He thought: That's probably her, that woman with the fish face is my aunt with the Negro daughter, I'm not curious, I really don't want to intrude in her private life.— He turned to his girl, he put his arms around her, and he kissed her. The girl thought: Ooh, I'd better watch myself, he's more passionate than I thought he would be, I was afraid he wouldn't kiss me till I was on the doorstep.— The girl's lips tasted of beer. Richard's lips tasted of beer also. It was very good beer. That's not him, thought Frau Behrend, he would never behave like that, even if he did grow up in America he would never behave like that.— She sat down on a bench and hesitantly ordered herself a beer. The beer was an unnecessary expense. Frau Behrend did not care for beer. But she was thirsty, and she was also too exhausted to take on the waitress and the beer hall without ordering something.

Carla and Washington had gone to the Negro club to celebrate the future, a future in which no one is unwelcome. On that evening they believed in the future. They thought they would experience this future for themselves, the future where no one, whoever he might be and however he wanted to live, would be unwelcome. Carla was musical. Before even clapping eyes on him, she had recognized her father, the old *Freischütz* conductor, from his way of playing jazz. Only the day before, Carla would have been embarrassed to meet the Trumpet Major in a Negro club, while being seen by him in Washington's company would have been utterly mortifying. Now she took a different view of the meeting. They were human beings. Human beings thought differently. During a break between sets, Carla went up and said hello to her father. Herr Behrend was happy to see Carla. He was a little sheepish, but he fought his sheepishness, and he introduced Carla to Vlasta. Now Vlasta was sheepish. All three of them were. But they thought no ill of one another. "That's my boyfriend over there," said Carla. She pointed at Washington. "We're going to Paris," she said. The music master might once have gone to Paris himself. During the war, he was supposed to be transferred to Paris. Instead he was transferred to Prague. Herr Behrend wondered: Is it all right for Carla to love a black man?— He didn't dare to answer his own question. The black man was probably a good man, because Carla was living with him. For a moment, the specter of doubt raised itself in all their heads. They thought: The only reason we are all together is because we have all lost standing in the world.— But because they felt happy on that evening, they had the strength to push away their doubts, and kill off their fear and their cynicism. They remained cordial and kind. Herr Behrend said: "Now I'm going to surprise you. You're going to see that your father can play it hot as well, a real hot jazz." He went back up on stage. Carla smiled. Vlasta smiled. Poor father. Thinking he could play real jazz. Only blacks can play real jazz. Herr Behrend's band started shaking the cymbals and bashing the drums. Then the trumpets joined in. It was raucous, and it was good. Susanne had found Odysseus. He had dared to come to the club. For her sake he had emerged from his hiding places and slipped past police cordons to get into the club, Susanne had known that Odysseus would come; they had communicated with a call, a word, and there he was. Susanne, who was Circe and the Sirens and perhaps also Nausicaa, held Odysseus in a tight embrace. To the Trumpet Major's hot music they snaked across the parquet together as one, like a snake with four feet. They were both excited. They were excited after everything they had been through that day. Odysseus had had to flee, he had had to hide, they hadn't managed to find him, the great and wily Odysseus had escaped his pursuers, he had turned the head of Susanne/Circe/the Sirens, or she/they had turned his head, and maybe he had conquered Nausicaa. What was that if not exciting? It was exciting. It excited them both. The snake with the four feet, the smooth and graceful, sinuous snake was admired by everyone. Never would they break from that embrace. The snake had four feet and two heads, one black face and one white, but never would the heads turn on one another, never would the tongues drip poison on the other: they would never betray each other, the snake was a creature against the world.

He was not Red Snake, he was Deerslayer. Deerslayer was stalking Red Snake. Heinz had climbed into the ruins of a department store. From the stump of a destroyed wall, he could see into the beer hall next door. The prairie was rippling, herds of buffalo were moving through the grass. The light of the lamps, bulbs fixed onto giant wagon wheels, grew dim in the reek of people and beer. Heinz couldn't recognize anyone. Deerslayer would have to leave the Blue Hills behind. He would have to move cunningly through the prairie. He ducked under tables and benches. Then he discovered an enemy he was not expecting to find. There, to his astonishment, was Frau Behrend, sitting in the Bräuhaus, drinking beer. Heinz didn't like his grandmother. Frau Behrend wanted to have Heinz put in a home. Frau Behrend was a dangerous woman. What was she doing in the Bräuhaus? Did she come here every evening? Or was she just here tonight, on the scent of Heinz? Had she guessed he was on the warpath? Heinz mustn't let her see him. But he was tempted to play a trick on Frau Behrend. It was a test of courage and skill. He mustn't simply turn his back on her. The band were playing *Fuchs-du-hast-die-Gans-gestohlen*. The hall had risen to its feet again. All of them had linked arms and were singing along. Frau Behrend had linked arms with a couple of bald businessmen and was singing *gib sie wieder-her*. Heinz thought of knocking over Frau Behrend's beer. He snuck up behind Frau Behrend and the fat, bald businessmen. But once he was directly behind Frau Behrend, he no longer dared to take her mug and pour away her beer. Instead he just took the full glass of schnapps that was next to her mug and emptied it into her beer. Then he snuck off. He was Deerslayer again, on the trail of Red Snake.

Ezra was sweating. He was sweating and trembling. He thought he couldn't breathe. Even his father had now turned into a giant, one of those German giants in the German magic forest. Christopher was standing with the others, singing *sonst-wird-dich-der-Jäger-holen-mit-dem-Schiessgewehr*. He didn't know the words, he couldn't say them, but he was trying to sing them, and from time to time his German neighbor would help him, give him a nudge and sing the words clearly separating the syllables and instructing, *Schiess-ge-wehr*, and Christopher would nod and laugh and raise his beer mug to his neighbor, and then Christopher and his neighbor ordered sausages and radishes, and they ate the sausages and the radishes together, and Christopher did not sense his son's fear. Deerslayer had tracked them down. He caught the eye of Red Snake and made a sign to him. It was time. Ezra could not back out of the fight. The German boy was the enemy chosen for him by the giants of the forest. He would have to measure himself against the boy. He would have to wrestle with him. If he defeated the boy, he would have defeated the forest. "I'm just going to the car," said Ezra. Christopher said: "What do you want to go to the car for? Stay here."—"I'd rather wait in the car," said Ezra. "Come soon. We have to go home. We have to go home very soon." Christopher thought: Ezra's right, he doesn't like it here, this is no sort of place for a kid, he's too little, I'll drink up my beer and take him back to the hotel, I can always come out later if I feel like some more beer, once Ezra's asleep I can come out and drink more beer.— He liked it. He liked the Bräuhaus a lot. He liked to think that he would come back later and drink more beer.

The Fama reached Frau Behrend. A Negro had killed someone, Negroes were criminals, the police sirens were wailing, they were chasing the Negro. "It's a disgrace," said Frau Behrend. "They're like wild animals. They're like wild, savage animals. You can tell just from looking at them. Ooh, the things I could tell you." The businessman on Frau Behrend's left silently suspected her of having drunk his schnapps. He thought: Well, how do you like that, the old bird has pinched my glass of schnapps and knocked it back, cool as you like.— But he thought Frau Behrend was displaying sound political attitudes. Even if she had drunk his schnapps, her politics were so sound, he would be happy to buy her another. Frau Behrend thought: I couldn't tell them, I couldn't make myself, but if I was able to tell them— She pictured the astonishment and the dismay on the two businessmen's faces. She thought: The father with a foreign floozie, and the daughter with a Negro.— And what about the American nephew? The nephew hadn't shown.

He hadn't come to the Bräuhaus. Frau Behrend took a deep and angry pull on her beer. It was hard to tell with foreigners. It was hard to tell with these beer mugs how much was still left inside them. Had she really finished her beer already? It was true; the beer hall, the music, the people, the singing, the excitement, her annoyance, and the Negro's crime—it all made you thirsty. The other businessman also admired Frau Behrend's thinking. Her mug was empty. He would treat her to another beer. She wasn't a bad-looking woman for her age. But most of all she had the right views. That's what mattered. What were the blacks doing here? It was a disgrace! The two businessmen had no black customers.

"Where is the dog?" asked Ezra, "I would like to see him." Red Snake wanted to see the dog. Deerslayer had been afraid of that. It could all fall apart over that damned runaway dog. Heinz had to play for time. He said: "Come into this building here. Then I will show you the dog." They were speaking to each other as if they had gotten the sentences from a phrase book for wealthy travelers. Heinz led Ezra into the ruined department store. He climbed up onto the stump of masonry. Ezra followed him. He wasn't surprised that Heinz was taking him into a ruin. Ezra too was playing for time. As yet he had no firm plans either. He worried whether Christopher would appear at the right time. He needed to come out to the car at the right time and drive off quickly. Everything depended on Christopher driving off at the right time. They sat on the stump of masonry and looked over the beer hall. For a while they liked one another. We could make a catapult, and shoot stones at the window, stones at the prairie, stones at the buffaloes, thought Heinz. From up here, the giants don't look so fearsome, thought Ezra. There's no point in dragging it out any longer, thought Heinz. He was terribly afraid. He shouldn't have gone ahead with this. But since he had gone this far, he would have to see it through. He asked: "Have you brought the ten dollars?" Ezra nodded. He thought: All right, here goes, I've got to come out on top.— He said: "If I show you the money, will you call the dog?" Heinz nodded. He shifted along to the edge of the wall. From there he would be able to jump down easily. He would grab hold of the money, and jump. He could jump onto a lower wall, and then run through the ruins to the Bäckergasse. The American boy wouldn't be able to follow him. He would stumble in the ruins. He would fall behind, and not see him in the Bäckergasse. Ezra said: "When you've called him, can I take the dog with me into the Bräuhaus to show my father?" He thought: Once I've got the dog, we're out of here, Christopher will burn rubber.— Heinz said: "First you give me the ten dollars." He thought: You can show me what you like, I've got your measure.— Ezra said: "First my father has to see the dog."— "You don't have the money!" shouted Heinz. "I have got the money, but I can't give it to you until my father has seen the dog." You lying dog, thought Heinz. He was a cunning adversary. Red Snake was more resourceful than Heinz had expected. "You're not getting the dog until I've got the money."— "Then there's nothing doing," said Ezra. His voice was shaking. Heinz shouted again: "You haven't got the money!" He was close to tears. "I have!" shouted Ezra. His voice cracked. "Then show it me! Show it to me, you stupid dog, stupid, stupid dog, show it me if you've got it!" Heinz could no longer take the tension. He dropped out of the lofty tone of the conversation and grabbed Ezra. Ezra pushed him away. The boys wrestled. They were wrestling on the ruins of the wall, which, under the movement of their embittered wrestling, with the effect of their violent shoving, began to crumble. The mortar, dried out from the heat of the fire, dribbled out from the cracks between the stones, and the wall collapsed and the fighting boys with it. They shouted. They shouted for help. They shouted for help in German and in English. The German policemen heard the shouts, and the American military policemen heard the shouts. The Negro policemen also heard the shouts. The sirens of the American police jeep wailed. The sirens of the German squad cars replied.

The sound of the wailing sirens made its way into the Bräuhaus and excited the beery spirits. Fama, the all-powerful, evil-wreaking Fama, raised her head once more and passed on her message. The blacks had committed a further crime. They had lured a child into the ruins and dashed its brains out. The police were on the scene. The mutilated body of the child had been found. The voice of the people now spoke up alongside that of Fama. They chanted together: "How much longer are we going to allow this to happen? How much longer are we going to sit idly by?" To many, the Negro club was an annoyance. To many, the girls, the women who went with blacks were an annoyance. The Negroes in uniform, their club, their girls, were they not just one more, black, symbol of defeat, of the humiliation of the vanquished, were they not a sign of obloquy and disgrace? For an instant the crowd hesitated. They didn't have a leader. A couple of youths were the first to set out. Then everyone else followed, with red faces, breathing heavily, and excited. Christopher was just on his way to the car. He asked: "What's the matter? Why is everyone running?" The man with whom Christopher had eaten radish said: "The niggers have murdered a child. Your niggers!" He stood up and looked provocatively at Christopher. Christopher called: "Ezra!" His call disappeared in the hubbub of excited voices. He was unable to push his way through to his car. He thought: Why are there no police here on the square? The entrance to the Negro club was unguarded. Red curtains glowed behind the large windows. Music was heard playing. Herr Behrend's band were playing "Halleluiah." "Enough of that nigger music!" yelled the voice of the people. "Enough, enough!" called Frau Behrend. The two bald businessmen were propping her up. Frau Behrend was slightly the worse for wear, but her attitude was exemplary. It had to be supported. The exemplary attitude had to be supported. In a crowd of people, you never know who throws the first stone. Whoever throws the first stone doesn't know what possessed him to do it, unless he was paid to do it. But someone throws the first stone. The other stones fly after swiftly and easily. The windows of the Negro club were broken by stones.

Everything breaks down, thought Philipp, we no longer know how to communicate with each other, it's not Edwin speaking, it's the loudspeaker speaking, even Edwin uses the loudspeaker language, or the loudspeakers, like dangerous robots, are holding Edwin to ransom: his words are only uttered through their metal mouths, the words become loudspeaker language, the global idiom everyone knows and no one understands. Each time Philipp heard someone giving a talk, he was put in mind of Charlie Chaplin. Every speaker reminded him of Chaplin, in his own way, he was a Chaplin. Even during the most serious lecture, there was a Chaplin who made Philipp laugh. Chaplin tried to express his ideas, to pass on information, to speak kind and wise words into the microphone, but the wise and friendly words blared out of the loudspeakers like fanfares, like lies and demagoguery. The good Chaplin at the microphone heard only his words, his wise and friendly words as he spoke them into the vocal sieve, he heard his ideas, he listened to the sound of his soul, but he failed to hear the roaring of the loudspeaker, and he missed its simplifications and its stupid imperatives. At the end of his address, Chaplin thought he had led his listeners to a new contemplativeness, and that he had made them smile. He was suitably embarrassed when they leapt up and chanted "Heil" and began to lay into one another. Edwin's listeners would not fight. They slept. Whoever was not asleep, would not fight either. They were the gentle ones who were not asleep. With a different Chaplin, the wild ones wouldn't have slept, while the gentle ones would have drifted off. The wild ones would have given the peaceful ones a rough awakening. In Edwin's lecture, no one would be awakened. The lecture would have absolutely no effect. The first one to drop off was Schnakenbach. Behude had led him away from the microphone. He had seated Schnakenbach between himself and the philosophical seminarians. He thought: Neither they nor I can help him, he is beyond our reach.— Did Schnakenbach even exist? In Schnakenbach's terms, the lecture hall, the speaking poet, and his listeners were a chemical-physical process that had failed to make the correct product. Schnakenbach's sense of the world was non-anthropocentric. It was completely abstract. His schoolteacher's course of studies had given Schnakenbach an externally intact sense of the world, the view of the world of classical physics, where causality operated and God lived in a sort of delivery office, pityingly smiled on but left to be. In this world Schnakenbach had been able to settle. His fellow students settled. They fell in the war, and left widows and orphans. Schnakenbach did not want to go to war. He was unmarried. He started to think, and he came to the conclusion that the picture of the world he had been given no longer held true. Above all, he found that there were already some scientists who knew and said that this world picture was inaccurate. To stay out of the barracks, Schnakenbach started gulping sleep deprivation pills, and studying Einstein, Planck, de Broglie, Jeans, Schrödinger, and Jordan. He was now gazing into a world where God's delivery office had been closed. Either God didn't exist, or else He was dead, as Nietzsche had insisted, or, as was also possible and this was timeless, He was everywhere, but He was formless, no God the Father with big beard, and the whole father-complex of humanity from the prophets to Freud turned out to be a self-tormenting error on the part of homo sap., God was a formula, an abstraction, maybe God was Einstein's general theory of gravity, he was the miracle of balance in an expanding universe. Wherever Schnakenbach was, he was circumference and center, he was the beginning and the end, but that was nothing special, everyone was circumference and center, beginning and end, every point was, every grain of sleepy dust in his eye, the lavishly measured gift of the sandman's, an assembled thing, a microcosm with atom suns and comets, Schnakenbach could see a nanoworld, full to bursting with tiny matter, and then it did burst, burst continually, exploded into space, leaked into indescribable, finally infinite space. The sleeping Schnakenbach was in continual motion and change; he received and emitted forces; from the farthest reaches of the cosmos they came to him and fled him, they traveled faster than the speed of light and traveled billions of light years, it depended on point of view, there was no explanation, perhaps a few data might be captured, one might write something down on a ripped pill packet, perhaps one needed an electronic brain to find an approximation, the true sum would remain unknown, perhaps man had thrown in the towel. Edwin was speaking of the summa theologiae of the scholiasts. "*Veni creator spiritus*, come intellect creator, stay intellect creator, it is only in mind that we exist." Edwin called out the great names of Homer, Virgil, Dante, and Goethe. He invoked palaces and ruins, cathedrals and schools. He spoke of Augustine, Anselm, Thomas, Pascal. He mentioned Kierkegaard, Christianity merely an illusion, and yet, said Edwin, this illusion, perhaps the last glimmer of the dying light of Europe,

was the only warming ray of light in the world. The fashion designers were asleep. Their models were asleep. Alexander, the portrayer of the Archduke, was asleep. His mouth gaped open; the
void streamed in and out. Messalina was fighting sleep. She was
thinking about Philipp and the green-eyed charmer and wondering whether Edwin couldn't be recruited for the party. Miss
Wescott was writing down things she didn't understand, but
thought were possibly significant. Miss Burnett was thinking: I'm
hungry, whenever I hear someone give a talk, I get incredibly hungry, there must be something the matter with me: I don't feel ele-
vated, I feel hungry.— Alfredo, the delicate aging lesbian, rested
her cheek on Hänschen's confirmand's suit and was dreaming of
something fearfully indecent. Hänschen was wondering: Does she
have money?— He was a little calculating machine; but he was still
inexperienced, otherwise he would have known that poor Alfredo
couldn't possibly have money. He would have pulled away the arm
she was resting on. Hänschen was cruel. Jack was trying to remember everything Edwin said. Jack was a parrot. He liked saying
things back. But the talk was too long for him. It was tiring and
confusing. Jack could only concentrate for a little at a time. He had
worries. He was thinking about Hänschen. Hänschen was wanting
money again. But Jack didn't have money either. Kay was numb
with the whiskey she had drunk with Emilia. She didn't understand her poet. What he said was beautiful and wise; but it must
be over her head, Kay couldn't understand it. Dr. Kaiser probably
could have understood it. She was sitting uncomfortably in her
fireman's chair, leaning against the shoulder of the German poet,
who was sitting on the hard policeman's chair. She thought: Perhaps the German poet is easier to understand, he won't be as
clever as Edwin, but maybe he has more heart, German poets
dream, and they sing about the forest and their love.— Philipp was

thinking: They're asleep, but there is greatness in his talk, wasn't the madman right when he wanted to wake us? he's one of Behude's patients, Edwin's persistence moves me, I respect him, now I do respect him, his talk is a vain attempt to invoke something, I'm sure he too must feel how vain the attempt is, perhaps that's what moves me, Edwin is one of those helpless tormented seers, he doesn't tell us what it is he sees, what he sees is frightful, he tries to draw a veil in front of it, but sometimes he pulls the veil aside a little, maybe there is no horror, maybe there isn't anything behind the veil, he's only talking for himself, maybe he's speaking for me, maybe for the priests, it's a conversation among augurs, the rest are asleep.— He pressed his arm tighter around Kay. She wasn't asleep. She warmed him. She was warm fresh life. Again and again, Philipp could feel Kay's freer being. It wasn't the girl, it was freedom that was seducing him. He looked at her necklace, a moon-pale ornament of pearls, enamel, and diamanté roses. It doesn't suit her, he thought, wonder where she got it from, maybe she inherited it, she shouldn't wear jewelry, this old jewelry takes something away from her freshness, maybe she should wear corals.— The necklace seemed familiar to him, but he didn't recognize it as Emilia's. Philipp had no eye for jewels, and no memory for their form and fashioning, and besides he avoided looking at Emilia's valuables; he knew that the stones, the pearls, and the gold drew tears from her, and those tears oppressed him; Emilia was forced to sell her jewels, she cried each time she took something to the jeweler's, and from the proceeds of the jewels and the tears Philipp also lived. It was one of the calamities of his existence that alone, without Emilia, he could live far more simply and get by, but since he loved Emilia and was living with her, shared bed and board with her, he robbed her of her possessions, and, like a bird on a twig, he was caught on the lime of the luxury bohème of the Commercial Councilor's inheritance, and could no longer move his wings on the short flights that were within his gift, and that would have got him his feed. It was a tethering, a tethering of love, the bands of Eros, but his life had led him to dependency on a poorly managed fortune sunk in ruins, and that was another form of tie, an unintended one, that weighed oppressively on the feelings of the lover. I will never again be free, thought Philipp, all my life I've sought freedom, but I've lost my way.— Edwin brought up freedom. The European mind, he said, represented the future of freedom, or else freedom would have no future in this world. Here Edwin turned against a line of an American writer, wholly unknown to his listeners, by the name of Gertrude Stein, of whom it is said that she taught Hemingway to write. Gertrude Stein and Hemingway were equally unsympathetic figures to Edwin, he took them to be second-rate popular writers, and they in turn reciprocated by calling him an epigone, and a sublime imitator of the great dead poetry of the great dead centuries of the past. Like pigeons on the grass, said Edwin, quoting from Stein, and so something of hers had lodged with him, but he was thinking not so much of pigeons on the grass as of pigeons on St. Mark's Square in Venice, certain civilization theorists tended to look on mankind as pigeons on the grass, endeavoring as they did to lay bare the meaningless and apparently random aspects of human existence, to depict people as free of God, only to let them flutter freely down into the void, meaningless, worthless, free, and threatened with traps, a victim for the butcher, but proud of their imaginary freedom from God and divine origin, even though it left them nothing but misery. And yet, said Edwin, every pigeon knew its roost, and every bird was in God's hand. At this, the priests pricked up their ears. Was Edwin working their ground? Was he nothing but a lay preacher? Miss Wescott stopped taking down notes. This thing Edwin had just said, had she not heard it earlier today? Was it not similar to the thoughts that Miss Burnett had expressed on the

National Socialist square, had she not also compared people to pigeons or birds, and described their lives as fortuitous and imperiled? Miss Wescott turned in surprise to Miss Burnett. Was the thought that man feels himself under threat, an object of chance, so widespread that her revered poet and her much less revered fellow teacher could express it at almost the same time? Miss Wescott felt confused. She was no pigeon, nor any other sort of fowl. She was a human being, a teacher, she had a job that she worked hard at, and duties that she tried to discharge. Miss Wescott thought Miss Burnett looked hungry; a strangely famished expression lay over Miss Burnett's face, as though the world, as though Edwin's illuminations had made her terribly hungry. Philipp thought: Now he's going to turn to Goethe, this is almost German, the way Edwin now brings in Goethe, the law-by-which-we-have-presented-ourselves here, and like Goethe he's searching for freedom under the law: he hasn't found it.— Edwin had spoken his last word. The loudspeakers crackled and squawked. They went on crackling and squawking after Edwin had finished, and the wordless crackling and squawking in their toothless mouths tore the listeners from their sleep, their dreams, and their private thoughts.

The stones, the stones they themselves had thrown, the shattered glass, the flying shards frightened the crowd. The older ones among them felt themselves reminded of something; they felt themselves reminded of another blindness, of a previous action, of other shards. It had all begun with shards, and it had ended with shards. The shards with which it had ended were the shards of their own windows. "Stop this! We'll only have to pay for it," they said. "When things get broken, we're always the ones who end up paying." Christopher had pushed his way to the front. He didn't know quite what it was all about, but he had pushed his way through. He stood up on a rock and called out: "Hey, people, be sensible!" The people didn't understand him. But seeing him standing there with outspread arms to protect them, they laughed and said it was Saint Christopher. Richard Kirsch had also run up. His girl had begged him, "stay out of this, don't get involved, it's nothing to do with you," but he too had run forward. He was ready with Christopher to defend America, the black America that was at their backs, the dark America that was hiding behind the broken windows and the blowing red curtains. The music had stopped. The girls were screaming. They were calling for help, even though no one was doing anything to hurt them. The draft that came in through the windows seemed to render the black soldiers immobile. It wasn't that they were afraid of the Germans. Their destiny, which pursued them, the lifelong persecution that didn't let them go, even in Germany, darkened and immobilized them. They were determined to defend themselves. They were determined to defend themselves on the territory of their club. They would fight, they would fight a battle in their club, but their immobilization kept them from plunging out into the sea, the sea of white people, the white sea that was boiling for miles around their little black island. The siren cars of the police drew up. The piercing shouts of the police were heard. Whistles, shouting, and laughter were heard. "Come," said Susanne. She knew a way out. She took Odysseus by the hand. She led him down a dark passage, past some garbage cans across a yard to a low, collapsed wall. Susanne and Odysseus scrambled over the wall. They groped their way through a ruin and emerged in a deserted alleyway. "Hurry!" said Susanne. They ran down the alley. The sound of their footsteps was drowned out by the sirens' wailing. The police pushed the crowd back. A cordon of military police positioned itself in front of the entrance to the club. All those leaving the club were checked. Christopher felt a little hand pulling him down from his rock. In front of him stood Ezra. His suit was torn, his hands and face were scratched. Behind Ezra stood another boy; his clothes too were torn, and he had scratches on his face and hands. Ezra and Heinz had fallen on the stones of the collapsing wall. They had hurt themselves. In their initial panic, they had cried out for help. But then, when they heard the police sirens, they had helped each other up off the stones, and had fled into the Bäckergasse together. From there, they had gone back around into the square. They didn't want to have anything more to do with each other. They avoided looking at the other. They had awoken out of their Märchen and their Indian stories, and they felt ashamed. "Don't ask," Ezra said to Christopher, "don't ask. I just want to go home. It's nothing. I fell." Christopher pushed his way through the crowd to his car. Washington and Carla emerged from the club. They went to their car. "There he is!" exclaimed Frau Behrend. "Who?" asked the bald businessmen. Frau Behrend was silent. Should she shout out her disgrace? "Is it the taxi-killer?" asked one of the bald men. He licked his lips. "There goes the taxi-killer," called out the second of the bald men. "This woman says he's the taxi-killer. She's identified him!" The second bald head had perspiration on his face. A new wave of rage surged through the crowd. The broken windows had sobered them up, but seeing human prey, their hunting instincts were roused, the persecution frenzy and the bloodlusts of the crowd. Whistles shrilled out, "the killer and his whore" was called out, and once more stones were thrown. The stones were launched at the heavenly blue car. They struck Carla and Washington, they struck Richard Kirsch, who was defending America, free, brotherly America, by standing by people in danger, the viciously thrown stones hit America and Europe, they disgraced the oft-evoked European mind, they hurt humanity, they hit the dream of Paris, the dream of Washington's Bar, the dream of NONE UNWELCOME, but they couldn't kill the dream, which is stronger than any stone-throwing, and they hit the little boy, who, crying "Mama," had gone running to the sky-blue car.

The little dog cuddled up to Emilia. He was still nervous. He had still not gotten over his fear of the other dogs in the villa on the Fuchsstrasse, and of the cats and of the squawking parrot, and he was afraid of the cold and dead atmosphere of the house. But the other animals didn't hurt him. They had purred and yowled and squawked, and they had sniffed at him, and then they had calmed down. They knew the new dog would stay with them. He was a new associate, a new colleague, let him stay. There was enough for the animals in the house to eat, even if there wasn't always enough for the humans. The dog would get accustomed to the cold and dead atmosphere, while Emilia was a guarantee of friendship and warmth. Emilia felt cold. She had hoped she would find Philipp at home waiting for her. She was still Dr. Jekyll. She hadn't had very much to drink, she wanted to remain Dr. Jekyll. Dr. Jekyll wanted to be nice to Philipp. But Philipp wasn't there. He had taken himself off, somewhere else, away from her. He didn't love nice Dr. Jekyll. How Emilia hated this house she would never leave! The house was a tomb, but it was the tomb of the living Emilia, and she could never leave it. How she hated the pictures Philipp had put up! A centaur—a copy of a Pompeiian fresco—carrying a naked woman on its horse's back, stared at her with mocking grin. In reality, the centaur was pretty expressionless. It was as expressionless as all the faces on Pompeiian wall paintings, but to Emilia it seemed to be mocking her. Had Philipp not whisked her away, maybe not on horseback, but young and naked he had torn her away from her property, from her beautiful, innocent faith in the eternal rights of ownership, and led her to the realm of the intellectual, of poverty, doubt, and guilt? In a dark frame, there was a Piranesi print, the one of the walls of the old aqueduct in Rome, an insistence on decay and dilapidation. Nothing but mold surrounded Emilia, trophies of the Commercial Councilor's estate, dead books, dead mind, dead art. The house was unbearable. Didn't she have any friends? Didn't she have any friends among the living? Couldn't she go to Messalina and Alexander? At Messalina's there was music and drink, at Messalina's there was dancing, at Messalina's there was oblivion. If I go there now, she said to herself, then I'll come home as Mr. Hyde.— So be it, she said to herself, Philipp isn't here. If he had wanted to be, he could have been here. Shall I sit and wait for him? what am I, a widow? do I want to live like a hermit? and what if Philipp was here? what then? Nothing then! No music, no dancing. We would sit and gloomily face each other. Love would be a possibility, erotic despair. Why shouldn't I drink, why shouldn't I be Mr. Hyde?— Philipp led Kay out of the auditorium. Behind him, he could still see Edwin bowing, the face to the floor for a long time, modestly closing his eyes, as though the accolade that was now being given him, the applause for which he had envied the actors and stars of our day, were something visible and nasty, created out of a misunderstanding, a brutal precipitation, following on the heels of incomprehension, a liberation of listeners who had understood none of Edwin's words and who now, with their hands, were brushing off—as if they had been spiders' webs—the last vestiges of his soft and delicate words, coarsened through the loudspeakers, and, by the time they had reached their hearers, already dead, already turned to ashes and dust: it was a humiliation, and because it was interpreted by him as mockery and humiliation and bustle and gross display of naked convention, of discreditable celebrity and mindlessness, the poet modestly sealed his eyes. Philipp understood him. He thought: My unhappy brother, my dear brother, my great brother.— Emilia would have said: "And what about my poor brother? You didn't say anything about that."—"Of course. And my poor brother too," Philipp would have replied, "but that's not important. What you describe as poor is the heart of the poet, around which the joy, love, and splendor of a poet's life form themselves, like snow around the heart of an avalanche. A chill metaphor, Emilia, but Edwin, his words, his intellect, his message, which made no visible impact in this hall, and left no repercussions, still is included among the great avalanches to roll into the valley of our times."—"And wreck it," Emilia would have added, "and spread further chill." But Emilia wasn't there, she was probably at home, creating out of wine and schnapps the terrible Mr. Hyde, who bewailed the loss of property, who over the loss of his property had become a drunk, and with his own microcosm of destruction, with the wild rampaging of the drunk, opposed the greater devastation of the time. Philipp led Kay out of the hall. They got away from the schoolmistresses; they gave Alexander and Messalina the slip. The nicely made-up, well-dressed, and comparatively well-off American schoolteachers stood around in the lecture hall as if they'd been poor timid little German schoolmarms. They had written dead phrases in their notebooks, a series of dead words, funereal markings of the intellect; words that they would not awaken to life, that they would not rouse to any meaning. They could look forward to a coach ride back to the hotel, a cold snack in the hotel, writing letters to Massachusetts we-have-been-round-a-German-city, we-got-to-listen-to-Edwin-he-was-majestic, they could look forward to their bed in the hostel, and it wasn't much different to the beds in other places they had visited.

What remained? The dream remained. And also the disappointment over Kay; Kay the charmer, Kay the shameless, she had run off with the German poet whose name they didn't even know, and they wondered whether it might not be worthwhile calling the police, but Miss Burnett was against the idea, and she cowed Miss Wescott by imagining the probable scandal of the military police in a siren car going to look for unfaithful little Kay. The Amerika Haus, a construction in the Führer's style from the National Socialist era, lay behind Philipp and Kay. With its symmetrically ranked windows shining out into the night, the building looked like certain museums, like a colossal mausoleum of antiquity, like an office block, where the leftovers of antiquity are administered—the intellect, the heroic tales, the gods. Kay didn't especially want to go with Philipp, but there was something in her that didn't want to refuse, and that something pulled the Kay who didn't want to go with him along with it, that was how strong it was, and what it was was a yearning for romance, a yearning for the out of the ordinary, a yearning for experience of a particular type, for adventure, for antiquity, for degeneration and destruction, for sacrifice, devotion, and the myth of Iphigenia, it was stubbornness, it was being fed up with the schoolmistresses, it was the stimulus of being abroad, the hastiness of youth, it was Emilia's whiskey, it was that she was tired of the heavy and awkward adoration of Miss Wescott and Miss Burnett. Kay thought: He'll take me back to his apartment, I will get to see the apartment of a German poet, that will interest Dr. Kaiser, maybe the German poet will seduce me in his apartment, Edwin didn't want to seduce me, of course I would much rather have been seduced by Edwin, but Edwin's talk was boring, to be honest, it was cold and boring, I will be the only member of our group who will be able to tell them back home what it's like being seduced by a German poet.— She rested against Philipp's arm. The city was full of the wailing of police sirens. Kay thought: This is a jungle, I'm sure there must be lots of crimes committed in this city.— And Philipp thought: Where can I take her? I could take her back to the Fuchsstrasse, but maybe Emilia's already drunk, she's Mr. Hyde, when she's Mr. Hyde she's in no fit state to receive any visitors, should I take the American girl to the Lamb? the hotel is seedy, it's depressing, I'd be taking the little lamb to the Lamb, what do I want with her anyway? do I want to sleep with her? maybe I could sleep with her, for her that would be travel romance, an *amour de voyage*, to her I must be something like an elderly gigolo, that poem of George's about the Porta Nigra: do I feel the arrogance of an old gigolo? Kay is charming, but I'm not set on it, I don't even want her that much, I want the other country, I want the distance, the different horizon, I want youth, the young country, I want the easy and unburdened, I want the future and the transitory, I want the wind, and since that's all I want, wouldn't the other thing be a crime?— After a few more steps, Philipp thought, and I want the crime.

They lay together, white skin, black skin, Odysseus and Susanne/ Circe/the Sirens and possibly Nausicaa, they were entwined, black skin white skin, in a room that perched shakily on a couple of beams, almost like a balcony hanging over a drop, because the foundations of the house had been torn away on that side, a bomb had blown them away, and they would never be rebuilt. The walls of the room were stuck with pictures of actors, the most looked at, the representative faces of the time, stared down on them with their bland features, their empty beauty, as they lay on the pillows, black and white, on the pillows, formed like animals, like devils and long-legged vamps, naked white and black, they lay on a raft, in the delirium of union they lay as on a raft, naked and beautiful and wild, they lay innocently on a raft, sailing into infinity.

"An infinity! But an infinity assembled from minutest finite particles, that's the world. Our bodies, our form, the thing we think of as us, are just a lot of tiny particles, tiny tiny tiny particles. But those little dots, they have such power: they are power plants, miniature power plants of intense power. The whole thing can go up! But for the briefest nanosecond, for the duration of our life, those billions of power plants have been blown like sand into the fleeting shape we call us. I could write out the formula for you." Schnakenbach was reeling home, half asleep, propped on Behude's arm. His poor head looked like a plucked bird's. This is stupid, thought Behude, but what have I got to counter him with? It's stupid, maybe he's right, both ends of material physics, the very big and the very small, are equally mysterious to us, we are no longer at home in this world, which Schnakenbach wants to set out in a formula, and was Edwin's version any better? It wasn't, his talk left me cold, it too only led up a cold, dark, and blind alley.

Edwin had withdrawn from all society, like an old eel he had wriggled clear of all invitations, he had even ducked out of the ride home in the Consular automobile; and had disappeared down the steps of the Amerika Haus, down the wide marble staircase of the Führer building, into the night, and strangeness and adventure. A poet doesn't age. His heart beats youthfully. He had gone into the alleyways. Without a map, he was merely following his nose, his big nose. He found the gloomy alleyways by the station, the parks around the law courts, the alleyways of the old city, the precinct of Oscar Wilde's golden adders. Just then, Edwin was Socrates and Alcibiades. He would have liked to be Socrates in the body of Alcibiades, but he was Alcibiades in the body of Socrates, albeit he walked erect and well dressed. They were waiting for him. Bene, Kare, Schorschi, and Sepp were waiting for him. They had been waiting for him for a long time. They didn't see Socrates and Alcibiades. They saw an old client, an old perv, a well-heeled old queen. They were not aware of their own beauty. They had no idea that there was such a thing as an addiction to beauty, and that in the beloved, in the body of a rough youth, the lover can be in love with the reflection of the eternally beautiful, the immortal, the soul as Plato once worshiped it. Nor had Bene, Schorschi, Kare, and Sepp read Platen, who-ever-has-beheld-beauty-with-his-own-eyes-must-die. They saw a smartly dressed rich client, a strange transaction they didn't quite understand, but that, as they knew from experience, was quite profitable. Edwin looked into their faces. He thought: They are proud and beautiful.— He was not unaware of their fists, their big, cruel fists, but he looked instead at their proud and beautiful faces.

It was a party without pride or beauty. Was it even a party? what was being celebrated? were they celebrating nothing? They said: "We're celebrating!" But they only gave free rein to their murky senses. They drank champagne, and they toasted cheerlessness, they filled the emptiness of their lives with noise, they chased away fear with midnight music and hysterical laughter. It was a horrible party. There was no atmosphere; not even an atmosphere of desire. Alexander was asleep. He slept with mouth gaping. Alfredo slept as well, a pointy-mouthed, disappointed little kitten with bad dreams. Messalina was dancing with Jack. Jack reluctantly lost out in a bout of freestyle wrestling. Hänschen was talking business with Emilia. He wanted to know whether the occupation dollar was about to be withdrawn. He was thinking of getting into scrap gold. He knew that Emilia understood something of these matters. The little adding machine Hänschen was purring. Emilia was drinking. She drank champagne and sharp burning gin, she drank high-proof cognac and heavy Spätleses from the Palatinate. She filled herself up. She drank everything. She was building up Mr. Hyde. She was wickedly and deliberately building him up. She drank, so as to do harm to Messalina. She didn't dance. She didn't let anyone touch her. She was a chaste little tippler. She filled her tank. What did she care about the people around her? She had come here to drink. She lived for herself. She was the inheritor of the Commercial Councilor. That was enough. The inheritress had been robbed; people had taken from her inheritance. That was enough. That was enough of people. That was all she needed to know about them. When she had drunk enough, she would go. She had drunk enough. Orgies didn't interest her. She left. She went home to her animals. She went home to rage and accusation. Cowardly Philipp wouldn't be there to confront Mr. Hyde, he would steer clear of her raving, she would have to rave at the janitor, she would have to scream at the locked doors, against the doors behind which dwelt only coldness and calculation.

He shut the door of the room, and he saw that she was cold. The ugly room with the single bed, the nasty room with the cheap glossy furniture, the tasteless factory furnishings, was that the poetic habitation, the home of the German poet? He looked at her, he thought, she's thinking this is a dump.— He mustn't now attempt to be tender with her; he must throw her down, like a calf in an abattoir; he must throw her down, so that she feels where she is.— Withered. Frozen. He felt old, and he felt his heart cooling. He thought: I don't want to become bad: not stone-hearted.— He opened the window. The air in the hotel was musty and sour. They breathed in the night. They stood by the window in the Lamb Hotel, and they breathed in the night. Their shadow vaulted down onto the street. It was the shadow of love, a fleeting, ephemeral apparition. They saw the electric sign of the Ecarté Club flash up, and the four-leaf clover of fortune unfold. They heard the siren cars of the police. A shrill English voice called for help. It was just a brief little scream, and then it died. "That was Edwin's voice," said Kay. Philipp said nothing. He thought: That was Edwin.— He thought: What a scoop for the *Neues Blatt*. Even the *Evening Echo* would put an attack on a world-famous poet on their front page.— Philipp thought: I'm not a good reporter. He didn't move.— He thought: Am I still able to cry? have I still got tears? would I cry if Edwin was dead?— Kay said: "I want to go." She thought: He is poor, look how poor he is, he's embarrassed because of how poor he is, how poor this room is, he is a poor German.— She unfastened her necklace, the moon-pale necklace of pearls and enamel and diamanté roses, the old grandmother ornament that Emilia had given her. She laid Emilia's attempt at a free and motiveless action on the window seat. Philipp understood the gesture. He thought: She thinks I'm destitute.— Little Kay looked out and saw the clover leaf, the flaming neon light, and she thought, there's his forest, his grove of oaks, his German forest where he walks and writes.

The church tower sounds midnight. A day is over. A page of a calendar is torn off. Next, please. The newspaper editors yawn. The printing blocks of the morning papers are shut. Whatever that day had happened, been said, lied, murdered, and destroyed, lay set in lead like a flat flan on the trays of the typesetters. The flan was hard on the outside, and slippery in the middle. Time had baked the flan. The editors had made it up into pages, the calamity, misfortune, desperation, and crime; they had squeezed the lies and screams into their columns. The headlines were fixed, the bewilderment of the governments, the consternation of the scientists, the fear of mankind, the lack of belief of the theologians, the reports of the deeds of the desperate were ready to be multiplied, they were immersed in the bath of printer's ink. The presses were running. Their rollers pressed the words of the new day onto the stream of white paper, the beacons of folly, the questions of dread, and the categorical imperatives of intimidation. Only a few hours, and poor, tired women will carry the headlines, the phrases, the beacons, the fear, and the feeble hope into the homes of readers; chilled, grumpy vendors will hang the morning pronouncements of the augurs on their kiosks. The news will not warm. *Tension, Conflict, Deepening, Threat.* In the sky, the planes are droning. For the moment, the sirens are quiet. Their tin mouths are rusting. The old bombproof bunkers have been blown up; the new bombproof bunkers will be built deeper and better. Death conducts maneuvers. *Threat, Deepening, Conflict, Tension.* Come-gentle-sleep. But no one can escape their world. The dream is heavy and restless. Germany lives in a force field, Eastern world/ Western world, broken world, two halves of the world, uncomprehending and hostile to one another, Germany lives on the seam, on the crack, time is precious, it's no more than a span, a brief span, done, a second to draw breath, to draw breath on a bloody battlefield.

New Directions Paperbooks—a partial listing

Kaouther Adimi, Our Riches
Adonis, Songs of Mihyar the Damascene
César Aira, Artforum
  An Episode in the Life of a Landscape Painter
  Ghosts
Will Alexander, The Sri Lankan Loxodrome
Osama Alomar, The Teeth of the Comb
Guillaume Apollinaire, Selected Writings
Paul Auster, The Red Notebook
  White Spaces
Ingeborg Bachmann, Malina
Honoré de Balzac, Colonel Chabert
Djuna Barnes, Nightwood
Charles Baudelaire, The Flowers of Evil*
Bei Dao, City Gate, Open Up
Mei-Mei Berssenbrugge, Empathy
Max Blecher, Adventures in Immediate Irreality
Roberto Bolaño, By Night in Chile
  Distant Star
Jorge Luis Borges, Labyrinths
  Seven Nights
Coral Bracho, Firefly Under the Tongue*
Kamau Brathwaite, Ancestors
Basil Bunting, Complete Poems
Anne Carson, Glass, Irony & God
  Norma Jeane Baker of Troy
Horacio Castellanos Moya, Senselessness
Camilo José Cela, Mazurka for Two Dead Men
Louis-Ferdinand Céline
  Death on the Installment Plan
  Journey to the End of the Night
Rafael Chirbes, On the Edge
Inger Christensen, alphabet
Julio Cortázar, All Fires the Fire
  Cronopios & Famas
Jonathan Creasy, ed: Black Mountain Poems
Robert Creeley, If I Were Writing This
Guy Davenport, 7 Greeks
Osamu Dazai, No Longer Human
H.D., Selected Poems
Helen DeWitt, The Last Samurai
  Some Trick
Marcia Douglas
  The Marvellous Equations of the Dread
Daša Drndić, EEG
Robert Duncan, Selected Poems
Eça de Queirós, The Maias
William Empson, 7 Types of Ambiguity

Mathias Énard, Compass
  Tell Them of Battles, Kings & Elephants
Shusaku Endo, Deep River
Jenny Erpenbeck, The End of Days
  Go, Went, Gone
Lawrence Ferlinghetti
  A Coney Island of the Mind
F. Scott Fitzgerald, The Crack-Up
  On Booze
Jean Frémon, Now, Now, Louison
Rivka Galchen, Little Labors
Forrest Gander, Be With
Romain Gary, The Kites
Natalia Ginzburg, The Dry Heart
  Happiness, as Such
Henry Green, Concluding
Felisberto Hernández, Piano Stories
Hermann Hesse, Siddhartha
Takashi Hiraide, The Guest Cat
Yoel Hoffmann, Moods
Susan Howe, My Emily Dickinson
  Debths
Bohumil Hrabal, I Served the King of England
Qurratulain Hyder, River of Fire
Sonallah Ibrahim, That Smell
Rachel Ingalls, Binstead's Safari
  Mrs. Caliban
Christopher Isherwood, The Berlin Stories
Fleur Jaeggy, Sweet Days of Discipline
Alfred Jarry, Ubu Roi
B.S. Johnson, House Mother Normal
James Joyce, Stephen Hero
Franz Kafka, Amerika: The Man Who Disappeared
  Investigations of a Dog
Yasunari Kawabata, Dandelions
John Keene, Counternarratives
Heinrich von Kleist, Michael Kohlhaas
Alexander Kluge, Temple of the Scapegoat
Taeko Kono, Toddler-Hunting
Laszlo Krasznahorkai, Satantango
  Seiobo There Below
Ryszard Krynicki, Magnetic Point
Eka Kurniawan, Beauty Is a Wound
Mme. de Lafayette, The Princess of Clèves
Lautréamont, Maldoror
Siegfried Lenz, The German Lesson
Denise Levertov, Selected Poems

Li Po, Selected Poems

Clarice Lispector, The Hour of the Star
The Passion According to G. H.

Federico García Lorca, Selected Poems*
Three Tragedies

Nathaniel Mackey, Splay Anthem

Xavier de Maistre, Voyage Around My Room

Stéphane Mallarmé, Selected Poetry and Prose*

Javier Marías, Your Face Tomorrow (3 volumes)

Bernadette Mayer, The Bernadete Mayer Reader
Midwinter Day

Carson McCullers, The Member of the Wedding

Thomas Merton, New Seeds of Contemplation
The Way of Chuang Tzu

Henri Michaux, A Barbarian in Asia

Dunya Mikhail, The Beekeeper

Henry Miller, The Colossus of Maroussi
Big Sur & the Oranges of Hieronymus Bosch

Yukio Mishima, Confessions of a Mask
Death in Midsummer
Star

Eugenio Montale, Selected Poems*

Vladimir Nabokov, Laughter in the Dark
Nikolai Gogol
The Real Life of Sebastian Knight

Pablo Neruda, The Captain's Verses*
Love Poems*

Charles Olson, Selected Writings

Mary Oppen, Meaning a Life

George Oppen, New Collected Poems

Wilfred Owen, Collected Poems

Hiroko Oyamada, The Factory

Michael Palmer, The Laughter of the Sphinx

Nicanor Parra, Antipoems*

Boris Pasternak, Safe Conduct

Kenneth Patchen
Memoirs of a Shy Pornographer

Octavio Paz, Poems of Octavio Paz

Victor Pelevin, Omon Ra

Alejandra Pizarnik
Extracting the Stone of Madness

Ezra Pound, The Cantos
New Selected Poems and Translations

Raymond Queneau, Exercises in Style

Qian Zhongshu, Fortress Besieged

Raja Rao, Kanthapura

Herbert Read, The Green Child

Kenneth Rexroth, Selected Poems

Keith Ridgway, Hawthorn & Child

Rainer Maria Rilke
Poems from the Book of Hours

Arthur Rimbaud, Illuminations*
A Season in Hell and The Drunken Boat*

Evelio Rosero, The Armies

Fran Ross, Oreo

Joseph Roth, The Emperor's Tomb
The Hotel Years

Raymond Roussel, Locus Solus

Ihara Saikaku, The Life of an Amorous Woman

Nathalie Sarraute, Tropisms

Jean-Paul Sartre, Nausea

Delmore Schwartz
In Dreams Begin Responsibilities

Hasan Shah, The Dancing Girl

W. G. Sebald, The Emigrants
The Rings of Saturn

Anne Serre, The Governesses

Stevie Smith, Best Poems

Gary Snyder, Turtle Island

Dag Solstad, Professor Andersen's Night

Muriel Spark, The Driver's Seat
Loitering with Intent

Antonio Tabucchi, Pereira Maintains

Junichiro Tanizaki, The Maids

Yoko Tawada, The Emissary
Memoirs of a Polar Bear

Dylan Thomas, A Child's Christmas in Wales
Collected Poems

Uwe Timm, The Invention of Curried Sausage

Tomas Tranströmer, The Great Enigma

Leonid Tsypkin, Summer in Baden-Baden

Tu Fu, Selected Poems

Paul Valéry, Selected Writings

Enrique Vila-Matas, Bartleby & Co.

Elio Vittorini, Conversations in Sicily

Rosmarie Waldrop, Gap Gardening

Robert Walser, The Assistant
The Tanners
The Walk

Eliot Weinberger, An Elemental Thing
The Ghosts of Birds

Nathanael West, The Day of the Locust
Miss Lonelyhearts

Tennessee Williams, The Glass Menagerie
A Streetcar Named Desire

William Carlos Williams, Selected Poems
Spring and All

Louis Zukofsky, "A"

*BILINGUAL EDITION

For a complete listing, request a free catalog from New Directions, 80 8th Avenue, New York, NY 10011
or visit us online at ndbooks.com